I0671397

Ruby Gold

By

Ron Bell

The Ronnie Campbell Series, Book 2

This is a work of fiction with historical facts mixed in to make a good story. Many of the names are of persons I have known over the years and have placed back into the 1860 time period. None of these people lived in this time but, if they did, they may have found themselves riding for or with Ronnie Campbell.

ISBN: 9780692839782

ACKNOWLEDGMENTS

I would like to thank some of the people who helped me get this book published. First is my wife Susie Bell, who is my editor and supporter on my projects. I am a poor speller and have no idea of how to put the little marks in the proper locations so things read correctly.

Dennis Doyle, Medium Photography

In this book you will find many different photos, some I took and others were pulled from a Pony Express photo shoot from a few years ago. Ruby Gold's cover is a special photo. Dennis Doyle (Ducilla) is showing Dandy and me working our way down the mountain with the wind blowing. Thanks for a great picture and allowing me to use it as my book cover.

Kristen Kabrin Photography

Kristen has many photos published and is well known around Carson City, Nevada. It was so much fun riding past Kristen and Melissa at full speed with rocks flying. They held their ground and got some great shots.

Melissa Knight, Faith Photography of Nevada

The third photographer was Melissa Knight, who was also on the same photo shoot that the book cover was taken. I would like to say that so many pictures came from that same shoot, some of the pictures even made it into many other publications.

Thanks for your photos I hope the readers enjoy them like I do.

FORWARD

The first book in this series was THE PONY EXPRESS RIDER. I started this book off at the point that the last one left off with many projects starting. I would like to tell you that this book has many twists and turns, with new people riding into the story, taking it in different directions. I have no idea as to how this process works, but I was told that I am a person who GHOSTS tell their story to.

If this is true, I may have many different stories to tell with many un-expected endings. Why I feel this could be true? When I am telling the story I have no idea as how it is going to end or what direction it is going. At one point, this book just came to a stop. I read it three times with no place for it to go. I was on a business trip heading to Texas, just outside of Tuscan, Arizona. I am driving at 80 miles per hour. I heard a voice saying, "I am Spike Martin I have come to finish your book".

When I returned home, I went back a few chapters and put Spike in the book. When I started the next chapter, the book just flew with many new twists and turns. At one time I had a direction I wanted the book to go. Well, not so, within two pages the book just make a right turn and this part of the story had its own story to be told.

I have been told that the last book gave a true picture of the human experience during that time period. My hope is that this one will give enjoyment to those who read it. When I had people pre-read The Pony Express Rider, I received some interesting comments like, "your women seem to be very independent and somewhat forward". I felt that real life offered the western women very little in choices of who they would spend their life with. When a real man would offer them and their children support and a chance to have a better life, they took it and moved on with life

CHAPTERS

Author Ron Bell, on Diamond in 2015, ready to ride.

Chapter 1 **Trip to Mr. Brown's Store**

Early Summer 1861

With everyone back at the ranch except for Juanita, Juan and their two young boys Little Juan and Hector, things were moving along at a breakneck pace. Ronnie and Sean were heading out to the mine site to see what timber and equipment was needed to start getting the mine into operation. They planned to be at the mine site for a few days. Ronnie had brought Diamond back in from the range to ride. He would need a horse that can cover some ground over the next few months. Ronnie had sent a letter to Bolivar Roberts asking if he could buy Buster and Lightning after the Pony Express shut down in the coming fall. Ronnie had also mentioned in the letter that Andy Sams would have a job on the ranch if he wanted it, also saying that Andy could bring the two horses to the ranch when he came to start work if that would work. Ronnie felt that Andy could help with the ranch operations and assist in getting the mine started. Andy had a way of working the steel few men could ever accomplish in their lifetime. One time Ronnie had asked Andy how he knew when to start working the steel. Andy would just look at him and said, "it is the eye, you either see it or you don't".

During the past few weeks White Bird and Tee had been learning to speak some English and Tony was learning Paiute as they worked around the ranch. The Indians were helping with the horses and riding with Tony to move the cattle onto new grass each week in the upper meadows. The two Indians had started to teach Tony how to track but it was a slow process. When moving cattle, one of the Indians would ride into the hills and have Tony try to follow the trail. This trip both Indians rode off into the hills leaving Tony to handle the cattle. After Tony finished moving the cattle to another meadow he turned back to look for the trail. He picked up the trail leading into the timber after some time looking, but after only a few feet the trail was gone. Tony got off his horse and started looking really close for any sign of tracks. Making a circle, he found a broken twig. After a bit he found a rock out of place. Tony was getting the idea that this was going to be a real test, not just for fun.

He was walking his horse now and was starting to see just small things out of place. Tony was finding his way but it was slow work. Most of the afternoon had gone and he was getting ready to make a camp but pressed on searching. The sun was setting now and he had worked his way into a small draw. As he cleared the trees, he found his dinner. White Bird and Tee had camp set up and food on the fire. They both smiled when he rode up.

White Bird said, "you did good, but you slow".

This was the first time Tony had been able to work out the trail without the help from either Tee or White Bird. Dinner was looking and smelling powerfully good. They had three sage hens cooking over the fire on green willow sticks. As the fat from the birds was dropped onto the coals, it was spitting small flames up into the air. Picking up the birds with their roasting sticks, they all went to work on them. It is hard to find a better meal around any campfire, Tony told his helpers.

With the sundown and the three sitting around the small campfire, Tony was getting White Bird and Tee to tell him about their family, if they had one. After a bit Tony found out that they did have wives and some children on the other side of the mountain from the ranch. Abby had been after Tony to find out and have them bring their families to the ranch so they could be part of the ranch family. After eating the birds they kept talking about if they would move their families over or not.

The next morning both Indians told Tony they would ride over the mountain and talk it over. Tony headed back to the ranch to tell Abby he had asked. Only time would tell if they would move to the ranch headquarters.

Tony had moved the cattle to some good grass with plenty of water the day before but before heading back to the ranch he made a final check, and all was ok. The cattle would have plenty to eat for weeks so he could work on other things for a while around the ranch headquarters. When he reached the ranch it was late in the day. Dinner would be ready soon so he put Teddy up and went out behind the kitchen and washed up. When he walked in, Maggie was working at the stove with her back to him. Easing up, he kissed her neck. Maggie said, "I sure hope that is you Tony, and now go find someone to talk to until I get finished. Dinner will be ready soon".

Tony was sitting on the front porch when Abby came from the barn and asked him if he had talked to Tee and White Bird about moving their families over to the ranch. Tony told her about what they said and told her about them going over the mountain to talk it over, and said "your guess is as good as mine". Abby asked Tony if he would drive the wagon into town so the girls could ride the two standard bred horses on the trip to Mr. Brown's store. They would like to start in the morning, so they could get some ranch supplies and order some wedding items. The trip would take five days to get into Mr. Brown's and back to the ranch. Abby said that Ronnie was going over to Sam Applegate's ranch in the morning to talk about getting a freighting company started to supply the mining operation they were starting. If Sam liked the idea they would bring all of the wagons and draft houses back to the ranch and would start making repairs to the equipment they would take on the trip.

The next morning Tony was on the way before light, going to pick up ranch supplies and items needed with a wedding to plan. Abby and Maggie will head to Mr. Brown's store to look at some books to place orders for the wedding. Maggie also had to pick out some items for the new house that was being worked on. Abby and Maggie were riding fast to catch up with Tony by dinner time. Tony had left the ranch yard at a stiff trot with a team and wagon. Tony would push the team hard to make it harder for the girls to catch him. He knew they would wait a while so they could have a hair blowing ride to catch up with him. Abby and Maggie had been pushing their horses hard all day with only a short rest at noon and still no sight of Tony, they both started to worry. Tony had pushed on past the normal stopping spot along the trail just for fun. He had started a fire and had the coffee boiled by the time the girls came riding in on two sweating horses. When the girls stepped down, Tony asked what happened to their hair. It seems to be a mess. Tony asked "did you have a nice ride"? Abby and Maggie walked their horses down to get a small drink then came back to camp and pulled the tack and gave the two horses a good rub down. They put each on a picket rope so they could graze along the stream bank and have water. The two-day trip was better now that they had two camping locations along the trail. The men had built a lean-to cover so they could be out of the weather at night. When the three reached the first campsite, the girls were ready for a rest. Tony set about building a fire and tending to the horses. The girls got out the food box and they soon had a meal ready.

About midday the next day they arrived at the store, Jim asked Tony if he had seen the two men who had stopped to pick up a few supplies. They said they were looking for work. "I gave them directions to Ronnie's ranch and told them to ask for Ronnie".

Tony asked, if the girls heard that. Both said "no, why? Jim, we didn't see anyone along the trail during the last two days. What did they look like"?

"Well, they were riding some good-looking horses, looked like thoroughbreds by their size". Mr. Brown added they had saddle guns along with 44 pistols. They picked up two boxes of the 44's for their Henrys and some primers, powder and balls for their pistols. "Another thing, one of them had a hideout gun under his left arm. I think the one with the hideout gun was called Joe. When he leaned over, I got a look at just the butt end of a pistol under his left arm behind his vest".

Abby said, "when we get back, we need to tell Ronnie to keep an eye out for these two men".

"It sounds like they are riding too good of a horse to be ranch hands looking for work," Jim said.

The girls asked, Mr. Brown for some catalogs, they wanted to spend some money.

Abby asked Mr. Brown to send a message to Carson City and get a preacher heading this way. "When you hear back could you send someone to let us know when he will be here. We will pay to have the things we are ordering today delivered out to the ranch". They sat down and started going through the books and taking notes. Tony came over and said that he needed to start back if he was going to make the first campground by sundown.

With the ranch supplies loaded, the girls told Tony to just head home with the wagon.

"We will see you at the campsite by dark", Abby said. "We are spending money and do not need your help to do so". Maggie went over to Tony and gave him a little kiss and sent him on his way. As Tony was walking out the door he turned and said, "keep an eye out for the two men Jim told us about, and don't stay too long, it's a long ride. You will mess up your hair if you wait too long".

With a message sent for a circuit preacher and a lot of girl things ordered, the girls were ready to go. Both were looking forward to a fast ride to catch up to Tony.

Stepping up into the saddle, Maggie said "Tony is going to be a little mad at us for not getting started sooner". Leaving the store, the two horses were nose to nose in a hard run. After a few miles they dropped down to a hard trot for a bit, then back to a canter. After a couple of hours of riding hard, the girls stopped to let the horses get a drink and eat some grass along the stream as they worked on a cold biscuit, after a half hour they headed on to the campsite to meet Tony. They were making up time but it would be close if they made it to the campsite by dark. Both girls were good riders, and the horses were in great shape, so they could be pushed hard for the next few hours.

Tony was pulling out of a wash and the front wheel hit a rock with a jerk. He lurched forward in the wagon seat. That's when he felt the whip of a bullet pass by his head. He then heard the rifle report. Ducking down in the seat he slapped the reins down on the horses' rumps and they were off at a hard run. Looking back, Tony could see two men firing from behind some trees. Bullets were hitting the back side of the wagon seat that he was hiding behind as he raced for cover of the trees at the campsite.

With the campsite just ahead now, he knew when he reached it he would have some cover. Reaching the trees, Tony pulled the team to a stop, jumped off the wagon and pulling out his Henry. He started to return fire. He fired six quick shots and stopped. Whoever was shooting at him might think he had a Spencer rifle. It worked. As he was feeding the six shells back into the rifle he saw the men mount and start toward him running hard, thinking his rifle was empty.

His Henry was reloaded now with all fifteen rounds. Moving to a new position, he was starting to return fire at the two men. Then he heard shots coming from further down the road behind the men. Looking up, he saw Abby and Maggie firing at the men with their horses at a dead run.

Abby and Maggie had heard the shooting from about a mile out from the campsite. Pulling their rifles, levering a shell into the chamber, they were ready. Both girls were leaning forward in the saddle, taking the reins in their left hand, using their legs to guide their horses and smooth out the ride helping to aim their rifles. They came in at a full gallop, both rifles were talking. With 44 bullets now coming from two directions Joe and Bob turned back into the trees covering the hills, but not before Joe was hit by the girls. Maggie pulled her horse to a sliding stop and jumped off to see if Tony was ok. Abby asked Tony.

"What was that about"? Tony said, "I was just pulling out of the wash back down the road a bit when a bullet went past my head. If it had not been for that rock bouncing the wagon I would have been killed. I keep telling myself I am going to get a team down here and pull that rock out of the way. I am never going to move it now. That is what saved my life".

Abby said. "We need to get Ronnie and start tracking these two. I wonder who they were". Maggie was talking to Tony about what could have caused someone to shoot at him. Tony used Maggie's horse to ride back to the last place the men had been seen. When he got to the little draw they had rode into, Tony found some blood on the ground. "So, one of them is wounded". Walking along their tracks he could tell that the horses were large with a long stride, they could be thoroughbreds and one had a special bar shoe on the right rear.

Riding back to the campsite, Tony found a fire going and some dinner being cooked. The girls asked if he thought they should push on all night to get back to the ranch earlier so they could warn Ronnie about the shooting. "No, let's just keep watch tonight and hit the trail early. Why don't you cook some extra so we can just get up and start early? Those must be the men Jim was talking about," Tony said.

Everyone was up early. The sun was still behind the hills, just beginning to show some light. The wagon was loaded and horses saddled. They started back to the ranch. They would stop at the Applegate ranch to inform them to keep an eye out for the two men. They all knew that Ronnie was going to ride over to see Sam about hauling equipment after he and Sean got back from the future mine site, but they all figured he would have headed back to the ranch by the time they get there.

Dandy loaded with my HENRY RIFLE ready to hit the trail.

Chapter 2 **The Jail Break**

Bob Stanton and Joe Harding were to have their day in court today. They were facing many charges like cattle rustling, altering brands, stealing horse, just to name a few. Sheriff Johnson had been called out of the office on a shooting, leaving his deputy in charge of getting the two men to court.

When the deputy went in to get the two men out of their cell, Harding was hanging by a bed sheet. The deputy unlocked the cell door and ordered Bob Stanton to move back to the far side of the cell so he could enter. When he started to cut Harding down, Joe grabbed his gun and shot him. Joe removed the deputy's gun belt, swinging it around his waist. Grabbing the other end, he buckled the belt and slipped the pistol back into the holster.

"Let's go Bob. We need to go to court like Sheriff Johnson said, but let's just steal the best horses we can find at the courthouse hitching rail".

Having just broke out of jail, and stealing a couple of horses by the courthouse, they headed north out of town. After swimming the river they turned back east, heading into the foothills. The horses they stole were good ones, each having a Henry rifle in the scabbard. Joe and Bob were still mad over losing their gambling house and being put in jail by Ronnie Campbell.

First they needed some money and three more pistols. They rode back south to pick up a trail leading over the Sierras to Nevada. Bob had picked up that Ronnie had a ranch in the eastern part of Nevada. They felt that Sacramento was not a good place for them to hang around. Sheriff Johnson would start looking hard for them.

Joe Harding had shot the guard during the jail break, so the sheriff will be on their trail as soon as he picks it up. Skirting the low hills along the Sierras, they came to a trading post along the river, waiting for an hour or until they felt the time being right to rob it.

Pulling out their rifles, they both walked into the trading post and demanded all of the money, loading up on supplies. They started out to rob the store but when the owner pulled a pistol from under the counter, both men shot him at the same time. Reaching down, Bob picked up the pistol and walked behind the counter, getting what cash he could find. Joe picked two other pistols from the gun case, four boxes of 44 balls, 1 pounds of black powder and a box of primers. Bob and Joe turned and walked out the door to their horses and rode off.

Bob turned back the way they had come, hoping to lose their trail among the other traffic going north and south. After a few miles bob found a dry creek bed leading to the southeast, they tied flour sacks over their horse's hoofs. Bob had picked up the sacks behind the counter after they shot the owner. After a mile or so Joe removed the flour sacks, storing them in his saddle bags, we may need them later. Now they were riding back into the hills for a while, leaving no sign of hoof prints for anyone to follow. This trick had worked before, so they figured no one could find their tracks now.

The robbery had got them two hundred dollars and both now had two 44 Colt pistols each and plenty of powder and balls. Back on the trail heading southeast with some money in their pockets, they felt good.

Bob said, "Now we have some road money. Let's go after Mr. Campbell. I think his ranch is in Eastern Nevada. After shooting Sheriff Johnson's guard, we had better make tracks to Salt Lake City".

Joe said, "Look, Bob. We have not had much luck with Ronnie Campbell, and what luck we have had is bad. Let's just head to Salt Lake City".

"OK Joe, after we kill Ronnie and some of his men we will head that way. He needs to pay and pay he will".

After riding southeast for a few hours they picked up the trail over the pass leading to Carson City. So far things have gone very smooth. They felt sure that no one could pick up their trail when they used the flour sacks on their horses' hoofs. After picking up the Old

Pony Express Trail over the Sierras they started up over the mountain. It was getting late in the day when Joe said,

"we need to find a campsite. It will take a couple of days to reach Carson City so let's save our horses".

Harding turned to Stanton and told him about the barred shoe on his horse. He had seen it when he tied the bags on the hoofs after the robbery.

Stanton said, "not to worry, our trail is gone. No one would ever pick it up, the flour sacks never fail".

With Carson City behind them and keeping to the Old Pony Express Trail, they would keep heading east at a slower pace to give the horses plenty of rest. At Carson City they had picked up some oats to add a little extra strength to their horses. The trail east would be safe now and staying on the trail their tracks would be covered by other riders. They were also riding single file with Bob Stanton leading with Joe Harding following to help to cover the tracks left by the barred shoe on Bob's horse.

The two men felt that when they got beyond Carson City without any problems they would be in the clear. Sheriff Johnson should be back in Sacramento by now wondering what happened to them. Using those sacks was a slick way to lose the law. Moving along the trail, taking water at some of the old Pony Express stations along the way, no one had paid much attention to them. They were just other travelers heading east.

They rode past Spring Creek Station at night and camped just off the trail with no fire, not wanting anyone to see them in the area. They would turn a little south at a split in the trail sometime in the morning and head to Jim Brown's store that they had been told about. They felt that they could use a hot meal and needed some supplies along with some more grain for the horses.

Jim Brown greeted them when they came in the door. Stanton asked about getting a meal and told Jim what supplies they would need.

Jim told them to sit down, the cook would be out and take their order in a minute. "I will get your supplies ready and you can pay when you finish eating". Jim asked about the conditions on the trail coming from the west. Was there any Indian trouble? Bob Stanton told him that all was quiet. They had had no problems along the way.

"Mr. Brown, do you know of any ranch in the area that we might ask for a job? We are getting a little low on traveling money". Jim told them about the two ranches one was Sam and Beth Applegate and the other one farther north was owned by Ronnie and Abby Campbell. He used to ride for the Pony Express until about the time they shut it down, "I think he quit just in time".

Both Bob Stanton and Joe Harding thanked Jim and paid their bill and went out and climbed aboard and headed north. Thanks to Mr. Brown, they knew how to get to the ranch. Mr. Campbell is never going to know what hit him. "He should have left us well enough alone," Bob was telling Joe as they rode along the wagon road heading for the ranch. "Look, Bob, I still feel that we should just go on to Salt Lake and leave him alone". Bob said, "we need to get off the road now, so we won't leave any tracks".

Skirting along beside the hills, they would ride north and find a spot to camp for a few days and keep out of sight. After sleeping late the next day, Joe went to the point of the little draw that overlooked the flats. He was almost too late to see the wagon drive by, with two women riding beside it and a man driving. Joe was not much in favor of shooting any women but he was sure the man driving was going to be dead when they returned.

Bob had gone out and found the perfect location to make the ambush. When the wagon climbs out of the draw they would have a perfect shot at the driver. After waiting a couple of days under some trees they could see the wagon coming and the driver is all alone in the wagon. Joe and Bob waited until the wagon was in the draw before they pulled their rifles and waited. The team came out of the wash and the driver was just sitting there. Joe was going to make the shot he was the better shot of the two men.

Pulling back on the trigger, the Henry fired and when Joe levered the second round into the chamber the wagon was moving out as fast as the horses could run. Both men snapped another shot at the fleeing wagon, Harding and Stanton kept firing from behind the line of trees. After the wagon reached the trees, the driver fired six times, knocking some bark off the trees close to them. Then a pause came. Bob said to mount up. "He is out of shells. Let's ride in and kill this guy". As they spurred their horses after the wagon, they both started shooting as they came on in at a dead run.

From behind them they heard a rifle bark. Now they were being fired on from both sides, with bullets flying by them like angry bees.

Joe said, "damn it I'm hit" so they pulled back into a draw behind some trees. With their plan having gone bad, they rode up the draw and into the mountains away from the road. "We need to cover our trail so we can find a hideout. Then I will check your arm," Bob said.

Bob pulled up to let his horse blow after the climb to the top of a ridge. Joe joined him and they talked over what was going to be the best way to lose their trail. "I think we best drop over this ridge and come out back down toward the store. Then we will cross over the wagon road and work back into the mountains and find a good spot to lay up for a day or so. I will be able to patch up your arm and rest our horses a bit. We are going to need to replace the horses and soon, that rear hoof can start causing problems at any time and these horses are tired".

*

After the escape Sheriff Johnson picked up the tracks of the two men leading back into the foothills northeast of town. The tracks showed one of the horses has a special barred shoe on the right rear hoof. When he started tracking the two men he had one of his deputies go back and get his pack horse and assemble enough supplies for two weeks on the trail.

After picking up the trail, the sheriff turned back to meet his deputy just outside of Sacramento. Sheriff Johnson turned back to the tracks he had picked up of the two killers trail heading southeast. He planned on being on the trail for a long time. Both men had a lot of knowledge on how to hide their trail so he would need to take some time to work it out. What Harding and Stanton didn't know was that Sheriff Johnson had also been a scout for the army for ten years and was a skilled tracker himself so this may get interesting.

Sheriff Johnson stopped and talked to a man heading into Sacramento who told him about a shooting and robbery about twenty miles down the road. He said to himself, "they needed some road money and now they have it". Putting his horse into an extended trot he headed out to check on the shooting. When getting close, he found the tracks leading south and another set heading back north. Sheriff Johnson knew this trick of back tracking and then easing off the trail and losing themselves in the back country.

The sheriff rode onto the trading post that had been robbed, leading his horses up to the hitching post. He started asking questions but could not find out much. The best the wife of the owner could figure is they got some supplies, about two hundred dollars and some pistols along with two hundred rounds of ammunition.

After spending an hour getting as much information as he could, he rode out southeast heading back into the foothills to find the trail to Carson City. Johnson felt the two would be heading east and the best trail was leading into Carson City. The sheriff kept an eye out for the tracks. He was betting they would head east to Carson City. When he reached the Old Pony Express Trail he found their tracks again heading east into the hills. By making the decision to just head to the trail over the Sierras he saved a good day trying to follow their trail.

This hunt was still not going to be a short one. Both men would hang when he returned them to Sacramento, or he would shoot them for resisting arrest. The weather had been good so even with the lead the two men had on him he found a track or two ever so often.

Sheriff Johnson had a feeling that they were going after Ronnie Campbell for putting them in jail. He would send a wire ahead to Mr. Brown's Store when he reached Carson City, letting them know about Stanton & Harding's escape from jail and were heading in his direction and be sure to warn Ronnie.

Jim Brown received the telegram from a Sheriff Johnson a few days after Abby, Tony and Maggie had been in to pick up supplies for the ranch. Jim would wait and see if anyone came by heading out to Ronnie's ranch who could deliver this telegram, he just didn't have anyone who could deliver this message.

Sheriff Johnson was riding as hard as he dared, having only his one horse and his packhorse. He should have had his deputy bring him an extra riding horse so he could trade off every day. Sheriff Johnson stayed on the Old Pony Express Trail as he rode, he would be passed from time to time by a Pony Express Riders heading east or west. They never stopped to talk.

It was nice to have the stations along the trail so he could get water for his horse and ask the stage station managers if the two men had passed this way. With the horse traffic along the trail it was hard to find any tracks left by the men. Many of the managers had seen the men but he was told they had only watered their horses and moved on riding east.

Sheriff Johnson had not found anyone who knew the location of Ronnie's ranch but was told to turn off after Robert's Creek. He should find a trail leading a little northeast. That should lead him to Jim Brown's store. He would know the location of Ronnie's ranch.

Jim Brown was behind the counter when Sheriff Johnson pushed open the door and walked in. "Are you Mr. Brown"? he asked. "I am Sheriff Johnson. Did you get my wire"? Jim told him yes but that no one had came in so he could send the message.

Then he told him that the ranch was another two day ride northeast along the mountains. Being late in the day he asked if he could stable his horses and get them some grain. "Yah, just take them around back to the stable and come back and I will have some dinner on the table for you. I will have a fresh pot of coffee ready when you get back in".

After stabling the two horses he walked back inside. Setting down his rifle and saddle bags, he eased up to the table and started working on a steak and the trimmings. The coffee was black and hot, just to his liking. Jim came over and asked about the men he was looking for, getting a little history of how Ronnie had made a case about their stealing of cattle and running a crooked gambling house.

Jim was listening to how they had killed his deputy in their escape and how he had tracked them to the Sierras, when he got their direction set. He just started to push east along the Old Pony Express Trail. "I should be close behind them now. When I figured out where they were going I started to push hard, not bothering to take time tracking them".

Jim told him to come in and eat in the morning. Food would be ready before sun up so he could get an early start. Sheriff Johnson loaded his supplies in the saddle bags and paid. He asked if he could sleep in the barn. "That's all I have my two rooms are full, so go ahead".

Breakfast under his belt, he was off early, heading north along the wagon road. About noon he found the tracks of Stanton and Harding along the side of the road heading north also. I was now getting close "I just hope it's not too late". Later that day, riding out of a dry wash, he could see that the driver of the wagon had kicked up the horses into a hard run. After a short ride he could see tracks leading out from the timber falling in behind the wagon. "Yes, the horse with the barred shoe".

Riding along the trail he could see a couple of shell castings lying on the ground. Then two other horses came riding up from behind and more shell castings. Whoever came up from behind was firing at Stanton and Harding. Then he could see by the tracks that the two men had turned off into a draw leading off the wagon road to the left and the other tracks going on up the road at a gallop.

On up the road, he found where the wagon had stopped and the driver was shooting at the two men. "It looked like they found more than they had expected". Looking around the campsite he could see that the two riders were women. "Damn, they must be some tough women".

Early in the morning he was on the trail heading for the ranch, hoping he would be ahead of the men hunting Ronnie. His horse was starting to stumble, it's been a long hard ride from Sacramento. He would need to get fresh mounts soon or he would need to hole up and give his horse a few days rest.

Riding late, he came upon a ranch house setting back in some trees. Smoke was coming from the chimney and horses were in the corral, so someone was home. Riding up, he called out to the house. He was greeted by Beth Applegate and Little John. After finding out who he was they asked him in to eat and Little John put his horses in the corral and gave them some hay and grain.

Coming back in, Little John said to the sheriff, "Your horses are plumb wore out".

"Yah, they are. Could I make a trade for a couple horses from you? I would either pay or rent them".

"Na," Little John said. "We know about the two men. They shot at Tony on his way back from Mr. Brown's store a few days ago. Tony and the girls got them in a cross fire and wounded one of them".

"Ronnie, had rode over to talk to Dad about some freighting work, Ronnie had Dad drive our team and wagon to his ranch to get the wagons ready to make some trips. Ronnie then rode in to meet Tony and the girls coming back from the store. We should see Ronnie heading this way to pick up their trail by the morning. We have his horse Diamond getting some rest also. Ronnie is going to bring one of his Indians along to help track the two men".

*

Ronnie had ridden over to Sam's ranch to talk to him about hauling some lumber over from Genoa, a small settlement at the base of the Sierras just upriver from Carson City. Sam said he only had the one wagon and would need at least three to bring back the supplies he was ordering. Ronnie said, "I will have Mr. O'Reilly go with you, using Abby's freight wagon".

"After you get back with the lumber for the houses I will give you the money to purchase the extra teams and wagons in Sacramento. I have sent a letter to Juan to find the wagons and extra teams you will need for the trip back with the mining equipment from San Francisco. Now the question is, do you want to operate the freight business if I front the money"?

Sam said, "Yes. I should say hell yes. That would be a good deal for me. This country is growing and I would like to be a part of the growth. When do you want me to get started for Genoa"?

Ronnie said "let's get things ready to go in a week, that way we can have some time to make repairs. Bring your team and wagon up early in the week and we will go over all of your equipment".

Sam and Beth had been talking over the operation and what part Little John would need to play. Sam gave him half interest in the ranch if he wanted to run the operation when Sam was hauling equipment for Ronnie's mining operation. Little John said he was ready to take on the job for his Dad and Mom. Little John asked Sam if they could make the trips to Genoa and San Francisco and get back before the snow hits. Sam said he felt it would be close, but he would go, ready to sit out a bad snow storm if need be.

With business finished with Sam, Ronnie decided to ride toward town to meet Tony and the girls. He then would ride back to the ranch with them. He would camp out alone tonight and would meet them some time in the morning.

The next day Ronnie met them heading home, pushing the team hard. "What is going on, Tony? Why are you in such a hurry to get home"? Tony stopped the team and the girls got down and they told Ronnie about the shooting. Tony told him about the girls getting a bullet into one of them. Ronnie asked if they felt he was hit hard. None felt he was hit hard. They figured that it was just a flesh wound.

On the way back to the ranch Ronnie was making some plans. He would get one of the Indians to do the tracking for him. He would leave Diamond at Sam's ranch and ride the wagon back to the ranch to give Diamond a rest. Getting to Sam's ranch, he turned Diamond out in one of the corrals and asked Little Jon if he would give him some grain. Little Jon told Ronnie that Sam had headed for the ranch to get started on the wagons so they could be gone in the next few days. Walking up to the house, Ronnie told Beth to keep an eye open for two riders, and don't take any chances with those two.

"Little John, you keep a sharp eye out, watch your horses. If they look at anything you cannot see get out of there fast. They are going to need some fresh horses soon. If I were you I would go out and drive in all of the horses to the ranch yard corrals".

When Ronnie got back to his ranch, Sam had the wagons pulled into a good spot to remove the wheels and grease everything, making ready for the start of some long trips. All of the horses needed new shoes before the trip so Tony set about trimming and shoeing all of the teams. Sean was working on all of the harnesses for the teams and making other small repairs that could save a loss of weeks on the trail.

At dinner they all talked about the shooting and tried to think who would want to kill Tony. Ronnie laid out the plan. He would take Dandy for the pack horse and ride one of the other horses back down to Sam's ranch to pick up Diamond. Ronnie was sure that Dandy could outlast even Diamond on a long hard ride. He never seems to get tired. Just before dark the men went out on the porch so the girls could clean up. Walking into the yard, Ronnie looked up the river. The Indians were riding into the yard with everything they owned.

White Bird rode over to Ronnie and pointed to a spot along the river back into the trees and he told them that was a good place. With Tony along, they rode over to the new campsite for the Indians. Tony needed to talk to White Bird about going along with Ronnie to help with the tracking of the men who shot at Tony. Tony asked if White Bird could ride out with Ronnie in the morning to be the tracker and he said he could. Abby was on edge all evening thinking about Ronnie going after the men who shot at Tony.

When they went to bed Abby reached over and put her hand on him to see if he was awake. Most of the night they made love and talked about the ranch and who they thought could have tried to kill Tony. They didn't know, but with White Bird tracking they will soon know who it is and hang them if they don't die trying to escape. They will pick up their trail at the campsite. With White Bird along they will be on their trail in a day or so. Anyway, one of them was hit by you girls so that will slow them down some.

"Ronnie, I just don't like you going by yourself having only White Bird along. We don't know him that well and he can't even talk to you".

"Tony has told me how to talk using sign language and some words he knows. We will get along just fine," Ronnie said. Reaching over and pulling Ronnie to her, she asked,

"will you love me again? I am scared".

In the morning White Bird rode over saying he was ready. Tony asked White Bird if he needed anything extra for the trip and he said no. The sun was peaking over the mountains to the east when Ronnie and White Bird rode out of the ranch yard with Dandy and the extra horses.

Just after breakfast Ronnie and White Bird rode into the yard leading two extra horses along with the pack horse Dandy. When Sheriff Johnson walked out onto the porch Ronnie said,

"Well what are you doing out this way"?

"Harding and Stanton broke jail, they killed my deputy and stole the two horses they are riding".

Little John went out and picked out three horses for Johnson, two to ride and one for a pack horse. After a bit they were ready to start after the two men. Johnson had filled in Ronnie about the jail break and the other killings along the way. "Harding and Stanton need to be hung, and when we track them down, I will take them back to Sacramento, and do just that".

30

I hope you enjoy this poem, it is special to me.

THE MAGIC OF THE RIDE

The moon is setting high in
the sky my horse moves away
as the Mochila is placed
I step up, my toe searches for
the stirrup
Now my horses hoofs are
echoing in the night, I feel
The magic of the ride

With a cool night breeze in
my face
The trail is opening before
me, by the light of the moon
How many times, just how
many have ridden this trail
taking me back in time
The magic of the ride

As my horse floats across the
flats
The moon is lifting me into
the past
Has any rider ever felt what I
feel
My horse and I are feeling
The magic of the ride

Our new rider has the mail and
riding down the trail
The moon is aglow casting
shadows along his way
His heart is pounding as he re-
members the riders of the past
He is riding hard and feeling
The magic of the ride

I am up now and feel the night
calm my spirit
Shadows fly by as I canter
down the trail
I slow for the rocks, a shadow
moves across my path
my horse stumbles, but I go on
feeling
The magic of the ride

The last riders appear in the
dark, the mochila is passed
They canter out of sight, the
sound of hoofs are gone
Alone I stand in the glow of
the moon, my ride is done
As they ride to the next ex-
change do they, feel
The magic of the ride

Author & Cowboy Poet Ron Bell

Chapter 3 **Trip to Sacramento**

Juan had picked up a letter from Ronnie asking him to look around and find two freight wagons and two four horse teams to pull them. Ronnie was sending the gold to cover the cost of the wagons. He would also need two drivers along with two helpers and a cook. When pulling over the Sierras the extra men are a must to have to help with blocking the wheels when resting the horses on a hard pull. Juan would ask Juanita if she would want to ride into Sacramento and spend a few days. She would have time to do some shopping while he was looking for wagons and horses.

Juanita's father was doing better but still could not do any work. He just spent most of the days sitting on the porch watching the ranch workers coming and going. Juan had hired a lady to do most of the work taking care of Juanita's father, Don Jose Morales. Little Juan and Hector were running all around the yard playing and making a lot of noise. They now had other kids to play with on the ranch. When Juan and Juanita rode out of the yard both her mother and father, Victoria and Don Jose, were talking about how stupid they had been when Juanita wanted to marry Juan. Look at them now, they were thinking. If they had not gotten married what would have they done, they would have lost everything.

Juan had taken over the ranch operations and over the past few months he had gotten the cattle back and was making plans to start selling the fruit to a man in Sacramento who would then sell it to both Sacramento and San Francisco. That would make the ranch a lot of money. Some of the cattle could be sold this year but most would be a carryover to next year. Juan was looking over the young bulls he had so he could send some over to Ronnie in Nevada. He was thinking that five or six would do and he could have his men drive back bulls from the Nevada ranch.

As Juan and Juanita rode north heading into Sacramento, they got talking about what hotel they wanted to stay in. They had been told by Ronnie and Abby that the Gold Dust Hotel had just got in an extra large brass tub and had hot and cold water at the tub. Ronnie and Abby said they had enjoyed that a lot. As they rode, the idea of a large tub sounded better each mile they went. After checking in and having a nice dinner they retired to their room to see how well they fit in that big tub. Having this free time away from the kids and the ranch, they started to relax and enjoy washing each other. This was just the start of a long night of making love in a grand hotel along the Sacramento River. With the sun coming up they could see the boats on the river after taking some time to enjoy each other they got dressed for the day, going down stairs to find a restaurant. After a short walk they were eating breakfast on a deck overlooking the river.

Juanita said she thought they made a little girl last night, Juan said no way could you tell that soon.

"You just wait and see. I knew the night we made Little Juan". Juanita said she was going to shop for some things for the house today. She would have her purchases sent back to the rancho. As Juan started to head out the door he asked if Juanita had her pistol in her hand bag. He told her he would meet her later and have lunch.

Juan was heading for a wagon builder who had a shop just up the road along the river about a mile from the hotel. Going to the stable, he saddled up his horse for the short ride along the waterfront leading to the wagon shop. Sacramento was doing quite well with mining booming in the foothills not far from town. Each shop was building items for mining or ranching. Many of the shops were forging steel into tools or steel tires for wagons. As he rode along, Juan could smell the strong acid smell from the forging coal that was used to heat the steel white hot to allow the steel to join as one. At many of the shops he could hear the hammer on steel, the soft thud when the hammer hits the hot steel, then the ring of the hammer on anvil to rebound the hammer for its next blow on the white hot steel. After riding along the waterfront for a while he came to the large wagon shop he had been told about.

In a side yard he could see some finished wagons. They were too small for the task he had in mind. The freight wagons he needed would have large wheels with wide steel rims to carry the heavy loads, the wood needed to be strong and be able to last in the harsh sun and heavy wind they would see in Nevada.

Juan rode up to the hitch rail and tied off his horse. Walking into the shop, Juan could smell wood chips and heated metal on wood. He was greeted by the owner of the shop.

"Hi, I am Tom", he said. "Can I help you with anything in particular today young man"?

"Yes I think you may be able to build just what we will need. My partner in Nevada is going to need at least two large freight wagons to bring mining equipment back from San Francisco to eastern Nevada," Juan explained.

Tom reached up and rubbed his chin for a bit then asked Juan to follow him to the back wagon yard to look at one wagon that had been sold but the owner died a few weeks ago. Tom told Juan that the man had died about the time the two men killed the jail guard and stole two horses at the court house. Sheriff Johnson is tracking them now.

Reaching the back yard, he found a large freight wagon. Tom said this wagon was going to haul cow hides south to a small town called Manteca, there is a hide processing plant there.

"Well, Tom, this may just do for a start but I will also need another one but just a little bigger. Can you make the box about six feet longer with the bed a foot wider"? Tom said that would not be any problem but it would take a month to finish it. Juan told Tom that would be ok but no longer because his partner was sending two other wagons this way soon.

Tom asked why don't you have the equipment shipped by boat to our dock and we could load it here? That would save some time. Juan said that would be a great idea. He was sure Ronnie would like that.

"Now Tom, do you know of any draft horses I could purchase to go with the wagons"?

"I do know of a breeder that is north of here about a four day ride in a town called Chico. It's at the edge of the foothills. His name is Gary Gee, his ranch is just a bit east of Chico back in the hills". Tom Chancy turned to Juan and said, "You keep a sharp watch. There is a gang of about ten to fifteen men led by a man named James Barton. They have been involved with many holdups clear up to Oregon. Ask Sheriff Johnson about them-he can fill you in about their bad habits".

Juan asked, "Tom how much money he needed to get started building the second wagon".

"Well, why don't you just come back when it is ready, and you can pay for them both at the same time if you like.

You did say your partner was Ronnie Campbell. Is that right"?

Juan said it was.

"Look you can have all the credit you want in this shop, the two men he helped put in jail had caused a lot of problems for many of the people I know".

Juan pulled out a small bag of gold and said why don't we just weight this out and you keep it until we come back to settle our account.

Tom was quite happy with that part of the deal, not only did he get rid of a wagon for cash, but got a second one to build the same day along with a bag of gold that would cover most of the cost of both wagons. Being in the wagon building business was good this day. Saying thanks to Juan, he turned back into the shop to get started on the new wagon.

Juan started back to the hotel to have lunch with Juanita and send a telegraph message to the breeder of the draft horses to find out how many he had to sell. The sun was getting high and the dust was kicking up from his horse's feet as he rode back down the road along the waterfront. He was feeling just a faint breeze in his face and could smell the river as he rode to the hotel. Just as he got to the hotel, Sheriff Johnson's Deputy Crabtree was riding up the road. Juan said,

"Hi, Deputy. Do you know anything about the Barton Gang"? He told Juan that they had been causing problems to the north of Sacramento, but we have not had any problems in town yet. Juan told him about heading north to pick up some horses in a few days. Deputy Crabtree told him to go well armed and be ready at all times. They seem to know when someone is heading out of town with money.

"Good luck," he said.

Juanita was waiting in the hotel lobby when he walked in. She rose to greet him with a light kiss then moved up close suggesting more if he had a mind to partake. Juan leaned over and whispered that after a light lunch they may retire to talk about the day if she would like. Smiling, she found his hand and turned to lead Juan into the dining room for their lunch. Juan signaled to the desk clerk he wanted to send two telegrams. After filling out the telegrams he was sending to Ronnie and Gary Gee, Juan set back and started to read the menu, thinking of things to come.

Yes, this book is not about the Pony Express, but it does start after Ronnie is building his life, and the Pony Express is a large part of my life. This Mochila shows the support that we have from our community members and businesses. Squeeze In is a great place to eat, look for them in Reno NV and Las Vegas NV.

This Mochila has 1100 pieces of mail that will be carried 1,966 miles, then sent by US Mail to people like you. The names you see are riders who have already ridden to this point. Every rider signs his or her name.

Chapter 4 **On the Run**

Bob Stanton was leading, trying to find a trail down off the mountain so they could cross over the trail and hope to lose anyone who had a mind to track them. Joe Harding was still bleeding and needed some time to heal up a bit. After the shooting they had just tied a bandage to his arm and rode on. Bob came to a trail that looked like it was used by wild mustangs and other game leading back down to the trickle of water in the valley.

When they reached the bottom, Bob pulled out the bags they had used after the holdup in California. Placing them on their horses' hoofs, they rode on across the valley floor heading back south for a bit. Bob found what they were looking for, a trail leading up a draw. It also was another wild horse trail. When they stopped at Mr. Brown's store they had been told of a rancher closer to the store that was raising cattle and horses. Horses is what they needed now, their two were about done in and would not make any long run.

Bob had in mind to get up on the spine of the mountain and head north until they found the ranch. They will steal new mounts and then find a spot to hide. After about a mile Bob stopped and removed the bags from the horses' hoofs and replaced them in the saddlebags. These bags are done. We will use them to start our fire when we find a campsite.

Joe said, "I got to get the bleeding stopped soon".

"OK" Bob said, "I will find a spot to hole up soon. Then I can work on your arm".

"Look, Bob, if you would have just left that damn Ronnie Campbell alone we could have been well on our way to Salt Lake City by now. I now have a hole in my arm and who knows how many men we have on our trail by now. You know that damn sheriff will not take killing his deputy very well, he will be looking for us even now".

"Quit your whining. No one will find our trail".

Bob came up over the ridge and stopped. Turning to Joe, he said, "We have just found a little spot of heaven". The two men sat looking at a small valley with water and plenty of grass. They moved down into the valley to find a campsite. Turning out the horses on a picket line, they set up camp and started to heat some water to clean the bullet hole in Joe's arm. Taking off his shirt they could see that the bullet went all the way through so all they needed was to clean the wound and pack it with some moss after getting the two holes stitched up. The high elevation will help a wound heal faster than in the lowlands Bob had cleaned the two holes with some whiskey before and after his sewing job.

Bob told Joe to catch some rest. He would scout around some to see what he could find. After walking for a mile or so, he found a good spot to look out to see into the lower valleys. They needed to get some new horses and fast.

When Joe woke up he went out to check on the horses. He could see that they had plenty of grass and could reach the water. As he walked up he could see some trout just holding position behind some rocks in the stream. As he watched, the fish eased out to catch a bug coming down the stream then slid back behind the rock. Easing back from the water Joe pulled out his knife. He cut a willow stick and then removed all of the branches except one on the very bottom. This he would use as a gaff to pull the fish out of the water. Working very carefully, he cut the last branch off, leaving three inches of it connected to the main branch. Using his knife, he cut a point on this branch to hook the fish with when he pulled it back to him. This was going to be a problem because of his bad arm, but they needed some food to eat. Staying low in the grass along the bank, he eased up until he was a little behind the trout. Reaching out with the branch slowly, keeping the gaff behind the fish, he was able to get it past the first fish. Lowering the branch over the top of the first fish, then lowering it until the branch was just under the water, he was ready. Joe pulled as hard as he could. He felt the gaff hit the fish, the point entering its side. He pulled the fish up onto the bank beside him. Looking out over the grass he could see the other fish were still in the same spot. If he could repeat this a few more times they would have dinner.

When Bob came back Joe had the fish on a willow stick cooking over a small fire. "Well what do we have here? Are they ready to eat"? Bob asked. "Have at it, they should be done. We don't have any salt but they will have to do". "What did you find"? "Well I think I found the horse ranch. There are horses not too far down off this ridge in an upper canyon. We can ease down and take a look see. I think there are mares with a stallion in this small herd". After eating the fish and banking the fire, they turned in to get some rest and get ready for the next day trying to steal some new horses.

*

Sheriff Johnson had been sitting on the porch when Ronnie rode in with White Bird.

"Well, son, ready to put Harding and Stanton back in jail to hang this time"? Ronnie said, "I have plenty of rope, we may just need to hang them sooner".

"Well son, why don't just catch them and then we will see what we need to do with them". Little John was pulling stock and getting Diamond ready for Ronnie as they talked. Switching saddles to the fresh horses, they were ready to ride out when Beth came out with some road grub.

"This should hold you for a couple of days," she said.

Sheriff Johnson told Ronnie to raise his right hand along with White Bird and he made them both deputies. Now they could shoot those men legally. Turning south to hunt the trail, Sheriff Johnson told Ronnie he would lead them to the start of the trail leading up the draw that would lead up to the ridge. As the day wore on they were getting closer to the campsite and the location of the shooting. Just as the sun was going down they reached the starting point of the hunt.

White Bird set about making the campfire and putting on the coffee. Ronnie got out the food that Beth had sent along. After eating they brought the horses in close so they could keep watch as they slept. Dawn was still a bit away. Ronnie lay watching the horses to see if anything was around. Seeing that they were alone, he got up and got the fire going again and put on the coffee.

White Bird slipped out of his bedroll and was gone with no sound. If Ronnie had not seen him leave he would have never known he was gone. Sheriff Johnson was getting up and looking for some coffee and was glad it was made and waiting. The two men ate some of the meat and a biscuit Beth had sent then started to get the horses ready to travel. White Bird came in and told Ronnie about the trail the two men headed up and pointed to Diamond's right hind hoof and made a mark showing that one horse had a special shoe. Sheriff Johnson told Ronnie that one of the horses had a bar shoe on its right hind hoof.

Ronnie handed White Bird some food and they stepped aboard with White Bird leading. After a short canter to the trail he slowed down, following it at a trot, heading up the mountain. When he came to a bush alongside of the trail he stopped and showed Ronnie that one of the men had been shot in the right arm, some blood was still on one of the leaves. After a long climb they topped out on the ridge.

White Bird trotted along the ridge for about a mile. He found the trail leading down the back side of the mountain. After reaching the bottom, the trail led to the stream, at the stream the tracks just stopped. White Bird got down and walked a circle looking for the trail. After a bit he pointed to the other side of the valley and walking back, he picked up a front hoof on his horse and used a hanky to cover the hoof to show them what he had found. Walking slowly he could see just a faint mark now and then. Then the tracks turned south. He got back on his horse and led off at a trot.

After about a mile he found the wild mustang trail and started up, heading for the ridge. After a few miles he stopped and showed them the fresh tracks after they had removed the hoof covers. White Bird moved off at a trot, heading north back into the Rubies. Later that day they found the overnight campsite. They stopped and made camp at the same location. White Bird changed horses and told Ronnie he would scout the trail until dark. From the campsite it looked like they were about two days ahead of them.

As dark settled into the little valley, coffee was on and the last of the food Beth had sent was set out on a log. Ronnie and Sheriff Johnson sat back and waited for White Bird to return. White Bird came in and stripped the saddle from his horse and went out to put him on a picket line for the night. Returning, he started telling about what he had seen before dark. Using a stick he made a mark on the ground showing the location where Bob Stanton had seen the horses in a valley below. Then he told about the tracks leading down into the valley. He said, "they steal horses".

Ronnie asked him to get some food as they talked about what else he was able to tell by the tracks. Using sign language, he was able to tell them that the two had went down into the valley to steal the horses, but I think they will come back up and cross over to the other side of the mountain. I think they want to get away fast. Using a stick, he marked on the ground showing the valley and the location he thought they would come back up and cross over the ridge.

Ronnie turned to Sheriff Johnson and said he thought they have just gained a day on them. By the time they get the horses and make the climb back to the top it will cost them a day.

*

Bob and Joe worked their way down into the valley to steal two fresh horses. Reaching the bottom, they started moving down to where they had seen the horse herd. Keeping back in the trees, they eased along, hoping not to spook the herd. After a short ride they found them grazing in a small draw.

Bob told Joe, "let's split up a little and move in to block the opening so we can get a good look and pick out the two we want to take".

Riding up from both sides, they had them bunched into a small area. The stallion started to make a fuss, but they talked low and moved up closer, moving slow. Joe could not use a rope with his bad arm so making the catch would be up to Bob. He worked up close to two of the mares. Both had shoes on so they must be used around the ranch. Bob was able to get a rope on both without any problem. Moving them back into the trees, they changed saddles and started back up to the ridge.

Joe was following Bob up a game trail heading for the top and said,

"we need to get out of this country fast and head for Salt Lake and leave that damn Ronnie Campbell alone". Bob had also decided that was going to be the best thing. They could come back another time and finish the job of killing Ronnie.

*

Little John had some cattle to move so he headed back into the hills to pick some of his extra horses only to find two new geldings and two of his mares missing. Little John started to follow the tracks up into the mountains, figuring that it must have been the two men who had shot at Tony. Not knowing if Ronnie was on the trail or not he would track them and see if he could get his horses back. Working his way along the trail up through the trees with the sun getting high, he figured it to be about noon. He would need to rest his horse at the first water he found.

Riding along the spine of the ridge, he kept on the lookout for a spring. He had never ridden in this part of the mountains. The tracks of the men dropped off of the ridge heading down the back side. After a short ride he came to a spring hidden by a stand of trees. Easing into the trees he found the spring and it showed that the two men had also stopped to water their horses earlier in the day.

After getting a drink, Little John started to scout for the tracks leaving the spring. After searching for about an hour and not finding any he decided he would have to head back to the ranch. Turning back up the trail leading back to the ridge, he would have to hope Ronnie was on their trail. About the time he was getting ready to start the ride back down into the valley he saw a flash of light. It could be off a rifle barrel. He moved back into the trees to wait and see who was coming along the trail, hoping it was Ronnie and Sheriff Johnson.

After a bit, Little John could see a horse and rider came into view followed by two other men. As the first rider got closer he rode behind some trees and was gone. Little John was about ready to ride out into the open when he heard a noise behind him. It was White Bird with a rifle pointed at him. Little John called to Ronnie to say he was being covered by White Bird. Riding out into the open followed by a smiling White Bird, Ronnie said, "that will teach you to be sneaking around in the mountains".

Little John told about the two horses being stolen and the gildings that were left in their place. Ronnie asked him when he thought they were stolen. He figured by the tracks just a day or so ago. He then told of the spring and not finding any tracks leaving the spring. Ronnie said why don't you ride back to the spring and we will spend the night and you can start home in the morning.

"Little John when you go home pickup the two gildings and take them back to the ranch, Sheriff Johnson will need to take them back to Sacramento with him".

By the time they reached the spring it was getting late. Little John started the fire and Ronnie got the coffee pot on to boil. Ronnie started to cook some dinner. After getting the horses settled, Sheriff

Johnson returned but White Bird was working the trail before it got too dark to see. After a little bit White Bird returned saying he had found their tracks. When the coffee was gone Ronnie said,

"in the morning we are going to be on the trail that White Bird found".

With light just showing, White Bird eased out of camp to work the trail. After a bit he came back smiling. He asked Ronnie to follow him out of camp. After a short walk he pointed to a boot heal print by a tree. Picking up some pine needles, he sprinkled them over the tracks. Heading back to camp they saddled up and said good bye to Little John and started down the mountain with White Bird leading the way. Ronnie turned to Sheriff Johnson and said,

"do you think we would be on their trail without him"? They both just smiled and followed their tracker down off the mountain, heading northeast.

Chapter 5 **Gun Fight at The River**

Bob Stanton was letting his horse drink from a small spring in the foothills on the east side of the Ruby Mountains when he saw a flash high up in the mountains. When he turned to get a better look, it was gone. Turning to Joe he said,

"We have a problem, we have someone on our trail, I just saw a flash high up in the timber where we just came from".

"I told you to leave that damn kid alone. Now we are going to have a gun fight on our hands. With these horses we can't outrun anyone". Turning north, Bob said we will make a stand at the Humboldt River just north of here. The only chance we will have is to shoot their horses and leave them afoot.

*

Ronnie rode up beside White Bird and asked him how far ahead they were. White Bird pointed to the east and raised his arm to what would be mid-day. They reached the spring and it was almost full of water again. Ronnie watered their horses and watched the water start to come back into the pool. Sheriff Johnson was also watching the water.

"Yes, I do think we are only hours behind them now. What do you think about turning White Bird loose and sending him back to the ranch? I think we will be able to follow the trail now". After talking a bit, Ronnie tied the extra horse's halter rope to the horse's tail in front. With the horse's lead rope in hand, White Bird headed home.

Ronnie was mounted on Diamond and Sheriff Johnson was well mounted also. Ronnie led off following the trail north. Ronnie turned and told Sheriff Johnson that the Humboldt River was about six hours ride from here. We should be able to make it before dark today. Johnson turned and asked Ronnie if he thought that Stanton or Harding knew they were on their trail. Ronnie said there was no way of knowing but when we get close to the river we need to keep a sharp eye. They may set a trap for us.

Ronnie had Diamond at a good ground covering lope with Dandy by his side. Sheriff Johnson was dropping back some each mile they rode. Diamond and Dandy were hard to keep up with. Ronnie wanted to have some daylight left to scout around when he got close to the river. He didn't want to ride into an ambush, Stanton and Harding were both trail wise. Each mile Ronnie would drop back to a trot to give his horses a breather. Both horses could run miles at a time and recover quickly by just going back to a trot.

*

Bob told Joe when he got close to the river, he would find some cover and let them ride past him. Then Joe could kill the first horse as they reach the river and then he would kill the other one. Bob and Joe had reached some trees and brush about a quarter mile from the river, riding close. Bob slid off with his rifle and Joe rode on to the river without stopping. Whoever was following the trail would never know he was not on the horse in time to make a difference in this gun fight.

Joe reached the bank with the two horses and swam them over to the other side so he could make his stand. The sun was starting to set so Joe put the horses on picket lines so anyone who came up to the river would think they had made camp. Joe got the fire started and put on coffee to boil. After they kill whoever is following, they could lay up and relax for the night. Joe moved up river and a little east of the campsite to make his stand. He had been hit in the right arm so he could hold the rifle better using his left side to shoot from. Now all they needed was to have whoever's tracking them ride in following the tracks and this gun fight would be finished in a few minutes.

*

Ronnie was ahead of Sheriff Johnson by about a mile now as he got close to the river. Easing through the trees he would stop and look, then move forward slowly. He could see the two horses on the other side of the river eating along the bank and some smoke coming from a campfire. Just as he cleared the last tree he felt the bullet hit Diamond and heard two more shots thud into Dandy. Ronnie got Diamond turned back behind the trees for protection from the other side of the river. Looking back the way he had come, he could see another man holding a rifle trying to get a shot at him. Diamond was down, Ronnie had to get Dandy to lie down. This would be his only chance. He had ridden into a trap and he was on the losing side of it. With the two horses on the ground, all he could do was use the horses for his protection. The second man was working his way through the trees toward him and had not given him a target.

*

Sheriff Johnson had heard the shooting about the time he made it to the first trees along the river. Ronnie had had a good lead on him. This may work out ok, he was thinking. He eased into the trees and up ahead he could see a man with a rifle working his way toward the river, they have Ronnie in a cross fire. He eased off his horse and moved toward the man who was trying to get a clear shot at Ronnie. Working from tree to tree he was getting closer to the man, just a few feet more and he could get a good shot at Ronnie.

He could see the man raise the rifle getting ready to shoot. Now was the time. Taking the slack out of the trigger he felt the rifle jump and could see dust fly up on the shooter's back. He was trying to turn when he heard another shot coming from ahead of the shooter. Dropping his gun the shooter just lay there. Sheriff Johnson moved forward to see if he was dead. As he moved forward, he could see Ronnie with both horses on the ground. That was not a good sight. Turning the dead man over he could see it was Bob Stanton. Well, that would save him from hanging him later.

Sheriff Johnson walked back to his horse and rode up to see how bad things were with Ronnie and his horses. When he got up to Ronnie, they heard Joe Harding ride off at a gallop, heading northeast. Ronnie was getting Dandy up to check him over to see how bad he had been hit by the two bullets. Stripping off the pack saddle he found the two bullets had hit the pack frame causing no damage to Dandy.

He knew Diamond had been hit but could not tell how bad until they got the gear stripped off him and see if he could get up on his own. Undoing the cinch, he pulled the saddle loose and started feeling around to find the bullet hole. When they let Diamond up he was able to get to his feet. Ronnie could see the blood coming from his mane. The bullet had taken a chunk of meat out of the top of his neck. Diamond would not be able to move around too much for a few days.

Ronnie put the saddle on Dandy and was making ready to go after Joe Harding. He would cross the river and then track him until either Joe's horse dropped or Dandy did. Dandy was not as fast as Diamond but Ronnie felt this horse could run all day or night if needed. He was built strong and had a barrel chest. Ronnie had never seen Dandy tired, he had just not ever needed him to ride after getting Diamond. After climbing out of the river Ronnie started out at a ground eating canter. After a few miles Ronnie leaned over and talked to Dandy, telling him to take it easy, just keep this pace and we will be able to run Joe Harding down.

As the sun was going down the moon was on its way up. Ronnie could see the tracks of Joe's horse. He only had a mile or two head start.

Dandy was eating up the ground and Ronnie could see the stride of the other horse getting closer together, he was tiring and Dandy would take him. Dandy seemed to know he was on the run of his life. His pace never slowed. Mile after mile he ran on. Ronnie was talking to him and he felt Dandy could understand what he was saying. As the moon started to rise in the sky Ronnie could start to see the rider up ahead from time to time and he was getting closer each mile.

*

Joe could feel his horse start to slow after about five miles. He was using his spurs, blood was running down the horse's sides, but it was doing no good. Damn that Bob for trying to kill that kid, I told him to leave him alone but now he may be dead and I am only a short time from being the same. He could feel the horse coming up from behind and he knew he had only two choices-one to stop and fight or just stop, knowing he would be hanged.

Joe could see a wash coming up and started to slow so he could find a way in when a bullet whipped by his head. Joe just came to a stop and raised his hands as Ronnie came cantering in on Dandy. Ronnie told Joe to get off and drop his rifle and pistols and start walking his horse to cool him down. Ronnie stepped down and recovered the guns and started walking Dandy back the way they had come with Joe walking in the lead.

The other horse was in bad shape after the run but Dandy was ready to go after just a few minutes of walking. They walked about a mile when Ronnie told Joe to get aboard and keep walking back to meet his old friend Sheriff Johnson. Joe would have a little time to think on his harsh ways after Ronnie turned him over to the Sheriff Johnson.

A few hours later they rode back to the river and made the crossing. Sheriff Johnson greeted Joe and

Ronnie saying, "I figured you would have come back alone after he shot your horse,"

Ronnie said, "Na, I would have hated to take away your fun of watching him swing when you get him back to Sacramento".

"How is Diamond doing"? Ronnie asked. "I see he is up and eating. Is he having any problem moving around"?

"No, he has been down to get water and is laying his ears back at the other horses if they get too close to him".

"Well, that sounds good".

"Sheriff Johnson, how do you want to work this? I know you want to get back to Sacramento but that is a long ride with having to take care of Joe Harding along the trail. Why don't you ride back to the ranch with me and recover your horses and the two that were stolen at the court house"?

"Ok, when we get back I will figure things out," he said.

Ronnie asked Sheriff Johnson if he could wait another day to start so Diamond could recover a little more. Walking over to Joe Harding, he asked, "why did you come after me"?

"Well," he said. "I told Bob to leave you alone. We had had enough problems with you already, but he just had to try and kill you.

"How did that work out for you? Now you get to ride all the way back to Sacramento for a trial and a hanging with you being first in line". Sheriff Johnson walked up and gave Harding some dinner. When he finished he cuffed him with his hands behind a tree. Harding started to tell the Sheriff that he could not sleep that way with the wound he had in his arm.

"So what," he said.

At first light Ronnie went out to check on Diamond and walk him around a bit to see if he would be able to make the two day ride home. As it looked, he was moving ok so let's head home. It would be a month or so before he could be ridden hard, if at all. After a bite to eat they saddled up and started for the ranch.

Ronnie said, "why don't we take that canyon we passed after we hit the flats? I think it will lead us to the back side of my ranch. Tony said the Indians had a camp just on the back side of the mountain from the ranch".

Ronnie led off riding Dandy with the extra horses and Diamond on a lead line, with one of the stolen horses being used as the pack horse. "Dandy liked being in the lead. When they came to the canyon, Ronnie started up, following the stream that was lined with willows. As they worked up the canyon they started seeing deer and elk in large numbers the higher they climbed into the mountains.

Lunch time found them deep into the mountains Ronnie found what he had been looking for a small island of grass along the stream. He picketed the horses close to the water's edge with grass close at hand. Ronnie gathered some wood for a fire. Coffee was the first thing on his mind. Sheriff Johnson was getting Joe Harding off his horse and was not too gentle at it. Joe was whining about his treatment but I don't think Sheriff Johnson cared much, if any. "I wanted to give the stock an hour or so to get some grass and take a rest, in fact I will take two hours so I can scout around a bit. This land was about as good as my ranch". He was starting to come up with a plan for this side of the mountain.

After the noon rest, they started to climb higher onto the mountain, trees were getting larger, and they had crossed some other streams coming out of side canyons. This country could hold a lot of cattle if handled right, he was thinking.

Night was coming on when Ronnie stopped to make camp. He had been following tracks for some time left by White Bird on his way home. They looked like the trail was leading some place that had been used by people. Yes, this is where the Indians had their camp before moving over to the ranch. No wonder they had to talk over moving to the ranch - what a location. Water was close at hand, firewood and plenty of timber around for wind protection. The grass was like a carpet leading to the other side of the little valley with a stream flowing from pool to pool down the mountain side. "Yes, What a nice place".

Sheriff Johnson removed the handcuffs from one of Joe's hands and told him to gather fire wood. Joe started to bitch, so he was now shackled back to a tree and he would not eat tonight. We will see how things work out in the morning; he may be ready to gather the firewood. Sheriff Johnson turned to Ronnie. "So this is what you had been looking for". "Right", "he said, I figured the Indians that are working for me had a camp over on this side of the mountain some place. I now know where it is and what a nice place to have a small ranch headquarters.

Joe was ready to help in the morning when Johnson removed one handcuff. After eating, they saddled up and Ronnie led the way up and over the mountain following the dim trail left by White Bird and Tee going back and forth to the ranch".

Dark was settling in when Ronnie rode into the ranch yard, Abby ran out and about pulled him off Dandy she was so happy. Ronnie told Sheriff Johnson to show White Bird and Tee how to work the handcuffs. They turned over Joe to the Indians to guard overnight. As they headed to the storage shed by the barn Ronnie told them if he moved they could scalp him. They looked at each other and then to Joe. Smiling, they ran their fingers through his hair and both grunted. Joe was trying to get Ronnie to let him stay in the house.

"No way," he said, and walked off toward the house with Abby.

Anne and Fred getting ready to show their stuff at an event at the famous Dangberg Ranch in the Carson Valley. Buffalo Bill's Wild West show was a hit in 2016 and will be back in 2017. Go Pony Express go!

Thanks, Melissa Knight for this picture of three riders of the Pony Express.

Chapter 6 **Trip to Genoa**

Ronnie had sent one of the new ranch hands along with Sheriff Johnson to help guard Joe Harding. The new hand was one of the riders from the Pony Express, Larry McPherson. Larry helped Pony Bob Haslam set up the race for Ronnie and Buster at Fort Churchill. Larry had rode in just a few days ago looking for work. They all knew Joe Harding would try to escape the first chance he got. Everyone kind of wished he would try so they could shoot him.

Ronnie asked Larry to ride all the way to Sacramento with Sheriff Johnson and then report to Juan at the California rancho. Juan could use some help when he picks up the draft horses in Chico, "but don't get them into any races on the way back to Sacramento".

*

Sam Applegate had the wagons ready to roll when Ronnie got back from hunting down Joe Harding. Sean and Tony had been working with Sam to get the wagons ready for the trip. It was time for them to start heading to Genoa to purchase the lumber for the roof for Tony and Maggie's new home. Sean would also purchase the timbers needed to start the gold mine. Ronnie was walking around the wagons asking about the water and food they would need for the trip. They would need to stop at Mr. Brown's store and pick up the additional supplies. Sam and Sean would need to cook on the trip into Genoa. Ronnie told Sam he could hire a cook and two helpers when he got the chance. Ronnie asked Larry to check on Andy Sams when he got to Carson City, he hoped to have him join the crew and bring back Buster and Lightning.

Ronnie and Abby were standing on the porch when the two wagons rolled out of the ranch yard heading to Genoa to pick up the lumber needed to finish the roofs and out buildings for the ranch. The walls were starting to go up, you could see progress each day. Getting the boards for the floors and roof from the saw mill should be just about the right time. The two four horse teams were stepping high as they left the yard with Abby's extra mare tied to the back of the wagon. They had not been worked hard over the last few months so it would take a few miles for them to settle down.

Joe Harding still had his hair but was glad to be away from these Indians, it would be a long ride to Carson City chained to the end gate of the last wagon. Sheriff Johnson and Larry were following with the two stolen horses. The owners will be surprised when they get them back.

With the wagon it took the better part of three days to reach Mr. Brown's store, even without pulling a heavy load. With the supplies loaded they were off heading for Carson City. With the sun setting in the west, Sam had found the camping spot Ronnie had told him about that had some water and feed for the horses. Sam put hobbles on all of the horses so they could graze all night without straying too far from camp. Sam had purchased four bags of grain at Mr. Brown's Store, to feed the horses just in case the grass was gone along the trail.

Reaching Carson City, Sam stopped at the Pony Express Station. Sam and Larry went in and asked about Andy Sams. They said he is in the blacksmith shop-go on back. When they told Andy that he had a job if he wanted it at the ranch, Andy said let's go. Andy started asking about Ronnie and the ranch, he said that things were winding down and he could ride back with them to the ranch. Sam asked about the two horses, Andy told him to go see Bolivar Roberts about that. Sam walked in and found Bolivar sitting at a desk. Looking up, he asked if he could help him.

"Yes," Sam said, "Ronnie wanted me to check on the two horses he wanted to purchase from the Pony Express".

Bolivar said that they are in the stable and he would sell them. Sam asked how much he wanted for them.

Bolivar said, "you can tell Ronnie he can have them for $100.00 each if he would like them at that price".

Sam said he will take them with him today Sam pulled out the money and paid Mr. Roberts. "When can Andy come to work for us"?

"I will go out and tell him he can also go with you today if he would like". Damn, Ronnie will be one happy man. Sam asked if any tack went with the two horses, Bolivar said to have Andy pick out what he would need to get them to the ranch.

Sheriff Johnson and Larry had Joe Harding mount one of the two stolen horses and shackled him to the saddle and started west on the trail to Sacramento and Joe's hanging. Larry asked if he could just shoot Joe if he made any wrong move. Sheriff Johnson told Larry if the horse stumbles and it looked like Joe was trying to make an escape, yes, that would be just fine with him but just in case he does try raise your right hand. I am making you a US Deputy Marshal for this trip.

Andy told Sam, "why don't I just saddle up and head to the ranch now? You can get your lumber and start back in a day or so. I am ready to see this ranch and I have the two fastest horses in Nevada so why would I want to follow a wagon? I will be to the ranch by the time you get back to Buckland Station". Andy filled his saddlebags. Grabbing his rifle and pistol, he stepped up on Buster and turned east at a full gallop. After a few miles he dropped down to a canter. He was using Ronnie's trick of changing horses every few hours, he was making great time.

Andy stopped at Buckland Station to eat and then got back on the trail heading east. He would be stopping at different Pony Express Stations along his way heading east. Just east of Hooten Wells three Indians were blocking the trail. Andy rode up slow until he got close then spurred Buster. Andy, Buster and Lightning busted through the three Indians at a dead run. He fired at one of the Indians but missed. By the time they turned to chase him he was way down the road running flat out.

After a few days of hard riding he rode into Mr. Brown's store to get directions to Ronnie's ranch. Mr. Brown asked Andy if he would like to set up a blacksmith shop behind his store. Andy said thanks but he would be working for Ronnie. Eating an early dinner, he started up the wagon road leading to the ranch. He had slowed down some but the two horses still wanted to run most of the time. Mr. Brown had told him the locations of the two camping locations on the road to the ranch. On the second day Andy rode into the ranch. Ronnie was checking on Diamond in the corral to see how his bullet wound was healing.

Ronnie turned when he heard the horses coming into the yard, "Damn," he said. Andy was stepping off Lightning when he got up to the horses.

"Well, I see you found me all right,"

"Yes," he said, "I can see why you wanted these two horses. They can move right along". Andy turned to Ronnie and asked him. "What do you want me to do now that I am at the ranch"?

"Well, let's go get some coffee and talk about what is going on in this part of Nevada".

Chapter 7 **Horse's in Chico**

Sheriff Johnson and Larry had reached Sacramento without much trouble from Joe Harding. They rode up to the hitching rail in front of the jail. Larry walked over to Joe to help him down from the saddle when Joe spun his horse and put the spurs to him, he was at full speed in three jumps. Larry pulled his 44 Colt and fired at the same time Sheriff Johnson fired at the fleeing Joe Harding. Joe fell off of the horse and lay still, the horse was still running down the street heading somewhere only he knew. Sheriff Johnson turned to Larry and asked if he could go catch the horse. He would hate to lose him now that he is home.

Larry stepped up and galloped after the runaway horse that was heading who knows where, but was going there fast. After about a mile Larry found the horse was eating along the side of the road. He picked up the reins and led him back to the Sheriff's Office. Sheriff Johnson said that he could not tell who killed Joe but he would take the credit because he had only made Larry a Temporary Deputy Marshal and it would be less paperwork.

Larry said, "It was a shame he waited that long to make the run. We could have saved some food". Speaking of food, "I am hungry and you get to buy, I am tired of your cooking anyway".

Sheriff Johnson told his Deputy Crabtree to get Joe Harding in the ground and fill out the paperwork, he was going to go to dinner. "Also," he said, "Send a rider out to the owners of the two horses and have them come in to pick them up in the morning".

At dinner Larry asked for the directions to the rancho so he could start his new job. With dinner under his belt, he walked out and stepped up into the saddle and waved to the Sheriff. Down the road he went. He should make the rancho about dark. Juan and Juanita walked out onto the front porch of the rancho to see who had rode in at this time of day. Juan had one of his men take the horse and asked Larry to come in and tell him what he wanted.

Larry told them who he was and that Ronnie told him he was to help Juan with whatever he needed. He said that Ronnie asked him to go with you to Chico and bring back the draft horses. But whatever you need just ask, Larry said. Juanita came back in with a tray of lemonade for them to drink while Larry told them all he knew about Ronnie and the Nevada Ranch.

Juan told Larry that his clothes and rifle are in his room. It is the third room down the hall on the left. You will be staying with us. "Let's talk about going after the draft horses. The road to Chico has a lot of problems. Many people have been robbed traveling that road, a gang of about ten seem to know when someone is heading north. They watch for travelers. We will need to have a plan, do you have any ideas"?

The two men worked late to come up with a plan to remove some of the bandits along the trail. With things set for the trip, Juan and Larry set out for Chico just after sun up, they had one of Juan's ranch hands riding along, leading the pack horse. Juan figured that they would be watched the first day and would be robbed on the second morning just after sun up. Juan had sent one of his men along the trail a day earlier to find a good camping location that could be defended with just four men. This location was just an easy one day ride north of Sacramento along the river.

Juan and Larry set an easy pace during the day, acting like they had all the time in the world. They stopped to have a smoke ever few hours and talked. Larry had seen a rider in the hills a few times during the day and a little dust. They knew they were being watched. As the sun was setting they came to the campsite. Water was close with some grass for the horses. The two vaqueros set about making the fire and getting dinner on to cook. Juan and Larry went out and rubbed down the horses with dry grass as they grazed along the stream that joined the river by the campsite.

*

James Barton and his gang had been robbing travelers heading north from Sacramento for years without any problems. James had informants located in most of the towns located on trails leading from Sacramento and San Francisco. James and his gang had wanted posters in most of the western towns, they read wanted dead or alive. James' poster listed his reward at one thousand dollars, most of his gang would bring five hundred or better, depending on the member of the gang and how many people he had killed and women they had raped.

James had received some information from a stable hand working at a horse ranch just east of Chico telling of the possible sale of eight draft horses. This could be quite a lot of money waiting to be picked up. The Barton gang had hideouts in most parts of the west. James got the word and he moved back into the hills between Chico and Sacramento to the ranch to wait on the buyers to head their way.

James is going to take over a ranch back in the hills that belonged to a young couple, Ralph and Sarah James. Sarah and Ralph had been married for two years; Sarah had been given the two ranches by her father as a wedding present.

When James and his gang rode into the ranch they found only Sarah at the house, her husband was out working cattle back in the hills. James told his men to find the man and kill him, telling them this would be their new home. James went into the house and told Sarah that the gang was going to stay for a while and he would explain the arrangement to her husband when he came back.

Some of the gang went into the barn and started to fix up an area for them to sleep and the others went out to find Ralph and stage an accident. After riding back into the hills they found Ralph herding some cattle. Riding up on both sides of Ralph, one of the men held his horse while the others hit him over the head. When he hit the ground they put his foot in the stirrup then hit the horse on the flank. After about a mile the men stopped the horse and Ralph was dead. With Ralph loaded on his horse they started back to the ranch.

Sarah came out to find her husband dead after being dragged by his horse. The men said, they just came over a rise only to find a bear going after one of the cows. Ralph tried to scare it off but his horse threw him and ran away dragging him. The men dug a grave and buried Ralph. That night James told Sarah he was going to now be her husband and to get used to the idea. Sarah was forced to fix dinner for the gang, after all the men went back to the barn to sleep, James told her to go into the bedroom and get ready for bed. Sarah knew that the gang had killed her husband and she was now going to be raped by James Barton.

What could she do other than what James said? James sat at the kitchen table drinking a cup of coffee and thinking over the situation. Liking the location of this ranch and having a woman for his use any time he wanted he was feeling good. When he finished his coffee he opened the door leading into the bedroom where he had told Sarah to go and get ready for bed. Reaching the door he found it blocked by the dresser.

James kicked open the door and stepped in. Sarah was sitting in the corner on the floor hoping he would not come in. James reached down, grabbed her by the hair, and pulled her up onto the bed.

James said, "You best do as I tell you if you want to live". When he finished he told her that he was going to leave two men to help with the ranch and protect her, he was going out to do a job and would be back in a couple of days.

Sarah vowed that day that she would kill James the first chance she got and any of his men that she could. Having not had a chance to get a gun and never being alone at the ranch, she had to bide her time. James went right to sleep after raping Sarah. Later she got up to wash him off her body. She found James' saddle bags laying over a chair in the kitchen and found a loaded pistol along with a thousand dollars of cash. James woke up early and took her again and walked out the door with his saddle bags over his shoulder without checking them. Sarah figured she just may have a chance to get free after James rides off now that she had a weapon.

When the gang rode out James had left only one man instead of two to guard her, but this man she felt had an idea of raping her after the gang rode off. Sarah put the gun under her dress and went down to the barn to feed the horses, the guard followed along behind a few steps, never taking his eyes off her. She could feel his eyes on her as she entered the barn. When she entered the first stall she turned and could tell he was hard and was going to make his move now. She told him that James would not like him messing with her. He just looked and started to undo his belt. Sarah turned and walked to the back of the stall, looking away from this man, trying to get as far away from him as she could.

He was smiling as he started moving toward her, taking small steps because his pants were down around his ankles. When she turned and looked at him he was only a few feet from her. Raising the pistol, she shot him in the chest and cocking the pistol again, she shot him in the crotch. Grabbing himself, he died. Sarah saddled a horse and after putting a catch rope around this dead man's shoulders she dragged him back into the timber and left him to rot.

James had two of his gang waiting along the trail for the men from the ranchos south of Sacramento to ride by. When they spotted the three riders and a packhorse, they knew they had their target. The orders were for one of the men to ride back and the other to stay off the trail but keep watch until they made camp for the night.

James moved the gang down out of the hills closer to the trail and waited for his man to inform them as to the location of the campsite. The gang member stayed well after dark and waited until they all went to bed, then the rider left to go to the meeting point and gave James the location of their camp. With the campsite only an hour's ride, he had all of the men fix dinner and get some sleep. James and the rider who had been watching talked about how the campsite was located, so when they charged the camp the four men could be covered. James didn't want to kill anyone. He just wanted the money they were carrying.

James had moved the gang out from the ranch to a campsite close to the road leading north to Chico. He woke everyone about two hours before dawn, giving them the final instructions on how this robbery was going to be accomplished. He was going to lead in the attack. He would fire one shot to wake up the four men. "Remember, don't start shooting. With our numbers we should be able to wake them up and take their money and guns, then ride out to our next meeting point". With the plans set, they started the short ride to the campsite to relieve them of their gold.

When James was close to the campsite, he stopped to listen for any noise. Not hearing any, he put the spurs to his horse and made the charge straight into the campsite. When he was about 100 feet from the fire ring, he fired into the ground to wake up the sleeping men. James was thumbing back the hammer when he felt the bullet hit him, then another. That was the last thing he felt falling to the ground dead.

*

Juan had kept the fire going late. The men sat around talking late into the night, acting like they were going to sleep late in the morning. Juan used the last of the coffee to cool the coals and kicked dirt over them. He laid down, using his saddle for his head. With everyone sleeping around the fire, the trap was set. The moon had gone down about three in the morning. It was now pitch black, you could not see anything. Juan and Larry woke the two vaqueros. They all slipped back into the trees. The men that Juan had sent ahead had pulled some logs in behind the first row of trees, so they would have a good firing position and great cover if attacked. Now the trap was set. From what Juan had heard about the robberies was that the gang would charge the camp just after dawn and shoot anyone who resisted.

Juan and Larry looked at each other, it was time. They could hear the horses coming at a gallop. The sun was not up yet but you could start to see enough to pick a target. The leader had his pistol out and fired into the ground by one of the bedrolls. Larry and Juan fired at the same time. James took two bullets in the chest and went backwards off of his horse. The man next to him on his right was also falling off his horse. The two vaqueros were also emptying saddles. Horses were bucking and pitching. Some of the men had been bucked off and were on the ground and were being stomped by the scared horses. The bandits turned, trying to escape the deadly fire only to have their escape route blocked by ten vaqueros on each side of them with rifles aimed ready to fire. Pistols and rifles were dropping to the ground with hands in the air, they had had enough gun play for one day.

The gang had started out with fifteen men when they rode into the ambush. Only ten were left after the shooting was finished. Juan wrote a note to Sheriff Johnson about the attempted robbery and for him to do what he liked with the rest of the gang. Juan's foreman would deliver the men to Sheriff Johnson's office in Sacramento, then go back to the ranch to start the fall roundup.

Larry asked the men how they knew we were carrying money. No one offered any information. Larry pulled his pistol and shot one of the robbers in the leg.

"Now who wants to talk or I just keep shooting". Still no one would talk so he shot the second man in the leg. That got the conversation started in a big way. All of the men had heard that James had informants in many of the towns and they knew that James had received a message from one of the stable hands. They had heard the name of Barker and James' younger brother Wes, who was all they knew. Larry turned to Juan saying they are going to hang anyway and it was just the leg. What's the problem?

Juan asked the vaqueros to get the fire going, they were ready to eat. With the dead loaded onto their horses and tied down, Juan's foreman started back to Sacramento with what was left of the gang.

Juan asked Larry, "you think that was a fast start of a day or what"?

"Juan, they could have at least waited until we had time to eat. That is tuff work on an empty stomach. Let's go and saddle the horses so we can head north after we eat". Juan told the Vaqueros to collect the reward money from Sheriff Johnson and split it among all the ranch hands and their families' each will get an equal share.

After the rough start, things went just great the rest of the trip to Chico. Reaching town, they asked about the location of the horse breeder's ranch. Heading back into the foothills they found the ranch without any trouble. They rode into the ranch along a road lined with trees and a fence along each side of the road. As they rode along, some of the horses in the pasture came to the fence to take a look.

Larry said "they are some damn big horses, Juan. A man fall off one of them he would damn sure kill himself". Reaching the large house and barn, they were greeted by the owner, Gary Gee. He was coming from the barn as they rode into the ranch yard.

Juan and Larry got off of their horses and introduced themselves. Juan said he is the man who sent the letter saying he needed the two teams of draft horses. Gary asked them to follow him to the barn and they could take a look at the eight horses he had picked out for them. Larry walked up to one of the stalls to take a look see. He reached the stall and one of the big black mares stuck her head out, wanting to be scratched. Larry turned and asked Juan how they were going to lead them back to Sacramento with only our little stock horses.

Gary just started laughing. "well boys, they will follow you anywhere with just a lead rope". Juan told Gary about the attempted robbery by the Barton gang, and that they received some information about one of his workers. Gary asked what they knew about any of his workers, "Well," Juan said, "we received some information from the gang about a man with the last name of Baker and he is missing part of his little finger on his left hand. Do you have anyone working for you with that name or description"?

Garry said he did have but two days ago. Dave, yes, his name is Dave Baker, he never came to work and from what he found out he has left the area.

Gary turned to Juan and asked if they would like to have the horses delivered to Sacramento. He would need some supplies in a month or so. He was going to use his wagons and he could just tie the eight horses to it and deliver them in a month or so. Juan and Larry were going for that deal. Juan paid Gary in gold and they started back to the rancho. They were about to the site of the gunfight when they saw a women riding ahead of them. Riding up from behind they were greeted by a 44 pistol, Sarah said that is close enough or she will shoot.

Juan said to put that thing down. We are not going to hurt you. We are just going back to my rancho south of Sacramento. Sarah said that she was going to Sacramento to tell the Sheriff that she had killed one of the Barton gang and would need protection from James. She said that the gang had forced her to stay on the ranch after they killed her husband. Juan told her that she was safe because they had killed James Barton just a few days ago along with many of his gang. Juan told Sarah that she needed to give the description of the man she killed to the Sheriff when they got into town, she could get the amount that was listed on his wanted poster. Most of the gang was $600.00 to $800.00 dead or alive. Sounds like your man is dead.

Juan suggested that they all ride into Sacramento and talk to the Sheriff to give him your story-you just may have some extra money. Juan asked Sarah if she needed some Vaqueros to help with the cattle. She said she needed two men to start with. "After we talk with Sheriff Johnson, ride down to the rancho and you can talk to a few of my men. There may just be a couple who would like to work for you".

Riding up to Sheriff Johnson's office, Juan introduced Larry and Sarah to the Sheriff. Juan asked Sarah to tell him about what happened at the ranch starting with the killing of her husband by the Barton Gang. When she got around to the killing of the guard who was about ready to rape her after James left, the Sheriff was ready to go back into his cells and shoot the whole damn bunch.

Sheriff walked back into the cell block, asked who was left behind to guard Sarah. With the name, he went out to look at the wanted posters. He had hoped it would have been Wes Barton, James younger brother. Bill Simms was his name and he was listed at eight hundred dollars dead or alive.

"Well, Sarah you will be paid eight hundred dollars for shooting Bill Simms".

Sarah turned to Juan, asking if he really could let her have one or two of his men to help her get the ranch back into operation. Larry was standing back listening to Sarah and Juan talk about the need for some ranch hands. Larry asked Sarah if she would like him to go back and help her for a few weeks. He turned to

Juan saying, "what about that idea Sarah"? She did need a hand and Larry looked like he could do the job. Sarah asked Juan if he could ask some of his men if they wanted to come to the ranch and help. She had the thousand she got from James Barton's saddle bags and now the eight hundred. She would have enough cash to get the ranch back into operation.

Juan turned to Larry and asked if he was going to stay on the ranch or was he going to come back after getting Sarah settled. Larry said he would be back in time to escort the mining equipment back to Nevada. With Mr. Gee delivering the teams to Sacramento in a month he would have plenty of time to get Sarah settled and with some men you are going to send she should be just fine by then. See you in a month. Larry and Sarah turned back north so she could get the new start at life.

When Juan returned to the rancho he told Juanita about the gunfight by the river and what had happened to Sarah James. When he finished she asked if Larry would return or if he might just stay with Sarah. We will see in a month or so. The mining supplies should be delivered to Sacramento in eight weeks, let's hope the other wagons arrive about that time so we can get everything in one trip.

When Juan reached the bedroom he found a very large brass bath tub setting under a large window. Walking over, he could see it was full of water. Reaching down, he found it hot. Juanita closed and bolted the bedroom door and started taking off her dress. Juan asked her if she felt that he needed a little bath to wash off the road dust. Juanita told him to get ready because she was going to wash every bit of dirt off of him, and I think you have one part that will take some special attention.

Juanita was getting into the tub as he was finishing getting out of his clothes. After their baths were finished, they spent the rest of the night in each other's arms.

Juanita said, "Welcome home. By the way I am late this month. We will see if I am right about the baby girl. Mr. Juan Lopez".

In this book series The Pony Express Rider, Ruby Gold and Kill Ronnie Campbell there is many times I talk about hidden locations of water along the trail. In many of the canyons around Nevada you will run into a location just like this. Picture by Ron Bell

Chapter 8 **Wedding at the Ranch**

Mr. Brown had just received the last of the items that Maggie and Abby had ordered a few weeks ago. Now he would need to get them delivered to the ranch. With the gold mining starting up in Western Nevada and California, it had been hard to hire men to make deliveries and help around the store.

Late in the day Jim heard a wagon come to a stop in front of the store. Stepping down was a thin man dressed in a black coat, white shirt, black stripped pants. There also was a little lady with a pinched up kind of face. She looked like a lady who liked things all set in place, and a place for everything. When the man hit the ground he held out his hand for his wife to step down. Turning toward the store he could see a man standing on the porch. Reaching out he said,

"I am Zack Smith and this is my wife Betty. We are looking for the Ronnie Campbell ranch". Jim said, "I am Jim Brown. This is my store. Welcome". Zack said that he had been asked to come to the ranch to do a wedding, he is a preacher.

"Well, it is late, water your horses and park your wagon. I will have some dinner ready when you finish". Entering the store, they could see that Jim was good at his word. He had the cook set out the food. They all would sit and eat. During dinner Jim asked if they had any room in their wagon to carry some extra supplies that needed to go to the ranch. Zack said he would be glad to haul them when he left in the morning. He was happy that Jim was going to pay him to deliver the goods to the ranch.

The preacher and his wife would eat with Jim in the morning and then start for the ranch. Jim had told them it would take about three days by wagon. Zack and Betty finished eating and headed to the ranch. Jim had loaded the wedding supplies while they were eating. Jim also told Zack how to find the campsites along the way.

*

Tony was out by the barn checking on the progress that White Bird and Tee were making on the young horses when Maggie came up and rested her hands on his shoulders. Tony turned and put his lips on hers. The next thing he knew they were walking out to the river bank to enjoy the setting sun. Maggie had a blanket with her so they could sit down under some trees and talk a bit.

Tony and Maggie started to talk about what and where they would go after the wedding, Abby suggested that they go over to California and see Juan and Juanita for a few days and then go on up to Sacramento to one of the hotels for a few days. Ronnie had told Tony that he would like to get some gold over to Juan to pay for the wagons and they could take it to them. Maggie said, "why don't we just camp for a few days at the site White Bird and Tee found, they said that there was a hot spring just a short ride from the campsite. When we get back you can head over to Sacramento to help bring back the mining equipment".

Tony said, "when I go, we will both go, but the camping does sound like fun, we could take three of four days and then come back and head west".

A few days later, late in the afternoon, a wagon came into the yard. Everyone went out to see who had came to the ranch. Zack got down and helped his wife Betty down. Turning, they introduced themselves and asked for Ronnie. Ronnie grabbed his hand and started pumping it some. Turning, he introduced them to the rest of the crew. When he got to Tony and Maggie he said, "this is the two who are getting married". Maggie asked if he had stopped at Mr. Brown's store. Zack told them all of the wedding stuff is in the back of the wagon.

Maggie and Abby both ran to the back to start unloading so they could see if everything they ordered had come in. Handing things to everybody, they turned to the Smiths. "Come on in. We will have one of the hands park your wagon. Let's get some dinner on. After we eat Maggie and I are going to unpack the boxes".

Zack told Tony and Maggie that they would like to talk over what they had planned and set a date for the wedding. The two girls were like two little kids after dinner, digging into all of the boxes to see what everything looked like that they ordered. Maggie asked if they could get married at noon five days from now. Abby said that they would need to get Beth and Little John to come for the wedding. Tony was ready for that to be done with. "OK I will get the supplies ready to go over the mountain after the wedding. You and Abby get your plans ready".

The sun was just starting to show light when Tony galloped out of the ranch yard heading into the hills with Tee and White Bird right behind him. Ronnie asked Maggie if she knew what Tony was up to,

"Yes, he is getting two pack horses for us to use. We are going to make a short trip over to Tee and White Bird's campsite for a few days after we get married. Then we will go over to Sacramento to help with the mining equipment. Tony would like me to meet Juanita's family and he can spend some time with his sister". "Good plan," Ronnie said.

*

Sam and Sean found the sawmill just outside of Genoa along the river. As they pulled up to the small cabin in front of the mill, a large man walked out to greet them. "Hi, I am Tim Dobbin, the sawmill manager". Sam reached for his hand.

"I am Sam Applegate and this is Sean O'Rilley. Do you have our order ready"?

"Yes," he said. "I got the telegraph a few weeks ago". Tim called to some men and told Sam and Sean to pull the wagons over by the third pile of lumber and they will get it loaded in short order. With all of the lumber loaded, Sam turned back down the road heading east and to home.

The trip home should be no problem, Sam had hired two helpers and a cook in Carson City for the return trip to the ranch. The two helpers were young, but he suspected that they were younger than they said, they may be fifteen if that. Jack Jenkins was a small blond headed kid and his brother Billy had dark hair and a long face. Now the cook, Dave Baker, looked like he had been around a little more than he put on. His eyes seemed to check out everything, but said little. Sam asked him about his past. He said he was from around Sacramento, but he could cook a bit so Sam took a chance that he would work out.

With the help of Bolivar Roberts, Sam had picked up a small covered wagon to use as the supply and chuck wagon. Bolivar had used this wagon after the Paiute war to haul supplies and feed his workers when rebuilding the remote stations that were burned down. The team was Morgan's, they would weigh about 1,100 pounds each a good match for the supply wagon. During the noon stop Sam told Dave to pick up the pace and go on ahead to the first campground so he could get dinner ready by the time they got there.

Dave set out at a good pace. The Morgan's liked to move along so late in the day he found the campsite and set to making dinner. He had been stopped for just a short time when a rider came out of a draw and hailed the camp. Dave turned to see one of the Barton gang sitting on his horse just outside of the campsite. In fact, it was James Barton's brother Wes.

"Well," he said, "So Johnson failed to find you".

"Ya," he said, "I was off looking at another job for James when they got shot and some were captured".

"What kind of a game are you working on now"?

Dave said that he had heard about this job at a saloon in Carson City. They say this ranch is rich and they are starting a gold mine.

"My idea is to tag along and get paid for my time, I plan to steal their gold and head east to Salt Lake City for a change of scenery and change my lifestyle. Wes, would you like to lend a hand with this job? We could make a killing on this one I think".

"OK, let's do it, I am in. What do I need to do"?

"Well, take this chunk of meat it should hold you for a bit and ride out and wait until after dark. Then come in to the camp from the west. Sam will allow you to eat and then you ask about a job, I think they will need extra men at the ranch and mine. If that works we are on the inside. We will bide our time and then strike fast and make a run for the big city with some of their gold. Look, Wes, you need to take another name, Barton is too well known, why don't you go by Bart West"?

*

Sam and Sean pulled into the campsite just before dark, pulling the wagons around behind the fire pit. They set about getting the horses on water and feed. They would need to give each horse a quart of oats each feeding. After getting the horses on water and what grass there was, Sean started to check out the harnesses for all of the teams, making any small repairs each day. Sam had built racks to hang the harnesses on the side of each wagon before they headed west to get the lumber for the houses. This made Sean's work easy. This also helped in the morning getting ready to hit the trail.

Dinner was finished and all of the men were sitting around the fire talking when someone rode up and asked if he could come into the campsite. Sam and Sean picked up their rifles just in case they might need them. The man came in riding slow. When he got close, Sam told him to come and get a cup of coffee. Stepping out of the saddle, he dusted his pants off using his hat. He said, "I am Bart West heading east looking for a job".

Sam asked Dave to get him some food and a cup for coffee. Bart said, "thanks I could use a good meal for a change". As Bart dug into his food, Sam quizzed him a bit, Bart told them he was looking for some ranch work and said that he had been working around Stockton, California for the last year and wanted to see some new country.

After Bart ate his food, Sam told him to picket his horse and they would talk in the morning. Sam and Sean walked out into the night so they could talk some about this new man, Sean said he wonders some about him, he is riding a real good horse for a ranch hand. Sam said why not we just see what he acts like for a few days, we will just let him travel along with us and see what comes about but keep an eye on him.

Dave had breakfast ready by the time the horses were harnessed and hitched to the wagons. Bart helped with the work and seemed to know what to do around a team. Sam asked if he would want to ride along with them back to the ranch and talk to the owner. He said that would be great, he was short on road supplies, so if he can help out along the trail for his food it would be good for him.

The routine along the trail went off without any problems Bart was doing the jobs Sam asked him to do without any problems. With the ranch only a short haul in the morning it would be nice to get home and check out the ranch. Sam had not stopped by his ranch on the way in but would start back the next morning. Ronnie heard the trace chains long before seeing Sam and the wagons pulling into the yard.

Ronnie walked out to greet the wagons and look at the lumber they had brought for the gold mine and to also finish the house. Sam made a wide swing in the ranch yard and stopped by the corrals, Sean was right behind him with his wagon. Ronnie pointed to have the cook wagon pull around by the house to unload at the kitchen and storeroom.

Dave Baker pulled his wagon to the storage shed beside the kitchen and climbed down. Ronnie walked over and introduced himself to Dave.

"I am Dave Baker your new trail cook, Sam hired me in Carson City".

"Well, welcome to the ranch, help unload this stuff and we will talk later".

Sam was met in the yard by Beth,

"What are you doing here"? she said,

"You got back just in time, Tony and Maggie are getting married in the morning and I was asked to the big event".

Sam said, "What about me"? You can stay if you clean up a little, we can make a bed in one of the wagons if you like". Sam asked Bart West to come over and meet Beth and then go meet Ronnie and see about the job.

Ronnie and Sean were looking over the support timbers he had brought back for the mine shaft when Sam walked up with Bart West.

"Ronnie, this is Bart West. He is looking for a job. I let him ride along with us. He was good help on the trail".

Ronnie told Bart to come along and they would talk about a job. "I will need to ask some questions about what you know and what kind of work you have done in the past". Ronnie had looked at his hands and they were not callused and his pistol looked well used. Ronnie asked if he could work cattle, Bart told him he had in the past but it had been a while".

"What have you been doing the last few years, I see your hands are a little soft and your horse is too good for an everyday ranch hand".

"Well, you are right about that. I have been working around San Francisco as a gambler and my horse is one I won in a poker game. I felt it best to find another line of work when the past owner came looking to get his horse back without paying me for him. He pulled iron and missed, I didn't, so I felt it better I fine some other place to work so here I am. Do I get to stay or shall I hit the trail"?

Maggie and Abby were up at the crack of dawn only to find Dave Baker was in the kitchen with the coffee on and biscuits in the oven. "Grab some coffee. Breakfast will be ready in a bit". Shocked, they got a cup of coffee and walked out onto the porch and sat down looking at each other, this is not too bad.

Abby turned to Maggie and smiled. "Today is the day, are you ready"?

"I am so ready I hurt. Can you remember how you felt on your wedding day"?

"I think a wedding brings back all of the feelings I felt that day also. Are we going to have enough time to get ready by noon"?

"Yes we will get it all done, in fact we are going to let Beth help and get the new cook Dave to do the baking and you just take care of yourself, do you hear, Maggie"?

Breakfast was a loud meal, a long trip finished, a wedding to get ready for and everyone wanting to hear about the event. White Bird and Tee came over to check out the noise. Turning back to the barn, they started saddling two horses. Ronnie came over to the barn with Bart, telling them who he was and let him ride along with them to start moving the cattle out of the high meadows.

Bart asked, "I get to stay then"?

Ronnie said, "we will give you a look see". Ronnie turned, starting back to the house turning, He told Bart to watch his hair. White Bird and Tee looked at each other, then they reached out touching Bart's hair and smiled. Bart saddled up and followed the two Indians out of the ranch yard and headed back into the hills.

After breakfast was finished Dave Baker asked Maggie what she needed him to get ready for the wedding. With his directions in place he started to bake the cake and made plans to make a light lunch for the wedding party. Dave is now alone in the house. He had waited all morning, hoping to get a chance to look around to see if he could find the location of the hidden gold. Dave had just put the wedding cake in the oven and after calling out to see if anyone was around, he started to check out each room for a hiding spot for the gold.

He had just got back into the kitchen when Ronnie came in the front door to pick up some items from the small office area in the hallway leading back to the bedrooms. After picking up one of the order sheets from the lumber mill he spotted a small smudge of flour on the lower drawer. Ronnie came to alert. Taking his time, he moved back into the bedrooms and checked all of the rooms. He found small amounts of flour in both bedrooms. "We have a problem," he told himself.

Easing back to the desk area he made some noise then walked back out into the kitchen to ask Dave if he had any coffee left from breakfast. Ronnie sat down at the kitchen table to sip his coffee. After a bit Ronnie asked Dave how the cook wagon worked and if he needed to make any changes prior to the trip to Sacramento. Dave said that some of the storage areas are a little too small but he could fix that problem in a few days. He then asked Ronnie when we will start heading for Sacramento. Ronnie said that just as soon as Tony and Maggie get back from their camping trip. Sam will be getting the wagons ready this week. His best guess it will in be just about two weeks if all went well. Ronnie got up, leaving his cup on the table and headed out to the ranch yard where Abby and Maggie were going through the rest of the supplies delivered by Pastor Smith. Walking up to Pastor Smith's wagon,

Ronnie said "let's move around the back of the wagon, we need to talk, we have a problem," he said. He told the girls about finding the flour in the rooms, so Dave Baker was looking for something. "My best guess he was looking for the gold storage".

Ronnie and the girls talked about setting a trap to see if Dave was a thief or just looking over the house, either way they would need to get to the bottom of this quick. Abby made the point that with Maggie and Tony leaving for a few days after the wedding it would be her and Ronnie's problem to deal with, so let's have a wedding.

Pastor Zack Smith and his wife had talked to Tony and Maggie on how he would handle the wedding. The time had come, the wedding party was waiting under the trees beside the stream for Maggie and Abby to be driven there by Little Jon. With the proper waiting time past they could see the buggy come around the hill by the stream. Maggie and

Abby were in their new dresses they had ordered from Mr. Browns Store. Little Jon came to a stop and got down to help the girls out of the buggy. They were all smiles.

Sean came up and took Maggie's arm to escort her to Tony. Abby was walking forward a few yards ahead of Sean and Maggie. When Sean walked up to Tony he stopped and gave Tony her arm and walked over to watch the ceremony, stopping to stand by Ronnie.   With Tony and Maggie standing in front of Pastor Smith, the pastor turned to his wife and asked if she would sing a song to set the mood for this wedding.

When Betty started to sing, she came alive and her voice was like a voice from heaven clear and beautiful to hear. They were all amazed, how could anyone who looked like a prune sing like an angel. With the song finished, Pastor Smith started their vows. With I do's finished Tony was told he could now kiss his bride, and he for sure did kiss her. Tony and Maggie rode back in the buggy with Ronnie and Abby driving this time. Tony was still kissing Maggie when they reached the ranch house. Dave had the wedding cake and the lunch ready for the wedding party.

After a bit everyone was back at the ranch ready to see the cake cut. Maggie cut the cake and they fed each other a bite. Lunch was on the table. With everyone sitting, Ronnie asked Sean if he wanted to say anything to the new couple. Sean stood up and told the new couple to love each other and be kind to each other and all will work out in your life together. Ronnie gave a little talk about how when he met Tony, he was just a young man, being thought of as Juan's brother. Now look at him he is a key member of the family and is running this ranch. With everyone eating, Little Jon went out to the barn and saddled the horses and got the pack horse ready for Tony and Maggie to start over the mountain to their campsite to start their married life together.

Wedding dress changed to a split riding skirt they were ready to start their new life together. Well wishers watched Tony and Maggie start up the canyon that would lead over the mountain they were going to camp for the few days prior to heading to Sacramento for their honeymoon and help pick up the mining equipment.

Is this not cool, Pony Bob finished his ride at Fort Churchill or Buckland Station. This is Steve Nielson (Haslam)

Pony Bob was Steve's great, great, Uncle, riding Red.

Chapter 9 **The Young Widow**

Larry McPherson and the young widow Sarah James were heading back to her ranch to start her new life without her husband of two years, he had been killed by the James Barton Gang. This trip will take two days without pushing the horses too hard. Sarah had picked up the reward money for killing the outlaw that was going to rape her plus the money she took from James Barton prior to his death. As they were riding along Larry asked her what she would need to make a new start at the ranch.

Sarah figured with the cattle she had now the next thing would be to start raising some high quality saddle horses. Larry asked her why horses,

"Well," she told him, "I am a good horse trainer and I know more about ranching than my husband". Sarah said that she had been raised on a cattle ranch and she was her dad's son he never had, so she worked the ranch and broke horses until she got married. "My dad purchased my ranch along with a smaller one that is next to mine for a wedding present". Larry told her that they need to extend their trip a few days, to go up to Chico to look at a few horses that are for sale. He told her about purchasing some draft horses from Gary Gee and that he had some good saddle stock with two good stallions. "I think you can get them cheap, Gary is only interested in raising draft horses".

Sarah asked Larry why will Gary sell them to me cheap?

"Well," he said, "his ranch is not a very large ranch and his barn is full of draft horses. When I looked the mares over they all needed their feet trimmed along with the stallions. This means they have lost value to him; his focus is on his draft horses. What do you say"?

She said let's ride.

Gary was heading to the barn when Larry and Sarah rode into the yard, Gary stopped until they reached him. Looking at Larry, he said, "what are you doing back here, and you do have prettier company also".

Larry told him about Sarah losing her husband and having problems with the Barton gang over the past few months. Larry told Gary that Sarah is a horse trainer and she was looking for some cheap stock to the started and she has only a little money.

Gary told Sarah that he in fact had changed his operation and would like to sell his saddle stock. "Let's go and see what I have and see if you would like any of my horses". Gary told them to ride down to the barn and he would get his horse so they could ride out to take a look at the mares. "While I get saddled look at the two stallions behind the barn, remember they have not been kept up much for the past year". When they rode back to the two pens the stallions were in, Sarah told Larry these are some good stock. Both were over 16 hands by the looks. "When you were here before did you get a good look at the mares"? Larry told her that he had seen them when they came in for water at the tank and they all looked good to him but had not paid that much attention. He had been looking at the draft horses.

"I will get Gary to show you the ones that will be delivered to Sacramento next month".

Gary rode up and opened the gate to the pasture. They rode in and closed the gate. I think they will be back in the trees to keep away from the flies this time of the day. Sarah asked Gary how many mares he had for sale, "I would get rid of all but two, this one I am riding and one other so that would be eight plus the two stallions". Gary kicked his horse up to a nice lope and they rode around and over some low hills until they could see the line of trees about a half mile ahead. Gary headed toward a fence line. Turning in the saddle, Gary told them they will turn the mares back and drive them to the stock pens at the ranch yard.

Entering the trees, they found them all swishing flies in the shade. Moving up slowly, they started the herd moving back toward the ranch. The three spread out to keep the horses bunched, Sarah took the center because she wanted to get a look how the horses moved.

Reaching the ranch they pushed them into a corral that they had been watering in so they moved right in without any problem.

Sarah eased along through the horses, checking them all out to see if any were injured or lame. Finding all in good shape she rode out and closed the gate behind her.

Gary said, "let's go over to the barn and tie up our horses and then we can go up to the house and get some coffee from my cook. I am also sure he will have a bite to eat also". On the way to the house Sarah asked Larry what he thought about the horses and what he figured Gary would ask for them. Larry told her to let him do the talking, if that would be ok with her.

Reaching the house, Gary was right. His cook did have some food ready. As they drank the coffee and had some lunch, they got around to talking about the horses. Larry asked Gary what he would need for all except the two he was keeping. Gary told them that the one stallion was a standardbred and the other was a Morgan, and all the mares were mustang standardbred cross, he had not bred any mares with the Morgan yet. Larry told Gary that it looked like he was not going to have any use for the ten horses so why don't you just give them to Sarah. She will be able to use them and treat them right, in fact she would train and sell the first year's fouls and give you the money for payment.

Gary sat back and rubbed his chin for a bit. Then, turning to Sarah, he asked if she could pay him one hundred each for the stallions and still give him money for the first foals like Larry said. Sarah looked at Larry, swallowed, and told Gary she could live with that if he could. Shaking hands, they made the deal. Gary told Sarah that she could wait to pay for the two stallions after she sells the other horses if she needed to. Sarah pulled out some money she had received from the reward and gave it to Gary saying thanks, you won't be sorry about making this deal.

The next day Larry and Sarah started back to her ranch with the stallions on a lead line and the mares tied tail to tail behind the stallions. Larry wanted to make thirty miles if they could and camp at the spot they had camped on the way up to Gary's ranch. The first few miles were a test for both Sarah and Larry, they had started out at a lope to get the horses tired fast. None of the horses had been worked any for a year of two. Instead of stopping at noon they rode on so they could get in early to the camp site.

They reached the campsite early and had plenty of daylight left. They put the horses on picket lines so they could graze until dark. The campsite had a small stream coming out of the hills with willows lining both sides of the stream. On the way up Larry had seen that the stream had a bend in it just up from the campsite so after getting settled he told Sarah he was going up and take a bath in the pool at the bend of the river.

Taking his saddle bag with him, he started upstream. Reaching the bend, there was a nice size pool in the bend of the stream. Washing out his shirt and pants he hung them on the bushes to dry, taking out his clean extra shirt and pants. He got dressed and headed back to camp. Sarah asked if the water was too cold. Larry told her that it was cold but refreshing. She got her kit and went to test out the water for herself.

Larry got the fire started and started some pan biscuits. When Sarah got back from washing she walked up to Larry and kissed him saying,

"how did you ever get the idea of offering Gary so little money for all of his horse's? she asked". Larry asked Sarah if he could return her kiss to make them even. She smiled and turned her face up to meet his mouth. Stepping back, she smiled and said that was nice.

With the biscuits done, Larry started cooking some bacon. Sarah walked out to take a closer look at her new horses. She had been afraid to take too long of a look, thinking Gary would change his mind before they could get away from the ranch. Sitting on a log, they ate their dinner. Sarah walked down to the river to wash the dishes using river sand. With the fire down to coals, Larry said he was going to bed. Walking out, he pulled the picket pin on his horse, leading him back beside his bed roll to act as a watch dog. Larry's horse was a mustang taken from a herd in Eastern Nevada only a year ago. He would blow if anything came close. He had two other horses waiting for him in

Sacramento when he got back from this trip, they were part of the Barton gang's stock.

Sarah carried her bedroll over next to Larry's and unrolled it. Larry asked her if she felt that was a good idea. She said nothing at the time, just went about getting ready to go to bed. Larry was laying on his back trying not to get too excited or nervous about Sarah sleeping next to him. When she got in her bedroll, she looked over at Larry and asked if he would just hold her during the night. He told her yes but that he may not get much sleep. This was a new thing for Larry. After putting her back to Larry she said she needed to get rid of some of the memories of being raped and forced into things at the ranch.

"I want to just feel again, this may just help some". Larry rolled over on his side and opened his arms to her, she moved back and molded into him, Larry felt himself getting hard and pushing into her back. Sarah acted like she never felt anything and went to sleep. It is hard to hold a women without touching her breast with your hand, that added to Larry's problem as Sarah slept.

Early the next morning Larry had got up to let Sarah sleep late if she could. Larry had never just held a sleeping woman all night. The sun was just peeking over the hills when Sarah woke up to the smell of breakfast cooking. Laying in Larry's blankets she started to smile. She was thinking just how unfair that was to ask a man to resist taking a woman who was sleeping in his bed. Stretching out in Larry's bed, letting the morning come to her, this was the first night of real sleep she had since her husband had been killed by the James Gang. Thanks Larry, you must be tired.

Knocking out her boots, she got up and walked down by the river and broke off a small willow twig to then peal back the bark to clean her teeth. Breaking an extra one, she walked back to Larry and handed it to him. He took it and went to work on his teeth as he finished cooking breakfast. When he stood up to fill their plates, Sarah walked over and kissed him rather well saying

"I just needed to test your cleaning job. I would say you passed. Can we eat now? I am starved". After eating, Sarah went back to the river to clean the dishes while Larry got the horses ready to travel. We should be able to make the ranch if we push hard today, we can eat the extra biscuits for lunch instead of stopping.

The sun had been down for a couple of hours by the time they got to the gate that led to the ranch. Sarah told Larry that they would be at her ranch in a few minutes.

"We can just turn out the mares but I want to keep the stallions in the barn so I can keep an eye on them". Riding into the ranch yard, Sarah rode to the barn and stepped down to open the doors. She asked Larry if he would ride in first-she was still scarred. Larry rode in and released the two stallions into box stalls on opposite sides of the barn to keep them out of trouble. Walking the mares through the gate to the pasture behind the barn, with the eight new mares behind the gate, he stood with a foot on the rail of the gate watching them look around and, as horses do, test each other to see who is boss of the yard.

After a few bites and some kicks it was settled the little gray won the day. Teeth bared, head down, she pushed the herd out onto the side hill to graze. Sarah came up to watch the fun as the leader took charge. She told Larry that didn't take long to establish the leader. Larry enjoyed watching horses as they moved around just being horses. Turning to Sarah he said it is a shame that people can't settle issues with so little fuss.

Sarah said, "let's go up to the house and get a bite to eat, I should be able to find something if I look around".

Larry said, "just show me a place to sleep I can wait until morning. We can work on breakfast then if you like". Reaching the house, Sarah told Larry to bring his kit and follow her.

Walking up the stairs she led him to her bedroom, Larry turned and held her shoulder saying "are you sure you want this"? "Yes' she said, I need to be loved". Larry looked into her eyes and told her that he was still planning to meet Ronnie Campbell's crew to haul the equipment back to the ranch in Eastern Nevada. Sarah, looking back, closed her eyes and asked him to kiss her. He did. "Yes," she said, "I do need to feel loved and I know you like me a lot".

Larry asked about water to wash up after the long day,

Sarah said, "let's go down to the kitchen and wash there". Sarah looked at Larry and started to undress,

Larry was just one button behind her. The pump water was cold, he could see her body react with the cool air. After washing, they ran back up the stairs to bed laughing like two young kids. They both jumped into bed and found each other ready. Larry was more than willing to help Sarah get rid of some of her demons.

The next morning after breakfast they went outside so Sarah could show Larry her ranch. They saddled up and rode out into the hills to check on her cattle.

"How many acres do you have on the ranch"? he asked as they rode.

"I have three thousand deeded and I control over ten thousand by the way the ranch sets. Dad filed on all the land with access to water in the back canyons. I have some great water, all of the streams run year around so I can push the cattle back into the hills during the summer and bring them into the lower valleys for the winter months".

"My horse operation will be kept on a small ranch my father purchased for me just west of here. It also controls many acres that we don't have a deed to, dad planned well. I want to show you a nice spot by the river. We can eat some lunch their if you like".

"You are the boss, so lead the way". Riding over the next hill Larry could see a line of trees that backed up to some hills. When they reached the trees he could see the river running along the side of the hill. Looking closer, he could hear some noise that sounded like a water fall.

"Larry, you are right, it is a waterfall". Riding up to the edge of a pool under the falls it was cool with a nice carpet of green grass. The horses went to work on the grass as they unloaded the food Sarah had packed. Laying down a blanket, she set out the food. As she started to raise up, she felt him behind her, she could feel a twinge low down, it felt good. Reaching between them she found him ready as she turned her head to kiss his lips. Lunch would wait, they were hungry for other things and food was not on the menu. Later, they went for a swim to cool off.

Walking back to the blanket they both lay down to let the sun dry them and nibbled on a biscuit and some cold meat. The sun had passed overhead with the trees making some shadows. Sarah reached over and put her hand on him. Larry was awake and pulled Sarah to him and they enjoyed each other one more time.

Riding back into the yard Larry asked her if they had time to look over the other ranch before dark, "yes we can do that". Turning to the north just past the house Sarah picked up a trail leading away from the house. After about a mile they came to a wagon road that turned back to the east leading into a canyon. Sarah told Larry we are now on the smaller ranch but this is one of the better streams in the area, even better than the ones on the other ranch.

The ranch house was small but there was a nice barn a little ways from the house. Riding in, he could tell this place needed some work to get it in shape. "Why don't you turn this house over to the new Vaqueros when they get here? One I think has a wife. She would do the cooking for anyone you hire. Let's go look at the barn, how many stalls do you have inside"?

"I think six down each side with a tack room in the front if I remember".

"This will make a good start for your horse operation. How are you going to handle the stallions? You remember Gary kept two of the mares, they were only fourteen hands, I think he likes a small horse".

Out of the eight we have three that are larger-just under sixteen hands. I will breed them to the Morgan stallion, they should give me horses that I can train for a light team or buggy horses. The others I will breed to the standard bred stallion, better saddle horses and faster I think. Let's get back and get ready to move some cattle out of the back canyons in the morning. Winter is on its way, I don't want to ride the back hills in the mud.

All of the next week they worked from dawn to dark eating by a campfire every night but they had gathered most of her cattle from the high canyons. In the morning they will take the cattle down into the lower valley to winter. They woke up warming up by the fire when they heard some riders splashing through the creek. Turning, three riders came into their campsite. Two of the men were men Larry knew from the ranch by Stockton the other one he had never seen before.

Julio rode up saying he tracked them from the ranch and came to see if they could be of any help. Larry introduced him to Sarah and Julio told them of the other riders. Sarah asked if they had had had breakfast. They all said they were ready to move cattle. Larry helped pick up the campsite and moved in behind the drive, they had little to do, Julio had it well in hand. Sarah and Larry just rode along behind enjoying the morning. Sarah asked Larry why don't we ride ahead and fix a meal for the noon stop. Loping over to Julio, they informed him of their plan. Loping past the cows they went to find a good spot to cook a noon meal for the new hands.

Late in the day Sarah rode into the yard only to find a wagon with a Mexican woman and two kids playing in the dirt by their wagon. Sarah rode up. Getting down from her horse, she asked the woman her name. She came back that she was Julio's wife and her name was Sonya Garza. "Well, we need to get some food ready. Would you like to help me"? They walked into the house. Sonya told the boys to play by the wagon until Papa got in with the cattle. Larry had stayed with the herd to help scatter the cattle in the lower canyons. They all rode into the yard about an hour later to find food on the table and Sonya and Sarah talking like they had lived together all of their lives.

Sarah had told the new crew to move over into the other ranch house and gave them directions. Sarah and Sonya would make a trip to town for supplies in the next few days. Larry would ride along for protection. This trip would take a long day each way using the team and wagon, the men would make repairs to the house and make a bunk room in the barn for the other two men. Jose Garza, who was Julio's brother, and his cousin Victor Garza went to work getting the repairs started. They had been working for Juan but wanted to be closer to their family in Chico. This was a good move for them.

Larry was lagging behind the wagon by about a mile just looking over different things along the wagon road. He had stopped to watch some salmon working along the river bank. When he came around the point of a hill he could see the wagon stopped and two men were talking to Sarah, as he eased closer. He was still behind some trees but he could hear Sarah tell the men to go away and don't come back. Then Larry heard one say that he may just take over where James Barton left off. Larry eased out of the trees taking the thong off of his pistol. Taking his time, he rode up beside the wagon on Sarah's side.

"Well boys, what would you be wanting now"? Both were watching Larry close but not making a move.

"Did I hear you say something about taking over where James Barton left off"?

"That is right, I am going to take over the ranch like James did". Larry just pulled his pistol and shot both men, they never got their guns clear of their holsters. Sarah was having a time holding the team but after a bit they quit trying to run, Larry asked her if she knew the two. She said that they had stopped by the ranch for a day or two a few months back. They are part of the Barton gang, or they were.

Both men were hit hard and were not trying to go for a gun. Larry stepped down and walked over saying this is just the way James Barton finished. I don't think you have long to wait, you will be joining James any minute.

"Sarah I think you just may have a bit more money for your bank account. These boys just died, what a shame don't you think? From what Sheriff Johnson told me there should only be two more alive from the Barton Gang, they may get the word about staying away from you and your ranch soon I think".

"Sarah did you look at the horses they are riding? Not many men ride them,"

"no," she said.

"Both are mares, and they are big. This will help your breeding operation some and at no cost to you, I think you may have made close to a thousand dollars in just seconds". With a flood of memories past now she was thinking about getting on to the store and getting supplies for the ranch.

Larry asked her if she could make it to the trading post and back to the ranch, he would like to take the bodies into Sacramento and collect the reward for her if it is ok.

"Yes I can make it. I don't think we will have any more problems with these two dead. I will see you back at the ranch in a few days". Sarah headed on to the trading post as Larry was loading the two dead men on their horses or should say her horses now.

Sheriff Johnson was pleased to mark off these two from his list. He said this only leaves Dave and Wes from the gang. Could you just go out and find them for me so I could close the book on that bunch of robbers? Sheriff Johnson asked Larry if he could be back to Sacramento a week early.

"Why" he asked.

"Well, I received a letter from Ronnie telling me that he has two men coming to Sacramento who he feels could be part of this gang, I have a feeling it could be Dave and Wes the last members of the Barton Gang. Ronnie feels that they will try to rob Sam and Sean south of Stockton on the way into Sacramento. I would like to have you with me when I ride out to meet the wagons". Larry asked if he could be a real deputy, Sheriff Johnson said he could.

"Well, I will be back in plenty of time to meet the freight wagons, Sarah will be settled with her new men on the ranch".

The reward was only five hundred on each of the men but an extra thousand will be nice, Larry and Sheriff Johnson walked over to the bank to make the deposit in her name. "Get that badge ready. I will be back in three weeks. Polish it up some so it will look good on my vest". Turning north, Larry was leading the two horses and thinking about getting to be a real live deputy and being able to shoot a robber legal like. Larry liked the Idea of hunting down outlaws as a fulltime job, he was an above average hand with a pistol so he felt this kind of work would suit him fine. The other part of being a deputy marshal would be he should have a lot of time off between jobs.

Reaching the ranch, Larry rode into the ranch yard. Changes were being made and they looked good, Sarah walked out to meet Larry and gave him a knee shattering kiss when he stepped down from his horse.

"Well, I see you made it back. Did you get to shoot anyone while you were gone"?

"No but Sheriff Johnson has asked me to help finish off this Barton Gang. He has a line on the last two men. Wes and Dave could be riding with a wagon train heading this way, they intend to rob Ronnie's crew before they get to Stockton, so I will be leaving in a couple of weeks. You now have an additional one thousand dollars in your bank account".

"I have a couple of weeks before I need to head to Sacramento so what I would like to do is teach you how to shoot both rifle and pistol.

"Sarah, you need to be able to protect yourself at all times, so in the morning we will get started".

Larry, "I would like to get better with both pistol and rifle, I remember only too well what can happen if you are not able to protect yourself.

Sarah, "Do you have enough work for Julio's crew to last the next two weeks"? Larry asked.

Sarah said, she had talked to Julio about going into the back country to see if there are additional cattle to be brought down to the lower canyons. When we did a count, I am about 25 cows short, I don't think they have been stolen, it is hard to get out over the canyons to the east.

Jim getting ready for the Nevada Day Parade in 2016, fun day to be a member of the Pony Express. The Nevada Division.

Chapter 10 **Ride to The Hot Springs**

Riding out of the ranch yard with Tony in the lead and Maggie riding behind the pack horse, Ronnie turned to Abby saying I hope they find what we did. I love you Abby and kissed her. They watched until they were blanketed by the trees. They walked back into the house to meet with Sam and Sean about the upcoming trip to pick up the mining supplies in Sacramento. Sam said he would like to go home until you want us to start for Sacramento. Sean could pick me up on the way if you keep Bart West on for the trip.

Ronnie said for him to go back to the ranch with Beth and Little Jon. That plan would work unless he had to make a change, then he would send someone to tell him.

"See you when you get back with the mining equipment". With Tony and Maggie gone for a few days on their short wedding trip, Sam heading home with his family, and with Zack and Betty leaving in the morning, they would be able to spend some time alone.

Sean came up to tell Ronnie that the two brothers would be helping Andy Sams in the forge until we head west, Andy was making some repairs on the wagons if that was ok with him. Sean was going to load some of the timbers and haul them out to the mine site if that would be ok. Ronnie asked him if he could use one of the brothers at the mine and have Bart West help Andy. "Great, that will work out just fine if I have some help if I need to move some dirt. Do you want me to bring back the ore or break it out and just bring back the gold"?

"Go ahead and just bring back the gold".

*

Tony worked his way along the bottom of a canyon winding its way back into the mountains. There was just a whisper of a trail beside the stream. As they climbed higher into the canyon the trail branched off to the left and started to make some switchbacks as they climbed up and over the spine of the mountain. Tony kept asking Maggie if she was doing ok. When Tony reached the top Maggie rode up beside him and touched his leg and smiled at him.

"Have you ever seen anything like this? It looks like the world is laid out at our feet," She said.

"No," he said and pointed to a valley below them. "That is where we will camp for the next few days. It will take about two hours to reach the valley floor".

"Ok let's get going. I want to find the hot springs the Indians told us about".

They reached the camping spot beside the stream and among the trees. Tony started to unload the pack horse and Maggie gathered some firewood for their campfire. Tony left the saddles on the two horses so they could ride over to the hot springs after they had the camp set up. With the camp ready, Tony joined Maggie in their bedrolls. "Maggie, are you ready to become my wife"?

"Yes, I have been so ready I hurt", Maggie opened the blanked and Tony joined her. After they finished showing their love for each other they lay talking about their future.

"Tony, I never could have thought loving you could be so wonderful".

"Maggie," he said, "you are the most wonderful person I have ever known, I am so glad we waited, our first time could have never been this good without the wait. Thank you for making my life whole. I love your red curls, all of them," he said.

Tony got up pulling on his pants and went over and started the fire. Looking back, all he could feel was his love for his new wife with flaming red curls. Walking down to the stream, he filled one of the cooking pots to heat water in so they could wash up before going to bed for the night. Maggie was lying on their bedrolls looking up at the clouds passing through the trees and thinking about how she had never had a day like this one. When Tony came to her with the warm water, they both washed up as the light was going away. When they had finished, Maggie moved close to Tony. Rapping his arms around her they both fell asleep.

The sun was peaking over the mountains when they woke up Tony looked out at the horses to see if they were ok. He could see them working on the last of the grass that they could reach. Tony got up and pulled the picket pins and put them on a new spot of ground along the stream. Walking back to the fire pit he found a few hot coals. Dropping some tinder on them he had the fire started in a few minutes.

Walking down to the river he used river sand to wash the pan, bring back water for coffee. Dumping the coffee in the coffee pot he set it on the corner of the fire to boil. He placed the frying pan on the fire then cut strips of bacon into the pan to cook. Maggie woke up to the smell of frying bacon. Maggie lay on her side just watching her man cooking breakfast over the open fire. Tony could feel her eyes on him and turned around to be greeted by a big smile framed by a ball of red hair.

Tony asked if she would like some coffee, it should be ready. She said yes and a piece of that bacon if it is ready.

"We kind of skipped dinner last night if I remember". Tony asked her if she would rather have had dinner. He got another big smile and she shook her head and said no, last night was the best it could have ever been.

Going over to one of the packs he removed a package of biscuits they had brought along and placed two slices of bacon between one after dipping each half in a bit of the bacon grease, then took it to Maggie.

"Can I eat right here? I am nice and warm. I might catch a chill if I get up like I am".

Tony said he could get their coffee and a biscuit and join her back in bed.

Maggie said, "how can a cold biscuit with some hot bacon taste so good to me today, it must be the mountain air, or it could be the lack of food last night".

Maggie laid back on the blankets and asked Tony if it would be too soon for him to make love to her again.

"No," he said, and removed his pants. Lifting up the blanket, he moved under to join her. Tony told her to take charge, so most of the day was filled with making love and talking about their future.

On the third day they rode out to find the hot springs the Indians had told them about. After a short ride they found it. Stripping off their clothes, they eased into the hot water. It smelled a little like Sulfur but the warm water was great. After a bit, they got out and ran into the ice water of the stream, Maggie's skin was pink from the water. They got back to the campsite late in the afternoon. Tony started to gather up the supplies and put them back into the packs, getting ready for the return trip back to the ranch in the morning.

With this being their last night alone for a few weeks they held each other and filled the night with love making and talking. After a light breakfast, they saddled up and started back to the ranch so they could get ready to ride to Sacramento to finish their honeymoon. Maggie asked Tony if Ronnie had ever told him about the big brass tub at the hotel.

Tony asked, what tub?

"You will find out when we reach Sacramento" she said.

Chapter 11 **Going to Find a Horse Race**

Ronnie turned to Abby saying, "we may have a problem with this new cook, I found out that he had been looking around the house".

"How did you find that out"?

"I found some flour at the desk and also in each of the bedrooms today. When I went in to look at the bill for the lumber there was some flour on the desk drawer. Not much but a few flakes. I am going to talk to Sean about what he saw on the trip back from Genoa. Now I also must think about Bart West, he is riding way too good of a horse and his gun is well used".

"I have not seen them talking much but Bart was in the high country most of the week, I think I will ask Tee and White Bird to keep a watch and see if they get together and talk. The letter I got from Juan said that they shot up most of the Barton Gang but Sheriff Johnson felt that two or three may have gotten away, one was James Barton's brother Wes".

Abby said, "I have been thinking if you reverse the name Bart West that could Wes Barton".

Ronnie said, "why don't we not get excited until we have some idea that things are not what they are now. If we have a problem they will need to get together soon because the wagons will be heading west when Tony and Maggie get back".

For the past two nights Tee had been watching inside of the barn and White Bird was watching from the trees behind the house. Tee was sitting with his back to the wall waiting to see if the two men got up to talk outside. The Jenkins brothers were also sleeping in the barn. It was getting on midnight when they crept past Tee, they had no idea he was watching. Moving outside the barn they walked out to the creek to talk. White Bird had moved up behind some trees so he could listen to what they had to say, Tee was watching from a spot behind one of the wagons in the ranch yard only a few yards from the two men.

*

Bart was asking if Dave had found out the location of the gold, he was saying he had found nothing that looked like a storage area. They knew that Sean had returned with a small bag of gold from the mine site a few days ago and neither had seen the hiding location in the house. Dave was asking what will we do if we can't find the gold before we start west with the wagons. Bart told Dave that he was thinking on this some and Ronnie could be sending the gold to the bank in Sacramento in one of the wagons. Bart said let's get back before we are found out here talking, Dave said that he would go back and Bart could follow in a few minutes.

The next day Tee and White Bird found Ronnie and said that the two men had walked out to the river and talked some then. Dave went back to the barn Bart came back later. Ronnie saddled Diamond and Dandy, leading them up to the house. Ronnie called out to Abby, asking if she would like to go out and look at some of the horses. Walking out, she stepped up on Dandy and they headed out north along the river. Riding only a mile or so from the ranch, Ronnie stopped. They got down and found a log to sit on so they could talk about the two men.

"Abby I think I have a plan to put these two men in jail if they are who we think they are. This is how it will work".

*

Tony rode into the yard with Maggie beside him holding hands as they came into the ranch yard. Abby and Ronnie met them at the corral. Ronnie called for Jack and Billy to remove the tack and put the horses in the corral. Abby and Maggie walked back to the house to talk about the short honeymoon at the hot springs. Maggie looked around to see if anyone was around. Seeing none she whispered to Abby that she could have never thought making love could be so good. Abby told her that it is still so good even after the time Ronnie and I have been married.

Abby whispered to Maggie "I am going to have a baby. I have missed two months now".

"Does Ronnie know"?

"No, I am going to tell him after you leave for Sacramento. I want to be alone when I give him the news, you can tell Tony after you leave also, I just don't want a big fuss".

Maggie said maybe she could be also though she doubts it.

Abby said you just don't know when it will happen. "I hope I have a baby soon so they can grow up together".

Ronnie and Tony were sitting out by the river talking about the trip to Sacramento.

"There could be a problem with Dave and Bart," Ronnie said. "We don't know for sure they are together in a plot to steal some gold but I think they are the last of the Barton Gang". He went on to tell Tony about the letter from Juan on how Larry McPherson laid a plan and killed most of the gang and put the rest in jail to wait trial for murder and robbery. "This is how I want you to deal with Dave and Bart," Ronnie said.

Two days later the wagons would be heading west to Sacramento. The job would be to pick up the mining equipment Ronnie had ordered. Ronnie had taken the suggestion about shipping the equipment to Sacramento to be loaded on the wagons at the wagon shop because he had a dock and lifting equipment. Ronnie and Tony had slipped out and opened the secret compartment in Abby's wagon and hid the gold in there. The next day Ronnie and the men loaded a strong box into Sam's wagon and bolted it to the floor. Andy Sams had fixed the bolts so it would take another blacksmith to remove the box.

Both Bart and Dave helped with this task. The two Jenkins brothers were happy to be on the road again, another adventure for them all the way to Sacramento. Bart was not too happy when he found out his horse was lame on his right front hoof, Bart had planned on using his horse as a getaway mount after he and Dave stole the gold from the wagon. Wes had Andy check him and he told Wes that he had a bad stone bruise and would not be able to be ridden for two weeks. The wagons left the yard the next morning at daylight with Sam's wagon in the lead, Bart would drive it to the Applegate's ranch to pick up Sam. He would lead the crew to Sacramento. Tony and Maggie were riding out about a mile in front of the wagons. This way they could keep out of the dust from the wagons and keep an eye out for trouble along the way. What Bart didn't know was that Ronnie had Andy pull two nails and replace them but get them a bit deep so Bart's horse would have a sore hoof, Ronnie wanted Bart to be afoot without his horse and Bart was not very happy about leaving his horse at the ranch. After the wagons pulled out Andy removed the two nails and then he pulled all of the shoes to let the hoof grow out for a few months.

*

Abby turned to Ronnie saying, "I have some great news to tell you if you would like to hear,"

"Well what could that news be"?

"You are going to be a father". Ronnie grabbed her and spun her around, kissing her soundly.

"When did you know, does anyone else know".

"Yes" she said, "I told Maggie to tell Tony after they have left and when they get to California tell Juan and Juanita". When he asked her, Abby said it should be in the spring. 'Yes," she said, "early May I think".

"Do you think it would be ok for you to ride" I have an idea, why don't we ride over to Salt Lake City and take Buster and Lightning and see if we could find a horse race or two, Andy can watch over the crew putting on the roof and Tee and White Bird can take care of the stock".

"Let's go, she said. "When do you want to leave"?

"Why don't we start out in the morning just after the sun get's up.

Did Maggie tell you about the hot spring"?

"Yes, she did and I think we should give it a try to see if it can match the big brass tub at the hotel in Sacramento".

The next day they rode out with one of Abby's gildings, Diamond, leading Buster. Lightning was loaded with supplies.

"Why did you bring Lightning instead of Dandy"? Abby asked.

"Well, I think he can catch Buster in a longer race. This would be a great time to find out". Riding back into the hills, Ronnie found the trail leading over the mountain. As they climbed up along the creek Ronnie stopped to let Abby look back over the ranch laid out below with the stream winding along the valley floor. Ronnie told her that the next climb will be quite steep leading to the ridge.

As they topped out Abby could see both directions looking down into the fingers and upper meadows holding the cattle. Ronnie told her someday soon we will be able to look out and see thousands of cattle grazing, when our baby is 10 it will be that way. Ronnie turned to Abby saying to pull out her Henry slow and lever a round into the chamber. He was pulling his rifle as he spoke. Easing back, his hand took the thong off of the hammer on his pistol. He whispered to Abby to ease a little to the right and point your rifle at the leader when they walk out of the trees.

Six Indians eased forward into a small bench. They were just 50 feet from them. Ronnie raised his hand and spoke to them in Paiute.

Only one had a rifle, the others carried bows and the leader held a lance. The six Indians were looking at them with cold black eyes for what seemed like an hour.

When the leader spoke, he asked about Tee and White Bird. Ronnie asked why they wanted to see them. The leader said that he was a friend.

Ronnie told the leader he could follow their trail and it would lead to the ranch, Tee and White Bird are living at the ranch. Thinking for a bit, the leader touched his heals to his horse's flank and walked past Ronnie and Abby, heading down the trail to the ranch. Ronnie gave Abby a look and moved down off the mountain leading to the hot springs. When they reached the bottom Ronnie looked back and Abby was still white and was still holding her rifle.

"Abby, I am sure glad I started to learn Paiute from Tee and White Bird".

Abby asked if Andy would be ok. Sure, Tee and White Bird like him, he has helped them many times, he even eats with them sometimes.

*

Andy was shoeing one of the new colts when he looked up to see six Indians riding out of the trees heading for the barn. Andy dropped his tools and ran into the far side of his shop to get his rifle. By the time he ran back to the door Tee was coming out of the corral leading a filly he had been working. Tee came to a stop and raised his hand. Turning, he walked to their camp. The Indian kids came running out of the trees to join Tee. White Bird came galloping in on his horse to greet the small band of Indians.

All Andy could do was just watch from the forge shop to see what was going on at the Indian camp. After a short time Andy carried his rifle over to the forge, leaned it by the center post, and went back to work on the colt's feet. If Tee and White Bird were ok with the Indians at the ranch he would be too. The Indians stayed for two days then rode off into the mountains. Andy still had his hair, well, what was left of it anyway.

*

After the camp was set up, Ronnie asked Abby if she wanted to find the hot springs and get naked. After a short ride through the trees they found what they were looking for. Stepping down, they started getting rid of their clothes. After sticking a foot in to test the temp, they both jumped in feeling their muscles relax. After they were both pink from the hot water they jumped into the stream letting the ice cold water wash away the Sulfur smell from the hot spring. Putting back on their clothes, they rode back to the campsite to fix some dinner and get ready for bed. Ronnie was getting the horses set for the night while Abby was cooking steaks she had brought along for the first night out. The steak with onions and potatoes was ready when Ronnie returned. The sun was behind the mountain and the dark was settling in when they finished cleaning the dishes in the sand by the river.

Ronnie started to ask Abby if it is still ok to "you know". He smiled and pointed to the bedrolls.

"Would you like yours or mine"? After they finished, they lay talking about the baby. "Are you going to be ok having the baby at the ranch"?

Abby said that Maggie will help her deliver. "All you need to do is cover your ears and stay out of the way".

Both were up early. The leftover coffee was heated and they finished off the meat from last night's dinner. They were ready to ride. Ronnie said that they would pick up the wagon trail the next day sometime. They then will follow the trail on into Salt Lake City.

Abby asked, "how will we find some horses to race"?

Ronnie said, "We will find a real nice place to eat and tie all four horses up to the hitch rail for all to see".

"Then we will start talking to some of the men about our horses, they will want to take a better look at what we have. By the time we finish dinner we will have some leads or even a match race. When we stable the horses at the livery stable the owner will get a good look and he will also spread the word and help set up a race".

Riding up to one of the best hotels and restaurant, Ronnie tied all the horses up to the hitching rail then fussed over Buster and Lightning some before going in to eat. Abby just stood on the porch waiting for Ronnie to finish. She greeted some people as they came by. All were looking at the horses, as they came by on the porch of the hotel. When Ronnie finished with the horses they went in and got the best room they had. Ronnie asked if it had a large brass tub. He was informed they did and had hot water at the tub.

The desk clerk asked if they wanted the horses stabled. Ronnie said that he would do that after they cleaned up and had some dinner. Ronnie went out and unloaded the two carpet bags holding their clothes. With help from the porter they went up to their room. The sun was starting to go down when they jumped into the brass tub to wash some of the road dirt off. The road dirt must have been bad because it took a long time for washing to be finished.

Abby found herself making sure that everything still fit and was working fine and a good time was enjoyed by all. When they came down ready for dinner, Ronnie asked about the location of the livery stable. With that information, they went into the dining room to eat. They would have a small wait so Ronnie went into the bar to have a drink and Abby went to the sitting room just for the ladies. With a glass of brandy, Ronnie leaned back on the bar and was looking around when a man approached him asking if the two horses were for sale. Ronnie told him that they were two of his race horses and he would not like to sell either of them. The man then introduced himself to Ronnie saying that he is Jim Baxter, Ronnie introduced himself.

Jim asked if he could join Ronnie and Abby for dinner and talk about horse racing around Salt Lake City. Ronnie said why not, our table should be ready any time. Finishing their drinks, they went to find Abby and get to their table. When Abby came out to meet them, Jim told her who he was and hoped it would be ok for him to join them for dinner. At dinner they all three talked about ranching and fast horses.

Jim said that he would set up a few races around the area if that would be ok with them.

Jim then said, he just happened to have a racetrack at his ranch just outside of town.

*

Sam came out of the house to meet the wagons, Beth and Little John followed along with his travel supplies. Saying good bye, they drove off heading for Sacramento to pick up the mining equipment. Sam had Bart move over to help drive the other wagon with the Jenkins Brothers. Dave Baker was driving the cook and supply wagon, bringing up the rear behind the other wagons.

Tony and Maggie rode up alongside Sam. Tony stepped over onto the wagon seat beside Sam so he could talk with him about Dave and Bart and what Ronnie is thinking they will try before we get to Sacramento. Maggie had picked up Teddy's reins and was keeping up at the side of the wagon. After a mile or so they had a plan in place if the two tried to steal the gold or even try to find the hiding location.

When they crossed the Carson River, Tony and Maggie rode ahead on into Carson City to see if they could hire two additional men to help with the return trip from Sacramento. Tony also felt that Bart and Dave were thinking about finding the gold that was in the strong box in the wagon. Both men had been checking out the wagons during their time on guard duty each night. Ronnie, Sam, and Tony all felt that they would try to make a move when they got close to Sacramento because they both knew the area better and had some hiding spots picked out.

Tony and Maggie found two men that would make good helpers on the return trip. They felt it would be better to hire men in Carson City than try to find help with the gold rush going on in California. One of the men could cook some and would help Dave with the cooking duties and on the return trip. Marty Thomas would help Dave and Randy Jones would be a wagon helper. Both men had their own horses and were armed with the new Henrys and each had a 44 colt pistol. They said that they both had been over the trail a few times and their guns looked like they had been uses some.

Chapter 12 **Trying to Steal the Gold**

Tony, Maggie and the two new hands met Sam and the wagons at the general store in Carson City to pick up some extra supplies to feed the additional men during the trip on to Sacramento. Supplies loaded the wagons headed over the mountains to California. Tony had the two new men ride as rear guard behind the cook wagon.

Dave and Bart had tried to find a way to get into the strong box mounted to the floor of the first wagon, but Sam seemed to be close by every time they tried to get a good look. Dave and Bart knew of a couple of men they could get to help with the robbery when they got close to Sacramento, they would bide their time. Tony and Sam were talking about how edgy the two men were getting each day,

Tony said that they will need to keep a close watch on the horses each night from now on. Sam felt that they would make their move prior to stopping at the rancho just south of town.

*

Sheriff Johnson and Larry McPherson were at the rancho talking to Juan about when he figured to see the wagons from Nevada, they all felt it could be any day now. Larry and the Sheriff would ride south with two pack horses in the morning to meet the wagons and check out this Dave Baker and Bart West. They both felt that they were what were left of the Barton Gang. At first light they were saddled and heading out of the main gate at the rancho with food and supplies for a week. They would ride out to meet the wagons.

The main wagon road heading up the valley that passed by the entrance to the Rancho was about the only way to Sacramento from the south, Larry had come down from the ranch north of Sacramento where he had been helping the widow Sarah James get her ranch restarted. On the second day of riding south they made camp as the sun went down. After eating, Larry and Sheriff Johnson were talking by the campfire and they both felt that they would meet the wagons early the next day.

*

As night settled in at the wagons, Tony told Dave that he would stand watch at midnight and wake Bart at three to take over. Tony felt that they would wait another day before they made a try for the gold. Tony was thinking about how the two men would try to get into the strong box but could not come up with a good idea as how they would try.

Dave Baker had spent time around the blacksmith shop at the ranch watching Andy work the steel. One day when Andy went to get a horse, he picked up a steel pry bar that laid by the wall of the blacksmith shop. Later in the day he moved it to the supply wagon for use later if needed. The new men had their horses on the end of the picket line each night. The saddles all were stored on the wagon tong each night. Dave and Wes felt that everything was ready to steal the gold and make their escape Dave had the pry bar ready to break the lock on the strong box. They would make their move when it was his time to get Bart up for morning watch.

Dave moved over and touched Bart's arm telling him it was time to make their move. Dave had the pry bar in his hand. Moving over to the wagon with the strong box he eased into the darkness inside the wagon. Feeling for the lock, he slipped the bar into the lock's opening and eased his weight into the bar. With a snap the lock broke apart. Reaching into the box, he felt three bags. They were heavy, two were large and the third one was small, it was the one he had seen Sean deliver to Ronnie from the mine just over a week ago.

Tony heard a snap and woke up to listen. It must have been a limb breaking on a tree. He went back to sleep. Dave waited for about ten minutes before he moved the sacks onto the wagon seat, he eased out of the wagon to join Bart who had saddling two horses. Bart was still mad about not having his horse to make his escape when they got the gold, he knew that the only horse on this trip that could even think about keeping up with his horse was Tony's big stud. They found that neither saddle had a rifle in the scabbard. They would have to do with just their pistols until they could find some place to steal a rifle.

Stepping into the saddle they walked the horses up to the side of the wagon and eased the gold into their saddle bags and walked slowly out of camp, making as little noise as possible. About a mile down the trail, they clicked up the horses to a gallop heading north.

*

With the sun just making it over the top of the mountains Sheriff Johnson and Larry McPherson rode south to meet the wagons. They had ridden five miles when they came to the wagon campsite. Tony was mad as hell about not catching the two men when they were breaking the lock inside of the wagon. Tony had Teddy saddled and was ready to ride out when Larry and Sheriff Johnson reached their camp. Larry and the Sheriff stepped down and got a cup of coffee and started to talk to Tony about the men. Johnson asked about what they looked like and if they had any scars that were showing.

Larry talked Tony into heading for the ranch and letting them run the men to ground. Tony agreed and started the wagons for the rancho. He wanted to see his family it had been a long time. Larry talked to the new men about the horses Bart and Dave were riding then tossed out the coffee grounds and stepped into the saddle. Picking up the trail just outside of camp Sheriff Johnson and Larry started out at a canter, following the trail left by the two horses. Larry turned to Sheriff Johnson and asked him how long he thought it will take to catch these boys? Sheriff Johnson told Larry to raise his right hand to swear him in as a deputy, now you can shoot them legal like.

Larry found out by talking to Marty and Randy that both horses needed to be shooed, both horses would start throwing shoes with any hard riding. Dave and Bart were pushing the two horses hard and after about fifteen miles Dave's horse lost a front shoe. By the afternoon both horses had lost all their shoes and were bare foot. The two men needed to steal some new horses and fast if they were going to make good their getaway.

As the night started to overtake the outlaws, Bart told Dave to stop so they could divide the gold and then split up and go different ways. That would make it harder for anyone to catch them if they headed off in different ways. Under some cottonwood trees they found a spot with a large log to sit on as they divided the gold. Dave pulled the bags from their saddle bags. They sat down to have a look. Picking out the small bag of gold and looking he could see worth about fifty dollars. Taking the tie from one of the larger bags and reaching into the bag he found cast bullets for 44 colt pistols, not gold. Checking the second bag they found the same thing cast bullets.

Why would they lock up bullets"?

"Are you sure you got all of the sacks out of the box"? Bart asked Dave.

"Hell yes," he said, "what do you take me for a damn fool"?

Bart told Dave to hand him the saddle bags so he could look and see if he had more than he had said.

"Bart do think I would steal from you"? and went for his gun. He was just a second too late, Dave had two bullets in him before he could pull the trigger. Bart stood up and picked up the saddle bags and found some extra gear but no gold. Bart was now alone with two bags of 44 bullets and fifty dollars worth of gold. "When will I just trust someone? Now I will have that damn Tony and his big stud on my trail within a few hours".

Now Bart had to find a new horse because he was sure that Tony would be on his trail and gaining every mile. Riding a horse without shoes over rocky ground would put him afoot in hours. Bart crossed a small stream and found a trail leading northeast, not the way he wanted to go but the soft trail would save his horse. Keeping at a trot to save the horse he would ride until dark then make a cold camp, with no fire. He should be safe for the night. At first light he was headed more east along a trail that would help him meet up with the Pony Express Trail. Then he would double back and head back into Nevada, then on east to Salt Lake City. About midday Bart found just what he needed a ranch with horses in the corral by a barn. He was still mad about not having his own horse, now he was stealing a horse that could be just as bad or worse than the one he stole from Marty.

Riding into the ranch yard he called to the house. No one answered so he rode on to the barn, still no one was around. Leading his tired and sore footed horse into the corral, he put a loop over a nice bay gelding with one white stocking. Checking the shoes, they looked good. Switching the gear, he was on his way in just a few minutes, heading east, looking for the trail over the Sierras leading back to Nevada. Bart West felt he could now get away without any problems.

After a few miles he reached the trail, he was looking for, the Old Pony Express Trail heading east.

*

Ten miles behind Bart, Larry and Sheriff Johnson found one of the stolen horses and Dave Baker shot in the chest two times.

"Well, Larry you only have one man to chase down now". he said,

"What do you mean? I only have one to chase down"?

"Remember when I had you raise your right hand and say them words about following orders"?

"Yes, I did that before, when we were taking the last prisoner back to Sacramento".

Sheriff Johnson asked, "have you looked at the badge"?

"Well, no",

"Take a good look at it". When Larry turned up his badge, he could see US Deputy Marshal.

"I kind of forgot to tell you that you that now work for the US Government and you report to me. I am the US Marshal in charge of California and Nevada, so with that said I am heading back to Sacramento and you follow the tracks until you either shoot him or you take him into custody. Good luck and happy hunting".

Larry turned to watch Marshal Johnson pick up Randy's horse and ride back down the trail heading back to Sacramento and home. Larry pulled the body over to a sand bank and covered him with sand the best he could without a shovel.

As Larry followed Bart's trail leading east heading for the Sierras, after riding about ten miles, Larry found Marty's horse in a corral with two other horses. Finding no one at home he started to check the tracks of Bart's new horse. After a few miles Larry was getting an idea as to how Bart's new horse moved. Not too far down the trail Larry could see that the horse Bart was riding would not be hard to follow, each time he set his right hind foot it landed a bit outside of the front hoof track in the soft dirt along the trail. Since Larry knew what the tracks looked like he would take a direct route so to hit the trail over the Sierras leading his pack horse.

Larry was a big man, just over six feet four, weight going about 240 pounds in his sock feet. When he and Juan shot up the Barton Gang Larry picked up two of the better horses for his own to replace his mustang he had been riding for a short time. The two dead men would never need them again anyway. Both horses could be used as a pack horse or to ride. Many outlaws had the best horses in the west, all had speed and stamina, but most important thing is how fast they could walk. The only horse Larry had seen that could stay with these two he had now was Diamond, the big stud Ronnie Campbell rode.

Larry had renamed the two horses to suit him, both were bays. The one he was riding he called Jack. He was just under 17 hands and had one white stocking on his right front foot, and the pack horse he called Buddy-had a white blaze running from between his eyes down to his nose, one half of his nose was white. Larry had kept Jack in check until he established the tracks Bart's horse left in the trail. Then letting Jack have his head, he could feel him move out at a ground eating walk. Larry knew he would make up a mile or two each hour on Bart. Larry turned off the main trail and took a shortcut that led more south and to the east a bit. This trail was one Larry had been over when he rode for the Pony Express when he was picking up supplies for the express station he rode out of from time to time. Larry felt he could get ahead of Wes Barton by using this shortcut. He would find out soon when he hit the main trail leading over the Sierras.

Larry pulled up and eased off the trail by a small stream at noon to give his horses some food and rest. He pulled off the saddles and gave both a good rub down with some dry grass. With Jack and Buddy on a picket line, Larry went back to the pack saddle and got some grain. Larry then lit a small fire to boil some coffee a man had to have his coffee. Pulling out some jerky and a biscuit he moved over to a tree in the shade to let the horses eat. After an hour or so Larry saddled up and set out on the trail heading east. With a little nap and his horses fed, he was ready to get back on the trail. Larry figured that Bart would push on, not taking a break. Bart would not have any grain with him, nor would he take time to take a noon break to rest his horse.

*

Bart had stopped only to water his horse and heat some coffee, only taking 20 minutes, and then was back on the road heading east looking for the trail leading to Carson City to pick up the wagon road leading to Salt Lake City and freedom. Bart had made some effort to cover his tracks when any chance came along, riding up a stream for a mile then getting out on a rock shelf leading into some trees. The leaves would also help to remove the tracks. Moving back onto the trail, Bart kicked his horse into a canter for a mile or so but soon found out his horse was starting to tire. He had ridden his horse over twenty-five miles without any rest or food or water. Dropping back down to a walk, he felt the hair start to stand up on the back of his neck. Now he could feel that someone was on his trail and moving up. Due to not resting his horse, he started to get mad at himself for shooting Dave and not getting some grain from the barn when they stole the horses at the ranch.

Bart still had six hours until dusk and he had a tired horse and still had to start the climb over the Sierras. He had to find a spot to hide for the rest of the day and give his horse a chance to recover. Bart had passed a small stream coming out from the hills about a half mile back along the trail. Reining his horse off the trail, he stepped down and brushed out the track and sprinkled leaves and dirt over it to hide his trail. Bart turned back along the trail, working through the brush until he reached the stream riding upstream. He found a small clearing with some grass for his horse.

Stripping off the saddle and putting his horse on a picket line, He found a good spot to take a rest. He would stay here all night, just moving his horse onto new grass. Gathering some dry wood, he made some coffee and ate some jerky. Laying out his bedroll, he settled in for the night.

During the day Bart started to think about how things had started to go wrong over the past few months, James his brother was a planner and for the most part always kept ahead of the law. When James had been taken down Bart had been out scouting out a big pay role job for James, James had been looking at pulling this robbery for over two years. Bart had been in Virginia City when he heard that James and most of his gang was killed just north of Sacramento.

After hearing about James, Bart decided to drift out of the area to find a spot that he was not known. As he was riding through Carson City, he seen a bunch of wagons heading east and who was driving one of the wagons Dave Baker. Dave was always hanging around the gang but not really part of it, but Dave had a nose for money. Dave would know him by Wes Barton, but he was going to follow these wagons to see what Dave was up to.

*

Larry was getting close by using his shortcut. When he reached the main trail, he found the tracks and they looked fresh. No other horse had passed this way and the shoe print had sharp edges in the dirt, Larry felt he was within hours behind Bart.

Over the past few weeks Larry had been working on his holster so he could get his pistol out faster. The new cutaway holster seemed to work out better, but it still was hanging up, so Larry had soaked the holster in water and then molded the holster to fit his gun. After the holster was dry, he started working some oil into the leather, sliding his colt in and out of the molded holster. This seemed to be working. With the pistol sliding in and out with ease, he added a leather thong to go over the hammer to hold the pistol in when he was riding.

Just before dark Larry was looking for a spot to make camp when the tracks went away, Larry got off and could see that the tracks had been brushed out. Bart must have turned off the trail to find a spot to rest. Larry decided he would ride on a few miles to a spot he had camped before. It would be dark by the time he arrived at this campsite, but it had water and plenty of grass along the stream for his horses and hot coffee.

The sun had gone over the hills by the time he got to the campsite. There was enough light to gather some firewood and make some coffee, then take care of the horses. Larry settled in behind a line of trees just off to the north side of the trail. Larry planned to have some bacon on the fire by the time Bart would be riding by. Larry felt that Bart would never think anyone would be ahead of him. With the sun bringing the day into the low country, Larry got a fire going from the coals from last nights.

Getting the frying pan out Larry cut two strips off the slab of bacon into the frying pan. With the bacon sizzling in the pan, Larry kept watch on the back trail. Using his knife, he picked out the two strips of bacon, putting them on a cold biscuit. Setting the biscuit aside, Larry cut two more strips and dropped them in to the hot frying pan to keep the smell drifting down the trail. Larry just about finished eating the biscuit then turned the second two pieces over to cook the other side. Down the trail Larry could hear a horse coming at a soft trot. Easing the leather thong off the hammer on his pistol, he eased it in his holster. He moved over to stand part way behind a tree with the half-eaten biscuit in his left hand.

He could see a rider coming at a soft trot. Seeing the camp and for sure smelling the bacon, the rider slowed down and called out to the camp asking to come in. Larry told him to come in and have a bite to eat. Bart rode up and stepped down, keeping his horse between him and the fire. After looking things over and seeing the man with a half-eaten biscuit in his left hand, he walked to the fire. Larry told him to grab a biscuit and the bacon, and I will tie up your horse then I will put on some more bacon if you would like me to.

Bart walked up to the fire as Larry walked over to his horse and popped the last of the biscuit into his mouth and moved him over to a tree by his horse's so he could get a look at the hoof prints. Seeing that this was his guy, he moved back to the fire to offer him some coffee. Bart had the bacon and biscuit in his left hand. When Larry walked around the tree his jacket opened a little and Bart got a look at the badge, Bart made a play for his gun as Larry's right foot hit the ground. His hand slapped the butt of the colt and it came out in a flash, firing his first round and thumbing the hammer back and fired the second shot.

Bart felt he had him cold but as he was leveling the gun to fire, he felt the slug slam him in the chest, he fired into the dirt at Larry's feet and slid to the ground with his lights going out he never knew he was hit by the second bullet. With Bart's history, Larry removed the pan from the fire and set back and finished the bacon and had another sip of coffee. He reloaded the two fired cylinders then rotating it, so the hammer was over an open hole. He dropped the pistol back into his holster pulling the hammer strap in place then dumped the rest of the coffee on the fire to put it out.

Removing Bart's gun belt and checking his pockets for anything of value, Larry lifted him up and put him over the saddle and started packing /up his equipment, getting ready to head back to the ranch where Bart had stolen this horse. He would put Bart in the ground at the ranch where they would have a shovel. With Bart tied down he headed back down the trail. At least Bart's horse was rested so he could make good time. Larry made it back to the ranch just as the sun was going down. Larry rode up to the house and was met by the ranch owner.

Larry said, "as you can see, I have a load on your horse, if you can find a shovel and point to a location, I will plant this outlaw and you can get your horse back".

"Well, Mr. Marshal I have just the spot, I will join you". "By the way I am Willy Lincoln". Willy led Larry to a spot out by some trees after picking up two shovels. An hour later Larry and Willy were drinking coffee and Willy was getting the full story as to how he gained one horse and was missing a better one.

Willy asked Larry if he wanted to stay over until morning before heading back to Sacramento,

"That is a good offer, but I do need to get on my way I will camp after I make about fifteen miles".

"Your choice but you do what you got to do". Larry had roped Marty's horse and was ready to hit the trail as soon as the last cup of coffee was finished.

"Well Larry I will have something to talk about at the feed store next week".

Chapter 13 **Getting the Mining Equipment**

Tony finished getting the wagons loaded after Sheriff Johnson and Larry McPherson started out after the two robbers. Tony was telling Sam about the lead bullets in the two bags with the one bag that did have a little money in it. Little did they know what had happened over the last few days with Sheriff Johnson and Larry on their trail. Tony stepped up on Teddy and led the wagons north, heading to the rancho so he could see his brother and his wife and kids.

The rest of the trip on north to the rancho went smoothly. With Dave and Bart gone, the two helpers were moved up to driving and cooking. They sure would miss Dave some because he could cook. Tony and Sam were sitting around the fire talking about why someone like Dave would chose to be on the run when he could have made a good living working on the ranch, one can just never tell what makes a man the way he is.

On the second day after the Sheriff and Larry started the chase, they reached the rancho. Pulling the wagons into the yard, everyone was talking. Little Juan and Hector were climbing up on the wagon seat then jumping off, making the dust fly. Juanita got after them and told them to go play somewhere else. Kicking a stick, they ran back toward the barn to see what they could get into if they couldn't jump off the wagon seat.

Sam moved off and started to unhook the teams and take them to water. Two of the ranch hands came out to help him. Hector and Little Juan came flying out of the barn to see if they could ride on the horses after they were unhitched. Sam reached down and put them up on his team so they could ride. The two boys were sitting high, holding onto the collars as the team was taken to water and then to the barn.

Juan came out and told Sam to come on in to the house. His men could take care of getting the harnesses off the horses and putting the horses up. Jack and Billy were leading the teams back to the wagons so they could store the harness on the racks on the wagons. Sam went with Juan and told the Jenkins Brothers to come on into the house after all the gear was stored and Juan's men showed them where to put the horses.

Not long after the wagons got to the rancho Sheriff Johnson rode in leading Randy's horse. Tying up to a hitching post in front of the house, he was met by Tony. "I see one is dead. Who came out on top"?

"It was Wes Barton or Bart, Dave is under a sand bank with two bullets in his chest. I guess he was a little too slow on the draw".

"Sheriff Johnson said that Larry is still on the trail of Wes, He should have him in shackles by now or Wes is dead. "By the way, you may need to replace Larry, I never told you I am the US Marshal for Nevada and California and Larry is now a Deputy Marshal working for me".

"When did Larry find out he was a real Marshal"?

"When I started back with Randy's horse I told him, it was not we are going after Wes it is you". Tony said that may be just the right job for Larry.

"Ya, I think so and I have a lot of work for him to do, he will be on the road much of the time hunting down the bad guys. I also think he is sweet on the Sarah James girl, Larry has been helping her get her ranch restarted after her husband was killed by the Barton Gang".

Juan and the rest of the family were now on the front porch talking to the Sheriff.

"Will you spend the night? We have plenty of room and it is about dinner time. Why don't you ride back to Sacramento with us? We will be leaving in the morning to pick up Ronnie's mining equipment that we are taking back to Nevada".

"Why not, I like company on the road anyway". Juan asked one of his men to take care of the horses. Stepping up on the porch, they all went into the house to talk about the mining and cattle operation that was going on in Nevada.

Juan started to talk about the harvest coming off the fruit trees, Tony asked Juan why didn't we haul the fruit to Sacramento and deliver it to his contact? Have your men load the two wagons with all you can get on our wagons. We can bring back the money on the way back with the equipment.

"That is a great idea, let's go ask the men to get the wagons loaded. That will save me making two trips with my wagon". Juan and Tony went out to talk to the men and get the loading started.

Tony was up at first light to check on the wagons to see if they were both loaded and ready to go. Juan's men had the load. This would be the first fruit from the trees that Juanita's father had planted five years ago. Juan told Tony where to deliver the fruit in Sacramento, Sam and Sean would handle the loading of the mining supplies at the wagon yard, Tony and Maggie had other things to do. When they reached the wagon yard Tony paid Tom Chancy for the new wagon. It was really a big large wagon. On the way to the wagon yard they had delivered the fruit to the dock and collected the money to take back to Juan at the ranch. Tony said his goodbyes and rode back to the hotel to meet Maggie.

Tom Chancy gave the order to Spike Martin to help load the wagons and get any help he needed from the crew at the wagon yard. Spike asked Sam if he wanted to use the yard team to move the wagons off the loading dock.

"No, I will use the new team just to see how they do under a load". Spike talked to Sam and Sean about the ranch and mining operation, Sam told him they had a nice sized herd of cattle in the high country and were just starting the mining operation. Sam was saying it was going to be a hard trip back with these heavy wagons.

Sam and Sean figured it would take the better part of two days to get the equipment on the wagons and get them ready to start back to Nevada. With the equipment starting to be loaded, it was evident that they would need all three of the wagons. By far the largest load will be on the new wagon.

Sam was impressed by the new teams that Juan had purchased from Gary Gee out of Chico. With the first wagon loaded, it was time to see how well trained these new teams were. Sam had driven the new horses after they got the harness on, none seemed to have any trouble. Sam drove the wheel team into the wagon yard and eased up to the right front of the new wagon. Now would be the first test, he told Randy to just step over the tong and see if his horse would step over to his side of the tong without a fuss. Randy's horse just stepped over without any problem, Sam told them to back and they moved back and waited to have the tugs hooked. Randy and Marty finished hooking them up while Sam placed the lines on the wagon seat. "Ok, you boys, hold these two while I go get the lead team, we will see how they do right soon".

Sean had the second team waiting with the Jenkins brothers holding them on short lead lines just for safety. Sean eased the two horses in front of the two-wheel horses and asked them to back up, all went well with this team also. Sean ran the lines through the rings on the inside of the collars on the other two horses and handed the lines to Sam. Sam was thinking about what all could go wrong with having a heavily loaded new wagon and new team that he had never driven. "Damn, boys, be ready. If anything goes wrong you may need to get these big boys stopped".

Now or never, Sam thought. With two sets of lines in each hand he clicked them up, talking to them. "Easy now boys, easy now". The horses all seemed to hit the traces at one time, they just stepped into the load and the wagon moved forward. As he came off of the dock with the load there was a little downhill slope leading into the wagon yard. Sam started to get on the brake but he wanted to see if they would hold the load without spooking. When the front wheels started down the hill Sam eased back on the lines. With the back wheels starting over, Sam asked them to ease back. When the wagon started to push them from behind, the four horses just leaned back into the load, holding the wagon from gaining speed down the ramp.

Sam was a happy man. Sean eased up by the wagon box and told Sam it looks like this trainer is damn good. If all the horses work out this good, we will have some great teams. Sam set the brake and tied the lines around the brake handle. "Now let's get the other new wagon and hook up the other team and see if we can get the wagon onto the dock. If they handle anything like this team, I will be able to back the wagon onto the dock with the next new team hooked up to the other new wagon".

Sam climbed onto the wagon seat, taking up the lines. Sam asked everyone to give the horses their head and just follow along with the lead lines hooked up. They were ready to start. Sam asked the team to walk out and they just stepped out, he would need to make two hard right hand turns to get into the back of the wagon yard. With the first turn ahead, he asked the team to turn by saying gee and pulling on the right driving line. The lead team eased around the corner with the wheel team making the turn right behind with no problems. Up onto the loading dock they went. When they left the dirt and reached the wooden planks on the dock the team high stepped it a little then settled down. Sam pulled under the crane so the heavy equipment could be loaded onto the wagon Spike was ready with the crane to pick up the last of the heavy lifts. Now with the equipment loaded and tied down he would test the second team on the downhill slope leading from the dock down to the road. As before, the team held the load just as the first team did. Sam told Spike about how they had made a good deal by purchasing the horses from Gary Gee in Chico.

Sam now had the two wagons on level ground. He called for Randy and Marty to start pulling the tarp over the equipment so they could start back to the ranch in Nevada. Sean and Sam checked everything one last time and climbed up onto the wagon seats and clicked up the teams and headed back to Nevada. Sam told Randy and Marty to go on ahead to the camping spot they had picked out on the way in to Sacramento and get camp set up and have dinner ready when they get there.

Easing past the three larger wagons, they clicked the light team up into a trot and moved on ahead to the campsite. Finding the campsite by the river, they set about getting their work done. Marty started the fire while Randy went out and picked up the wood. Dinner was just about ready when the other three wagons pulled into the campsite. The sun had just eased down when the horses were taken care of and on grass for the night. With dinner ready, everyone got a plate and found a spot on a log around the fire.

Sam was the first to start talking about that Spike Martin and all of his questions about the ranch and cattle.

"I wonder if he was looking for a job"?

Sean said, "Did you get a look at his hands? They looked like a store clerk or banker". Sam asked Randy and Marty if Spike had talked to them about the ranch, Randy piped up telling about how Spike had asked how to get to the ranch and all about how many ranch hands did they have. He said that he might like to see if he could get a job working on the ranch or in the mine.

Sam came back with this guy may just be trouble coming our way, there is no way we can get home any faster than the horses can pull the load. It will be a couple of days when we reach the hills and the work will start. Jack and Billy, you will be earning your keep when we hit the mountains, you better practice jumping on and off the wagons for the next two days.

With this load you will need to block the wheels on each of the wagons so the horses can get some rest on long pulls. Sean, we need to find some good blocks along the way, Sean, look for a six-inch log about eight feet long. You remember the holes I had drilled in the support for the wagon box. We can tie the rope to the log and run the rope through the hole and tie it off at the back of the wagon box. This way we can hold up the log when we are moving.

Sam and Sean sat at the fire a bit after everyone went to their bedrolls. "I think we have a problem with that Spike. Here is a man with soft hands and way too many questions. He may be planning to try to steal the cattle and whatever he can find from the ranch. Ronnie is at the ranch with Andy, White Bird and Tee. They should be able to take care of any problem". "Let's just get this equipment to the ranch".

Breakfast finished, teams hitched, the three wagons started for the foothills of the Sierra Mountains. Today they may reach the rolling hills that will lead up to the long pull up and over the mountains.

Along the way, before reaching the hills, they found two straight trees to use as wheel blocks for the wagons, with both trees tied under the wagons just behind the real wheels. After being tested, they started for the long climb over the mountains. Sam had Jack and Billy to tie and untie the logs and drop them behind the wheels until they could do it in their sleep. By the end of the day the three wagons had reached some of the hills. At dinner Randy and Marty both talked about who would get to drive Abby's wagon and who would have to block the wheels on the steep grades.

Sam told them that they would need to take turns driving the chuck wagon and Abby's wagon. The chuck wagon had a brake so when they make a stop whoever was driving the chuck wagon would block the wheels on Abby's. Later the next day, when they got into the first real hard pull, Sam and Sean got a real surprise when all the teams made it up to the top without stopping. After about ten minutes the teams were ready to move on up the road. The small hills were no problem to the horses but they all knew what was coming. It didn't take long to see what looked like a mile of road climbing into the trees. Sam hollered back to everyone to be ready to get those wheel blocks ready,

"I will tell you when to get down and when to block the wheels". Jack and Billy had gotten down so they would be ready to set the blocks when Sam hollered.

Sam turned back and hollered back to the boys to drop the blocks and sing out when they are set.

Jack and Billy sang out "all set".

Sean and Sam stopped the team and let the wagon ease back to rest on the blocks. Marty was driving so Randy set the break on the cook wagon and got the log behind Abby's wagon's wheels. Sam asked if all was ok with all three wagons, Sean walked up to Sam's wagon saying "I think all of these big boys will need some extra grain tonight. Sean, go back and check on all of the horses and come back when they quit breathing hard so they can make the next climb".

At noon they pulled the harness off all of the horses so they could roll and eat some grass in among the trees along the road. They all took about a two hour break then. Putting the harness back on the horses, they set out for the top of the hill they had been climbing, Jack and Billy had been earning their money over the past few days but they both were having the time of their young lives. Sean came by and told them that they were doing a good job and that make their day.

The horses that Tony and Juan had purchased from Gary Gee were working out to be a better purchase as the days moved on, these teams could pull, and they liked the work. With everyone working as a team they were making a good trip over the Sierra Mountains. This went on for the next two days until they topped the Carson Pass overlooking the big valley.

"Ok men let's get the blocks moved to the front of the rear wheels on the three big wagons". We will tie the blocks up in front so we can drop them down to help break on the steep grades. Sam and Sean were both a bit worried about coming down from the top of the Sierra's the wagon road was steep in many places. Some of the road had very little space from the mountain side to the drop off.

By having the logs to block the back wheels of the wagons both men felt better after getting to the bottom of the first really steep section of the wagon road. Sam was in the lead as they climbed up a short section of the road, as he reached the top, he had Jack and Billy move the log to the front of the rear wheel so they could use it as a break on the down hill part of the road.

Sam had stopped to wait for the other wagons to catch up and

Stop to rest the teams.

Sean asked, Sam, "what he thought about this next part of the road   "?

Sean, "this is the part with the sharp turns, and it is very narrow, it is not as steep as some of the others I think we can try and see if the teams can hold the load without the log blocking the rear wheels".

Sam, "we will have both of the Jenkin Brother's walk down with you to drop the log if you need it".

Sam had the largest load and if he could make it through the sharp turns on this downhill section, they could save some time. Sam dropped the lines on the four horses and started down the hill with Jack and Billy walking beside the rear wheel ready to drop the log if needed. As the team started down the horses started to set back taking the load, Sam also had the brake applied and so far, the team could handle the load.

After reaching the bottom Jack and Billy walked back up the hill to help Sean if needed but as with Sam the team could hold the load so now, they knew when they needed to use the logs to hold the wagons or just let the team's do the work. With all the wagons Sam and Sean were very happy with the outcome. This had saved some hours and they could get further down the road before setting up camp for the night.

Jim got a jump on me on this photo, but he earned it, ride hard ride fast. The Pony Express is alive and well.

Chapter 14 **Going after the Cattle**

Spike Martin walked down the street to the first saloon along the river he could find. Walking up to the bar, he ordered a beer. He was only thinking about how to steal all the cattle on the Ronnie Campbell ranch. All he needed now was some help to pull this little job of stealing a herd of cattle. How many men will I need he was thinking when the doors swing open and an old friend walked in with four others, knocking the dust off with their hats. Seeing Spike, they all walked over and ordered a beer.

Turning to Spike, Jake asked if he had any luck lining up a job while working at the wagon shop.

"Well, I think so. It will take a few days of hard riding, but I think we can make it work if you guys are willing. Let's get a table and talk this out. Jake, who are the other three you are riding with? Can they pull their weight on a job"? he asked. "Spike, this is Bruce, Will, Doyle and Hank and yes they can get the job done". Jake asked Spike how many head of horses we are going to need on this job.

"Well, Ronnie Campbell raises horses along with running cattle. We will just take what we need when we get on the ranch. We are going to need to make some time because most of the ranch hands are tied up on a job of hauling some equipment back to the ranch".

"We will need to ride past the wagons and then hit the trail east to the Ruby Mountains in Eastern Nevada. I do not know how many men are still at the ranch and we may need to take care of Ronnie Campbell then get into the high country to round up all the herd. We will then need to drive them down into the valley and drive south to clear the hills and then we will turn them and head for Salt Lake to make a quick sale. Finish your beer and let's get on the road east, I will need to pick up my horse. Let's meet at the package store to pick up some supplies for the road".

Supplies in their saddle bags, Spike headed east to pick up the Pony Express Trail. This would allow them to pass the wagons without anyone knowing. Pushing hard, they were over the Sierras, heading for Buckland Station and points east in a few days. With Buckland Station behind them, Spike figured he was now at least a week ahead of the wagons and would be two weeks ahead when they reached the ranch. They knew not to stop at Brown's Store so they would not let anyone know they were in the area. When the hills started to close in, they figured they were close to the Campbell Ranch.

They should see the wagon road leading to the Applegate ranch turning to the right. They would not stop until they reached the ranch. When Spike felt they were getting close to the ranch he had everyone drop back to let him ride in to see who was at home, if Ronnie Campbell were home, he would get a drop on him and then they all would come on in to cover anyone else.

Spike rode in slowly, watching for any movement. When he reached the house, he could hear a hammer striking an anvil. No one came to the door of the house, so Spike turned to the blacksmith shop to see who was working. As Spike rode up to the shop, Andy walked out to see who was riding in. As he cleared the shed, he could see a pistol aimed at him.

"Well, old boy where is everybody"?

Andy shrugged saying "I just work here".

Spike said to turn around so he can tie his hands. After tying Andy's hands, he hit him with his pistol on the side of his head. Andy could hear others riding into the ranch yard. That was the last thing Andy heard before waking up in the storage shed.

*

White Bird and Tee watched as the rider pulled his gun. Each eased back into the trees so they could watch as Andy was tied up and locked into a shed by the blacksmith shop. White Bird and Tee gave the signal to their family to move back into the hills and hide. White Bird and Tee moved through the trees until they reached the stream easing along the bank. They reached the back of the blacksmith shop where Andy was being held. Pulling on the boards, they started to give. After a bit of work, they had enough room to get Andy out. Removing the ropes, they retreated back along the bank to the cover of the trees, moving along until they were in a small canyon were the women and the kid were hiding.

White Bird told the women to take the kids and go to the stash of food and their backup camp and stay there until we come and get you. Andy asked White Bird if they had any spare horses hidden so he could ride over to the Applegate's and tell Little John about the men taking over the ranch. White Bird led Andy back to a hidden corral that held some horses. Andy saddled up one and headed over a back trail leading to the Applegate ranch. Andy would take the better part of two days to get to the ranch.

White Bird and Tee waited to see what the men were going to do. They watched until the men had eaten and saddled Ronnie's horses and rode out.

"Tee lets go get our bows and arrows. We can give them an old time welcome if we get the chance".

Now White Bird said, "let's get those horses and drive them back into the box canyon". With the outlaw's horses hid in the canyon they went to drive all the other horses to join them. White Bird and Tee rode back into the hills to the back trail leading into the high meadows. The two Indians decided to move all the cattle that were in the lower meadows further back into the hills to hide them. They knew Andy would be three days getting back with Little John so they had to do what they could to slow up the cattle thieves any way they could.

The two Indians gathered about forty head, leaving the ones that were back into the timber.

"Let the cattle thieves get them out of the timber". White Bird said

"Tee you ride up the game trail to the left and move as many cows as you can. I will go over to the meadow by the spring and push all I can back to meet you. When we meet, we will push all of the cattle into the brush in those broken canyons".

Tee asked, "do you think Ronnie will get mad if we get an arrow or two into a few of those robbers"?

White Bird said, "no, he will be glad we caused some trouble". About two hours later the two Indians met and pushed about two hundred cows and calves back into the brush. Job done. "Now we can start having some fun with those men. They will have to split up to even find any of the higher meadows that will take them all day so we can kill dinner and give them a scare in the morning". Tee had a small fire going with a rabbit cooking when White Bird heard a horse coming through the trees. The rider called out "is that you Jake"? Picking up their bows the two Indians eased back into the trees out of site to wait. Hank had smelled the rabbit cooking and was riding into the campsite. Without knowing if Ronnie would like it if they killed any white man, they figured to put an arrow into his shoulder.

*

Spike had his men check the house and all the sheds to see if anyone was around. Jake rode around seeing the Indian camp, but found no one around, so he rode back reporting what he had found. Spike told Jake to take Doyle and find some horses and bring them into the corrals. James told Will to check the house and get some food ready". "Hank, you go find some halters for some horses. We will need to bring them into the high country to gather the cattle". Jake drove the horses into the corral, "OK, guys. It is time to get a bite to eat then we will saddle some of the new horses so we can give ours some rest.

Let's get into the hills and start rounding up the cattle so we can get them out of this country". Spike led the way back into one of the canyons looking for a trail the cattle were using. Having found none, he split up the men to see if they can find a way into the hills to find the cattle. With dark coming on, all the riders headed back to the ranch house to get some food and talk to the blacksmith some, he will talk, or he won't last long.

Spike and Jake were the first to return with Doyle, Will right behind. Spike said to Doyle, "go get the blacksmith we need to talk to him". Spike checked out the corral and none of his horses were there, in fact none of the stolen horses were there either. "Has anyone seen Hank? He must be lost back in the hills".

Jake came back to the house in a hurry.

"The blacksmith is gone, some boards were pulled loose, and he is gone. I looked by the creek. He had help from someone wearing moccasins. It could be two Indians".

Spike told Jake "I thought you checked the Indian camp and found no one there," "I did, and I found no one".

"Well, we have plenty of trouble, the blacksmith is gone, our horses are gone. What the hell else is going to go wrong"?

Hank was following some tracks along a ridge. He felt he was getting close to finding some cattle, so he just kept riding. Hank knew it was getting late and he should turn back and start another day. Just as he was getting ready to turn around, he got a whiff of smoke, so he kept riding hoping to find one of his gang cooking some coffee.

When Hank cleared the line of brush, he heard the twang of the bow strings. With an arrow in one arm and the other in his shoulder, Hank lit out back down the hill heading into the valley. When Hank reached the ranch, he could just barely stay in the saddle. The other men heard him come into the yard. Helping Hank out of the saddle and into the house, Spike started to rethink this cattle rustling plan. His horses are gone, one man injured, and no one had seen any cattle during the day.

Spike Martin had some real problems due to having his horses stolen and one man shot by the Indians. In the morning he would need to try and find his horses. He would need them to make a getaway if they got caught with the cattle before they could sell them. Hank is going to be of no help except to cook a little. That is if the arrows don't cause infection in his arm or shoulder. "Will you take the first watch, and I mean watch? We may be afoot if you don't keep the horses in sight. Wake Doyle and Doyle you wake Will about three. You men keep your rifle cocked at all times. Take no chances".

All had been quiet all night. After eating breakfast, he sent James and Jake to get the horses saddled and get ready to go hunt cattle. Spike told Jake to lead the search for the cattle and keep an eye out for the Indians. "Hank, you hang out on the porch with your pistol. I don't think you could fire a rifle". Spike decided that he would go after their horses that had been stolen from the corral. Spike eased out of the corral following the track of his horses and the others were heading east back into the hills. All went well for about one mile then the trail dropped from sight.

Spike rode on for another mile, checking each wash or small canyon leading away from the little valley. He was not even seeing any cattle tracks. Where in hell could anyone keep over a thousand head of cattle hidden. Spike worked a better part of the day and had not found any sign of his horse's, they just vanished into the hills. The little valley was getting smaller each mile he rode. When it looked like it was closing in, he rode around a little finger and was looking at an Indian lance sticking in the ground with a feather blowing in the wind, blocking the trail leading up the valley.

Spike could feel the hair lifting on the back of his neck. Reaching down, he pulled his Henry rifle and levered a round into the chamber, then reached down to ease the thong off the hammer on his pistol. Easing back on the reins and backing up slowly and not making a sound, his eyes were trying to look in all directions at one time. Turning slowly, he eased back down the valley the way he had come.

"This job is getting out of control".

One of our first-time riders, now she is an old hand with many miles riding the trail.

Chapter 15 **Race Day**

With Abby on his arm, Ronnie led the way into the dining room. Jim Baxter would be joining them for dinner to talk about a horse race or two. Jim had told Ronnie that he had a race course at his ranch just outside of town. Ronnie asked would it be ok if he just stabled my horses there. He will pay for the feed and grain. Jim asked if any of his horses needed shoeing. If so he could get his stable manager to contact their man.

"No, I just took care of that before I came over, but I would like to use you track to work my two boys out for a few days before I run them for real". Jim waited a minute until the waiter took their order for dinner and refreshed their drinks.

Then he said that anything at the ranch is theirs to use anytime.

"Do you want me to have one of my exercise boys lend a hand with your light workouts? I am sure they would love to ride some new horses".

"Well, Jim, we may give it a try, but my horse Buster is a handful even on a good day".

"I saw some fields of alfalfa growing along the road on our way in to town. Do you grow any on your ranch"?

Jim said, "yes, I do and will be planting another field this year. Ronnie, you do know that the seeds were imported from Chili back in 1850 to California. We started to grow it in this area not long after that". Abby asked Ronnie why don't we plant some in the big field along the stream, we could put a small dam up stream and irrigate it like Jim is doing.

"How could we get some seeds so we could get a field going in our ranch"?

"Well, I have plenty so I will get you enough to plant at least one hundred acres".

Dinner was placed on the table and the talk slowed for a bit. Jim asked Abby if she would like to go on a shopping venture with his wife during her stay. Abby said that she would like that but is not sure how much stuff she can buy, we kind of came with only a few changes of clothes.

"Well you can always pick up a pack horse to take home your purchases, I am sure Ronnie would not care if you picked up some nice clothes".

"I just may take you up on the offer if your wife is up the challenge".

"Jim, this is a great steak, I wonder who raised it".

"Well, we can meet the rancher who started a small feed yard out by my ranch. The ranchers figured if he started feeding the cattle in a small yard they would add weight and pack on some fat for a better taste".

With dinner over and Jim saying he would meet them in the morning to bring Ronnie's race horses out to the ranch, Ronnie said he would take the horses over to the livery stable and settle the horses and would be back in an hour. Abby started off heading to their room and gave Ronnie a look that said many things and Ronnie liked them all.

Ronnie put a halter on Abby's horse and tied the three together for the short trip over to the livery stable. Leading the horses into the stable, he met the owner walking out to meet him.

"Well son, looks like you could use some stalls for your horses".

"Ya," Ronnie said, "and I would like to give them all a good shot of grain, oats if you have them, with a little ground corn".

"No problem," "I will rub them all down if you like".

Let me put up Buster and you can get the others. This guy can be a problem if he takes a notion to get a bit out of control. Ronnie led Buster into his stall and gave him a good rubdown and put liniment on his legs. With the hostler working on the other three horses, Ronnie asked him to rub the other three horses' legs down.

With an ok, Ronnie headed to the hotel.

Ronnie headed up to the room wondering what he would find. Easing the door open he found Abby sitting reading a book with her back to him. Ronnie asked if we are going to read tonight. Abby stood up and turned showing an open bathrobe.

"Well that is what I was hoping for.

"You go get a bath, I will watch and may help if I see any spots that may need extra washing".

With the sun starting to show light, Abby stretched out greeting the morning. As she reached over and touched his chest, she found Ronnie laying on his back. Ronnie started to wake up, he was looking into Abby's eyes. Abby said you do know we need to enjoy each other now because I will be getting too large to play with the baby on the way.

Ronnie was in paradise,

"Abby, you do know how to wake a man up to get the day started". On the way down to breakfast Ronnie picked up a new paper, he knew Abby would like some time to get ready. Ronnie found a quiet spot to wait for her. Opening up the paper he started to read about the Baster gang. They just got out of town ahead of a hang man's rope. Jim walked by and stopped to talk. Ronnie showed the article to Jim, then saying he will meet him in the dining room as soon as Abby comes down.

Breakfast was interesting because the room was filled with people that Jim knew and also had race horses. Jim was making introductions left and right. Jim's wife Gail moved Abby off into the parlor with the other girls to talk about shopping and who had the fastest horses. All agreed to meet out at the stables to watch the show when each started to show off their horses and tell how fast they were, not to mention how much fun it is going to be to take the others' money on race day.

Jim had told Ronnie that he would wait to show his horses until last because he was the new man in town.

Ronnie asked, "how could you get so many horses and owners at the racetrack in such a short time"?

"Well", Jim said, "when I left you after dinner I sent riders out to contact the local owners. But we also have some owners on ranches that will take a few days to get them in with their horses".

"Ronnie," Jim said, "this is a real treat for us to have some new blood to take money from".

Ronnie came back saying, "it is going to hurt me to take all of your money with my three horses," "Whoo", Jim said, three horses, where was the third horse"?

"Oh, did I forget to mention that Diamond can also run a bit? Diamond is the stock horse I rode in on yesterday". Ronnie said.

"Well, Jim, I have never put Diamond in a race, but we just may find out how fast he is. I have never wanted to race my own horses. I don't think there is much money on it".

"We have some owners here. How do you want to set up the races? Are we going to do match races with just two horses or do you have another idea"?

Jim said "Why don't we all retire to the house so we can sample a bit of brandy and talk this out".

In the large living room at the ranch, the men and women were all sitting around the room talking when Jim said to the group,

"Why don't we just take a look at what we have here. First we all have raced each other and we kind of know what the outcome is going to be. Now with your three horses why not just divide up into three different races, all with a walking start. That way we can say run two, three or how many horses we want matched up to your three horses in a three race event".

Ronnie turned to Abby and asked her what she thought about that kind of a race, Ronnie got a big smile and a go for it.

Ronnie said, "how about I pick the order of horses I want to run then you match your horses with one of my three. What do you think about that"?

Jim came back with "ok, you pick your order and we will take until mid week to set our order. We would like to see your workouts".

Ronnie came back with "I will run Diamond last; he has never been in a race so I would like to give him time to settle down some".

Jim asked why have you not raced him?

"Well" Ronnie said "I need to take it back that Diamond had never raced before. He did have a race at Fort Churchill against a Major's horse and he did win by a half length that was about a mile run".

During the next week everyone was keeping an eye on the three new horses as they did some work on the track. Diamond was the first to take the track. Ronnie was riding him with his double snitch roping saddle. Some of the other racers were using the track at the same time and tried to get a little race out of Diamond but Ronnie just kept him at a steady pace, but that pace was eating up some ground. When he had a good two miles under him, Ronnie let him run for a quarter turn but no one had a chance to get much of a feel for just how fast he was or got a time on him from the three quarter pole on in to the finish.

Ronnie was giving all of the horses a good workout each day with a hard run at the end just to tease them a bit. Buster was getting more excited each day before he got to go out to get his exercise. Jim had sent some exercise boys over to help if Ronnie wanted but as of Tuesday he had kept the riding for himself. After the workout on Tuesday, as he was riding back to the hotel, a young man rode up to him and asked if he could ride a bit with him. Ronnie said sure. The kid said he was called Jingles and he would like to ride his horses in the race coming up.

Ronnie said, "I don't think I have seen you around the track this past week".

"Well you are sure right I have been hanging back just watching, you have some great horses and I am the one to win you some money".

Ronnie asked him how do I know if you can even ride.

"You don't know, but give me a shot in the morning I will just show you how I can handle that horse you call Buster. I have a feeling that horse has wings and I would like to fly with him. Oh, I have been riding in England and other places and I have just arrived into this area, I don't know anyone.

"Well, Jingles, meet me at the stable at 6:00 am we just may see how you handle Mr. Buster".

As the sun was coming up Ronnie was just getting Buster ready when Jingles walked up and asked Ronnie if he would just go over and take a seat for a bit so he could get acquainted with Buster. Turning to Ronnie he said, "I will be his new best friend, wait and see". Ronnie said he would be back in a bit, he would go over and get a cup of coffee so you can have a short visit with Buster.

When Ronnie got back Buster was walking out to the track and acting like an old pony horse. Well, that is a change but let's see if he can get some speed out of this boy. Ronnie walked out to the railing and called Jingles over to talk.

"OK, take him out and warm him up some then come back.

I will let you know what I would like you to do with him then". Jingles took him out for a soft canter and Buster was acting just fine with Jingles well in control. Ronnie looked around and none of the other riders were around and the other horses were still in their stalls when Jingles came around the back stretch. Ronnie walked down to the starting line with his stop watch and waiting for Buster to get there.

Jingles cantered up to Ronnie and asked what he would like to see.

"Well this boy has not had a good long run so ride him around and walk up to the starting line and I will tell you when to go and I want to see all he has for the mile". Buster came up to the line knowing he was going to get to run, Ronnie hollered go. Buster was gone in three jumps, Jingles had to hang on. He could feel the power in this horse. As he started, some of the owners were just getting to the track and rode over to see what this horse had. None had their watches out so they would just need to guess on the time Buster would run.

Jingles was getting in tune with Buster by the time they reached the back stretch, Buster was reaching out and driving hard. Jingles had ridden some fast horsts but this one had a little extra. Jingles reached Ronnie in short order. When Jingles was reaching the home stretch Ronnie had Jingles slow him down, he had seen enough. This horse could fly. He was wondering if Diamond could run with him for a mile.

When Buster was cooled down, he was on the back stretch at a soft canter. Jingles looked back and most of all of the other horses were either on the track or coming out of the stables. Jingles said to himself that they better get up early to see our boys run. When he got back to the open gate by the stands Ronnie was waiting with a smile.

"Well Jingles, you do have a job".

"Do you want me to take out Lightning for some exercise so we can tease some of the other horse owners"?

Ronnie said "yes, but just give him a good run, we will give him a hot lap in the morning early".

"When do I get on your big boy Diamond"?

"We will see how things work out, I am taking him out with a full stock saddle just for fun. I plan to give him a hard run with you today. Get Lightning ready to go. I will just ride Diamond out on the track and we will work them side by side".

"This will give all of the owners a bit to chew on during lunch today. What do you think"?

Jingles said, "I would like to be in the room when you have lunch".

"Well you will be sitting right beside me and Abby". Jingles turned to Ronnie and said that he had never had lunch with any owner he had ever ridden for. Ronnie told him that Abby would like to meet him and get to know some of his background.

Ronnie came out to the track with Jingles. Ronnie even had his rope on the saddle with a rifle in the scabbard. All of the jockeys could not believe what they were seeing, none had ever thought of riding a stock saddle to work out a horse. After a short warm up Ronnie said to follow him, they are going to make some time. Ronnie touched Diamond with a spur and off they went, Diamond got the jump but Lightning was gaining. Lightning moved a bit ahead and Diamond moved up to regain the lead. Around the track they went with the two horses neck and neck, at the three quarter pole Ronnie pulled Diamond back a little at a time until they were cantering down the home stretch with every owner watching.

Ronnie told Jingles to take Lightning back to the barn after he was walked out and Abby would be by the stables to pick him up to go to lunch in town. Ronnie rode Diamond back to town and put him in the livery stable in town. With a large scoop of grain and a good rubdown, Diamond was set. If Ronnie needed a horse, he could use Abby's standard bred gilding, or he could rent or buy one. He could use it as a pack horse for Abby's stuff he knew he would need to deal with. As it looked now he would be going home with a new man if Jingles wanted to take a job.

Jim told Ronnie that everyone had their horses at the track now and they would be picking what horse would run in each race. Ronnie had set up his race order, Buster would lead off in the first race, Lightning would be in the second and Diamond would run in the third. All of the owners wanted to know if Ronnie would race with a racing saddle on Diamond or would he use the stock saddle. Ronnie told Jim that they would find out at the time of the race.

With the race card set and bets made, it was time to see who had the best horse in each race, Jim was sure that everyone knew that the winner took all. Side bets were just that side bets. Jingles had Buster ready as all of the other six horses started to the track to warm up before the race. Buster was ready to run. Jingles had to hold him back this took quite a bit of effort. Ronnie had never seen Buster handled any better than with his new rider, Buster and Jingles had a bond, so it seemed.

The starter was ready, firing his pistol and off they went. Buster broke fast with two other horses, the big bay moved out to a full length with Buster and the gray neck and neck. The other three were only a length or so behind waiting for the right time to make their move. Buster was pulling at the bit wanting to go all out but Jingles held him in check. Jingles was worried about the big black stallion just a length behind. Jingles felt he would make a move at the three quarter pole just before the home stretch.

The time was coming to see if Buster could outlast the big black, Jingles felt the move by the way Buster tried to let all go and run for the wire. As the black got his nose at Jingles knee he let Buster have his head and the race was on. That black could run and Jingles was in perfect sync with Buster.

He was helping him all he could, but when the black got a nose ahead Jingles felt Buster find just a little more reach and with every stride he regained the lead on the black and just kept on moving forward. By the time they reached the finish line Buster had a three quarter length lead as they crossed the finish line. Jingles had not remembered seeing when Buster and the black passed the big bay that had been leading when they reached the home stretch.

By the time Jingles had cooled out Buster Ronnie had his money. The one thousand he had put up and the other five thousand the other owners had bet. Jingles was just leading Buster back to the stable when Ronnie rode up on Diamond,

"Well, it looks like you have earned some real money on that race," Ronnie said.

Jingles asked, "well, what do I get for the ride"? Ronnie handed him two thousand. "Is that ok with you". He said that is damn fine with me,

"let's just do it three more times".

Ronnie felt that the black was the best horse in the stable except for his horses and the next two races would be about the same outcome. Ronnie rode back to the stable with Jingles to wash Buster and get him some oats for his work. "I think I will leave Diamond here at the stable until the race in two days, Abby will be around in a bit to pick me up to head back to the hotel. We will come back before dinner and get you if that is ok with you, Jingles".

"Yes" he said, "I am going to take out Diamond for a little light workout just to get the feel of him if that is ok".

"Remember you don't need to tell this guy when to head for home, just drop the rains and hold on for the ride".

The next morning Lightning was going to get his test, Jim had his best horse ready to have a go at Lightning. Lightning still had a habit of bucking every once in a while and when Jingles reached the track Lightning went straight up and hit hard on all fours. Jingles jerked his head around to his knee and with two small jumps, Lightning was finished with the show. All of the owners were talking about the show when Ronnie told them how he did that the day he signed up to ride for the Pony Express.

The show was over and they all started to come forward to the starting line, with the horses all about on the same line. The starter fired the gun and they were off. Lightning crow hopped and then started after the other five horses. By the back stretch he was only three lengths behind and holding. Jingles could feel that he was ready to run but he held him back until he reached the start of the home stretch and let him go. Ears back and tail out, Lightning was a gray flash. Jingles had moved him to the outside of the pack and just into the final turn he was even with the last horse. Jingles urged him on with a touch of the whip.

Lightning kicked in mid stride and then let it all out. Jingles did not think he could catch the leader but it was up to Lightning and he was flying down the track passing the other horses. His last horse was also a gray and Jingles could tell the other horse knew that he was going to be challenged. He laid his ears back and now both horses were giving it all. Every stride Lightning was gaining a little, but would it be enough. The finish line was coming at a blur and Lightning just kept driving for home a little at a time. When Jingles crossed the finish line he could not tell who was ahead. Was it Lightning or the other Gray?

The crowd was going wild at the finish. Jim had three men judging the finish of the race. When the horses finished the slow lap to cool down all three men were talking, trying to come to a decision. After a long talk they all agreed that it was a tie. Everyone was mad but the decision had been made so Ronnie split the six thousand leaving three thousand each. No one was happy except the two riders. They both got a good payday for their work. Ronnie came back to the stable as Jingles was rubbing down Lightning saying always bet on the Gray, and paid Jingles his part of the winnings.

Well, all were waiting for the next race to see if Ronnie would have Jingles ride with the stock saddle or the racing saddle. Ronnie kept Diamond in the stable and saddled him in the stall so no one would know until the last minute what saddle he was going to be using for this race. Jim told Ronnie that this was the best three days of racing they had ever had since he built the track.

Diamond was the last to reach the track and Jingles had a blanket covering the horse and saddle when he rode out onto the track. Reaching down, Jingles pulled off the blanket and he had the racing saddle on Diamond. With the horses lined up and moving to the starting line, Jingles was wondering what kind of ride this would be, he had never had Diamond running flat out in a race before.

Jingles was thinking of the last two rides he had and wondered if this one would be a winner. With the shot, all of the horses broke fast and Diamond was a nose ahead of the horse to his left. Diamond was running free and not laboring at all and was still leading as they started for the first turn, on the back stretch Diamond was two lengths ahead and running well.

Turning on the back stretch, Diamond started to move away from the pack. He was just gliding over the ground and he kept extending the lead. When Diamond headed for home he was alone by ten lengths and still moving away. Jingles took a look back to see how the other horses were doing. About half way down the home stretch, seeing his lead, he just stood up and eased back on Diamond and crossed the finish line at a gallop.

After cooling Diamond down, Ronnie came over and walked back to the stables with Jingles. Ronnie asked, "how would you like to have a job working for me at the ranch working with my racehorses"?

Jingles turned back and asked how much freedom in the training would he have if he took the job.

Ronnie said, "you do as you see fit, but I would like to be involved with any major decisions". Jingles said that would be a good deal for him.

Racing finished and the money in the bank in Salt Lake, Ronnie purchased two pack horses for Abby's stuff.

Abby said, "well, it serves you right to force me to come to some old horse races".

"So, you will be ready to head home in the morning".

"Yes, I will but I have just one thing to do before we head home," Ronnie asked just what that would be.

"Well, I want to see you suffer a little when I show you just who is the boss in this family".

Ronnie said, "I don't have any part in this".

Abby said, "yes you do but I will set the limits".

In the morning Ronnie was all smiles and Abby was quite pert herself. Jingles had the horses ready for the trip home.

He said, "I hope you don't mind if I ride Buster, we do have an agreement don't you know". Jim was waiting for them at the porch of the hotel with two bags of alfalfa seed for Ronnie and wished him well. "Come back next year, I have some new horses that will be ready to test". He watched as they turned to the west heading for the ranch, and all were in a fine mood and looking to be home in the Ruby Mountains for some relaxing times.

Nevada Day Parade 2015, a fun ending for the year of events and school talks.

Chapter 16 **Spike Has a Bad Day**

Spike was chilled to the bone. He had never figured on being run through with a lance in the hands of an Indian. Reaching the ranch, he stopped in to see if Hank was doing ok. Just after he reached the ranch yard, Bruce and Doyle rode in to meet Spike walking out of the house.

"What did you find"? he asked.

"We only found a few head on the upper meadows we checked on. It looks like the cattle are back into the brush and we can't get to them".

"Well, let's wait until Will gets back. It was not long before Will came into the yard at a gallop and looking behind him.

Spike asked what was up.

Jake said, "let's get out of this place. I just had an arrow stick into a tree just a few inches from my head". Spike told of his being stopped by a lance placed in the trail he was riding on heading up into the hills looking for the horses.

"Ok men, the horses have to be up the trail I was on because there was no other branch with a trail the horses could have gone on. Let's go get our horses, we better be ready for a war".

∗

Andy Sams had just returned to the ranch by the back trail with Little John to meet Tee and White Bird coming down off the mountain. Andy asked Tee and White Bird what has been going on while he was gone. "Andy," White Bird said, "we didn't know if Ronnie would like it if we killed a white man on his ranch so we put two arrows into one of the gang and put a lance blocking the trail leading to the horses in the side canyon". Andy said he was sure that it would be ok if we killed all of this gang that came to steal his cattle. He asked Tee and White Bird what they did with the cattle up in the high meadows.

"We drove them into the brush so they could not round them up. It will take a long time for them to come back into the meadows to graze".

White Bird told Andy that he thinks the gang will figure out that we have the horses past the lance we put in the trail, so we better get into a good location to keep them from getting the horses. They will want the big fast horses they rode in on, our stock are good cow ponies, but not built for a long run. Andy asked White Bird to lead the way to a good spot to defend the horse herd. We can make a good fight just down the trail about a mile. The trail pinched down and they would be able to fire at the gang from behind rocks.

"Tee why don't you ride back and see if they are heading our way? You can beat them back here before they can make it here". Tee was off at a gallop. Sure enough they were all heading their way so he turned back to join in the defiance set up at the rocks. They came up the trail slowly looking around, taking their time, trying to find a trail leading to their horses. Andy stepped out and asked them to drop their guns and put their hands up. Spike pulled his pistol and fired at Andy and missed. Spinning his horse, he galloped back toward the ranch house leaving his men to fight for their lives, Spike was never a fighter, he was a leader who found it better to save himself first.

Will never got his gun aimed before he was falling with two slugs from Little John. Hank was in no shape to make a fight but died trying, Jake and Doyle both charged into a hail of bullets without getting off a shot. Andy stepped out from behind the rocks saying,

"Men let's go back to the ranch and pick up the shovels and plant them where they lay".

Spike pulled up and headed up a canyon, hoping it led over the mountains toward Salt Lake City. He wondered if he would be pursued by one of the ranch hands and for sure not by the Indians. He hoped not, he had enough of that bunch. This is one ranch he would never try to steal anything from.

Spike felt that if he could get over the mountains he would have a good chance to make it to Salt Lake and freedom. The horse he was riding was a good one but would not take a long run like his horse that vanished at the ranch. "I think I will call him Baldy because his head was most all white with a brown muzzle to match the rest of him". Spike was making good time because he had found a trail leading up and over the pass, he was for sure on his way. When he reached the flats he knew for sure he was well on his way. He had checked his back trail during the day and could not see any dust.

On the second day out, it was getting late. Spike started to look for a place to camp. He thought he could see a fire a mile or so up ahead so he rode on looking forward to having someone to talk with. Reaching the camp, he called out to ask if he could ride in.

Ronnie met him as he reached the light.

"Well, how are you doing? You seem to be traveling late. Do you want some food and coffee? Go on into the fire. I will put your horse with ours on the picket line. You can give him some grain after you eat if you would like".

*

Ronnie was the first to hear the horse coming their way. He got up, picking up his Henry as he did so. The first thing he saw was one of his horses Splash, being ridden by someone he did not know. Well, this should be interesting, Abby.

"Get your guns handy. I will meet him just to make sure about the horse, it sure looks like Splash, but I will make sure before I say anything".

'Say gent, what is your name"? Ronnie said as he rode up.

Spike, he answered back.

"Well you are riding late,"

"I could see your fire a long way so I just took a chance and came on".

When Ronnie led Splash to the picket line he knew for sure this was his horse. No other one could have the same markings on his head and muzzle.

Spike was getting some coffee when Ronnie walked back to the fire. He had his back to Ronnie when Ronnie asked him how he got his horse. Spike dropped the coffee and went for his gun. That was not a good option. As he started to clear leather he was hit and hit hard by Ronnie's 44 Colt and for good measure Ronnie thumbed another bullet just to make sure he could not get a shot off at Ronnie. Abby had her Henry ready and Jingles was hunting a place to hide. When the shooting stopped, Jingles came back to the fire. Jingles asked, Ronnie is that the way you greet your guests in the west.

"Well, no but this man was riding one of my horses. Horse thieves are not dealt with in a friendly way. If you lose a horse in this country you are a dead man. He should have never gone for his gun that was his second mistake". Ronnie went to the picket line and picked up Splash and rode over, dropping a lope on the dead man saying "I will drag him over to the sand bank and cover him with sand". Ronnie got him in place and started jumping on the edge of the bank when it broke off. He had the dead man covered.

Riding back to camp, he unsaddled Splash and gave him some grain.

"Well, I guess I will just bring you along back to the ranch".

In the morning, two riders were riding toward the camp.

"Look at this Abby, we have some other company to ride back to the ranch with. Hi, Tee and Little John. Are you two lost or what"?

"No, but we see you recovered your horse, and it looks like the rider must have went for his gun, my guess that was not a good choice for him".

Ronnie said. "Little John and Tee, meet my new race horse manager. This is Jingles he just helped me win a bunch of money and he could use a job".

Jingles said hi to Little John but kind of was a little scarred of Tee. Ronnie told Tee to check Jingles out and see if he would make a good scalp. Tee walked over smiling and holding his knife in his hand, Jingles started to move away when Tee rubbed his hair saying,

"Yes" "he would make a good scalp, my lance could use another".

Jingles was not too sure if he was kidding or what as he walked out and saddled up Buster. When mounted, he told Ronnie if that Indian wanted his scalp he would need a faster horse than what he rode in on. Tee smiled at Jingles then picked up the pack horses' lead ropes and they started for the ranch. Jingles kept an eye on Tee most of the day, still not feeling all that comfortable but he would wait and see how things went. He had never had anything to do with Indians so this would take a bit of time.

Ronnie rode up to Abby and asked if she would like to take a bit of a bath at the hot springs on the way home, all he got was a wide smile. The next day Ronnie took one of the pack horses with the camping stuff and told the rest to go on over to the ranch. They would spend the next day or two camping in the canyon. They reached the campsite about noon and by late afternoon they had camp set up.

"What do you think", Abby, "do you want to get a hot water bath before dinner"?

Abby said. "Dinner can wait if we find anything to do with our free time" and headed for her horse. Reaching the hot springs, they jumped out of their clothes and eased into the hot water. Laying back on the rocks enjoying the hot water, Ronnie kissed her, and her eyes opened with a smile saying, "is that all you got"? Dinner was some cold beef and a slice of bread, but they were both happy and not hungry.

With the sun starting up over the hills, Abby watched Ronnie start their breakfast. She was content to just lay back and enjoy watching her man. Ronnie could feel her eyes on him as he worked. They would take their time and relax the rest of the day and head home the next day. "This valley is sure pretty," Abby said. "Yes, I do like it. Do you think we should file on this part of the mountains"? Ronnie said that he had an idea that might work and what would she think if we filed on this for Tee and White Bird for a ranch for them. We could stock a few head of cattle from our herd. What do you think? "I like the idea. We would need to keep the title in our name until things change toward the Indians. Next time we go to town we will file the papers and hold them until things are all settled".

The next morning they started up and over the mountain to see what the rest of the story was on the stolen horse. Ronnie could not figure why anyone would ever steal a horse like Splash that no one could ever not remember. Early afternoon they rode into the ranch yard. They had heard Andy was working at the forge, the hammer was ringing up into the hills. When they rode into the yard they had it right. Andy was working with Jingles shoeing one of the new colts. Ronnie rode up and asked if Jingles still had his hair. Jingles just looked up and smiled.

"Well, Andy tell me what went on, you know, about the one I had to shoot". Andy went into how he was hit on the head and about the Indians pushing the cattle back into the hills so the robbers could not get any of the stock.

Andy said, "let me tell you about White Bird and Tee stealing all of the robber's horses and hiding them back in the hills in the box canyon. We did get a couple of real good horses and one is a stud you may want to have Jingles look at him, he looks fast.

You do know that Little John came over and helped to finish off the gang. Have you heard of anything from the mining equipment"?

"No but they should still be a week, maybe less".

"Andy what do you think of Jingles"?

Andy said, "he looks like a solid man. He just came in and started to help. Between the Indians and Jingles we will have some of the best horses in the territory.

"Andy, could you dig out some of that low bank and make a bunk house? I think it will be cooler than just building it out in the open. If you can get started on it before the wagons get back, we kind of have some time before all of the building gets started. I would like to take the two matched half brothers and make a team out of them, moving the dirt would be a good test for them. I want to make them into a buggy or light wagon team, Abby will need a dependable team she can get around with".

Abby was angry that someone had been in her house, she was washing everything she could find and when Ronnie found her stomping around he just eased back out the door and went back to the barn to find a project to last until about dark. Andy had all of the Indian kids digging dirt from the bank, Andy was using the light team Ronnie had asked him to work with to move it away from the bank, to beside the house, to make a good garden.

With dark easing over the ranch, Ronnie felt he may just take a look in and see if Abby was cooking dinner. When Ronnie stuck his head in he did smell some good smells. Walking on, he found Abby with the table about ready for the crew to come and get it. Dinner went well with much talk going on about the attempted theft of the cattle. Later the talk went to when the mining equipment would show up at the ranch.

Fun day at a photo shoot, riding in the hills near Carson City Nevada. The only reason this picture is in this book is because I was leading.

Chapter 17 **Picking up New Wagons.**

Tony and Maggie made a little trip to San Francisco and were heading back to Sacramento to pick up their horses and get ready for the trip home. They would need to push a bit to catch the wagons before they get to Carson City but they could catch up later if needed. After paying the bill and saddling up, Tony said, lets go take a look at a small wagon and a light team, Maggie asked what is up with buying a wagon for the trip home.

You had some of the fresh fruit and grapes from the rancho. "Well, let's just take home some root stock to plant. With the wagon we could carry a lot of trees. If we do this right we could also make a nice bed in the back, or would you rather sleep out on the ground"?

Maggie smiled and asked if he had seen anything that would work. Tony said that the wagon shop had one that would fit the bill and it already has a team with it if they have not sold it by now. "Let's go". He turned Teddy back to the docks along the Sacramento River to talk to Tom Chancy to see what kind of deal they can make on the team and wagon.

"If I remember, it had a canvas cover for the wagon".

Tom saw Tony and Maggie riding up the road and waited to say hello to them. When they turned into the yard he was surprised but pleased to see them, he knew they had been on their honeymoon for the last few weeks.

"Hi, Tony and Maggie. Is there anything I can do for you today? You know the wagons are about a week ahead of you heading home". "I think you can, I would like to purchase the wagon and team you purchased while I was here loading the equipment," Tony said. "You are in luck, I do still have it and would sure like to get it off my hands, I am not much into feeding horses every day".

"Tony do you have any price in mind you would like to pay"? "Ya, I could go $800.00 cash. Would that work for you"?

"I had kinda though that $1,200.00 would be a good price but I can think on it a bit".

Tony told Tom that that would be a good deal if he could get it, but he has had to feed the horses for over three weeks now and how long would it take him to get the higher price?

Tony told Tom that he would add another $50.00 if he would get some of his men to shovel the wagon box full of sawdust, that will keep him from paying to get rid of one load and make some money at the same time.

"OK, you have a deal. I have the need to get rid of a few loads of sawdust anyway. Come on in and I will make you up a bill of sale for the whole outfit, sawdust and all". "Thanks, this will save me some time chasing down another wagon for the trip home".

With the saddle horses tied to the wagon box, they headed for the rancho to say goodbye to everyone and pick up some trees and other stuff to replant at the ranch in Nevada. With a hand, Tony helped Maggie up on the wagon seat and clicked up the team into a ground eating trot, heading south.

Maggie turned to Tony and asked him what is up with the sawdust anyway. "Well, I can put the plants down into the sawdust and they will stay moist on the way home. Now the real reason is that our bed will be nice and soft, and I hope to spend plenty time with you in that nice soft bed". Maggie gave a little laugh and said she hoped not everything is soft in the bed.

Reaching the rancho, Juan and Juanita greeted them with the kids climbing all over everything and rode the horses down to the barn so the wagon could be loaded with the plant cuttings and small trees. Tony asked if he could have two additional barrels to carry extra water so he could keep the plants watered on the long trip home. Tony also had some burlap bags to cover the sawdust before making the bed up in the back of the wagon. After the bed area was made, Juan placed the two new barrels so the trees were separated from the bed and the water would be handy. Using ropes to tie the barrels in place, everything was ready. Juan and Tony told the girls to make up the bed so they would be ready to head east in the morning.

Little Juan and Hector wanted to go with Uncle Tony, they were ready for a big adventure, but Juan told them in a couple of years when you get better at riding you may just get a chance to ride over when we take some cattle over to the ranch in Nevada. Juanita and Maggie talked on the porch for a long time. With a hug, Maggie started to the wagon. Their horses were tied to the tailgate. Teddy and Maggie's horses were all saddled so they could take turns riding ahead to scout the trail.

Maggie and Juanita had found old grain bags and made a padded seat and covered it with some sheep skins for extra padding to make the ride better for the long trip. Tony waved and clicked up the team and trotted out of the ranch yard. "What is going on? I saw you and Juanita talking just before we headed out". "Well, she is pregnant, and she said it will be a girl".

She told me she knew the night they made love in the hotel when they purchased the wagons".

"Do you think she really knew when it happened"?

"Yes, I do," Maggie said. "In fact I am also pregnant and we are going to have a boy. If you remember the night, we made love all night when we were camping, the last time when I went nuts, I felt it then. I know we have not been married for very long but I have not had my monthly, I am two weeks late I think".

The trip home will be longer but with all of the trees it will be worth the additional time it takes to get home. The equipment wagons had a week lead on Tony and Maggie, but they should catch up in a few days. The pull over the mountains will make for slow progress with all of the stops to rest the horses on the way up the west side of the Sierras.

Maggie spent a lot of time riding ahead to check on the trail, but she knew her riding time was getting short with the baby on the way in eight months. Maggie was thinking that now all of the women were having babies, the kids should have fun growing up together.

On one of her rides scouting the road ahead she was about to reach some trees when she heard some noise and shouting. Walking forward, easing into the trees, she could see two men and a black woman, she was being tied up and part of her clothes were missing. Maggie could see her naked breasts. Easing back out of the trees she walked her horse until she was out of hearing and turned her horse loose, going to get Tony.

Reaching Tony, she told him what she had seen and he grabbed his riffle.

"We need to stop this rape and fast". Tony tied off the team and jumped on Teddy. Off they went at a full gallop. Maggie slowed him down when they got close. When they got to the edge of the trees, they could see the men were taking their time and cutting off the girls dress and were having a great time. Tony and Maggie levered rounds into the chamber of their Henry rifles, walking slowly out of the trees.

The girl was the first to see them. Her eyes had a pleading look in them, she knew she was going to be raped and then killed. Both men had their backs to what was coming to end their day, Maggie moved a little off to one side and Tony eased up so the men could see him. The men dropped their knifes and went for their guns, they had only seen Tony coming at them. Both men never got their guns cleared when they were hit with 44 cal. slugs. With both men dead, Tony turned away from the girl and told Maggie to take care of her and he would go bring up the wagon.

Maggie cut the girl free and went over to the two men's horses to check for any clean clothes for the girl. Finding a somewhat clean shirt she took it to the girl and asked her what was going on with the two men. After putting on the shirt, she told Maggie that she was traveling with her husband, heading to Sacramento to find a job, when the two men came up and killed her husband and took her captive. The two men killed one of her team and burned her wagon earlier today.

"My name is Rose Braxton. I was a slave on the Braxton cotton plantation. As soon as we could my husband took the team and wagon from the Braxton plantation after the owner was killed in the war. We just grabbed what we could and headed west until these two killed my Isaac. He was a good man. "

When Tony gets back I will find you something to wear, and you can travel with us if you would like to, we are heading to a ranch in Nevada". Rose hugged her and then asked if they could go and bury her Isaac proper.

Maggie said, "that will be the first thing we do. How far have you came with these two"?

"It is not far. They wanted to rape me saying they had not had a woman in months, so they wanted to take their time and enjoy it".

"Rose, here is Tony. We can get started. You can ride in the wagon and one of us will ride one of our horses. We can take your workhorse along and you can figure out what you want to do with it when we get to the ranch". Rose was a slight built woman about Maggie's size so her clothes would do. Loading up and tying the three horses to the wagon box, they started to the sight of the killing and Rose's burned wagon. After about two hours they found the burned wagon and Rose's husband. He had been shot two times but was not burned.

Tony dug a grave by a tree while Rose and Maggie searched the wagon for anything Rose could salvage. A few things did not burn so she had some of her clothes and other personal items but not much was salvaged. Tony wrapped Isaac in a blanked and covered him up, saying a few words. They headed back to the trail leading to Nevada Tony helped Rose up to the wagon seat and started to climb up when Rose said "why don't you ride with Maggie I can handle the team. I need to be of some help". Maggie and Tony walked their horses out in front of the team and moved off at a canter. After a mile, they slowed down to talk. "I think Rose wanted some time alone to get herself settled after this terrible day".

Late in the day Tony found a good camp spot that they used on the way over to Sacramento. He tied off the horses on some grass after giving them a drink. When Rose pulled in with the wagon they had a fire going and were ready to start some dinner. Rose pitched in to help Maggie cook while Tony tended to the horses and the cargo in the wagon. Tony checked each root ball for moisture and added water to the ones that needed some.

With dinner about ready, Maggie went about to get Rose some blankets to sleep on. Tony was relieved to hear Rose say that she would like to sleep out by the horse's, she liked to hear the horses move around at night.

With dinner finished and dishes cleaned Tony took the horses down to water while Maggie was getting ready for bed. Tony washed up in the stream and headed to the wagon to test out the new bed again. After shucking his clothes he found Maggie ready, Maggie whispered to Tony saying that she is sure glad Rose didn't want to sleep under the wagon.

With the sun taking away the shadows, Tony eased out of the wagon to get the stock ready for the day's travel. As he walked toward the horses he could see he was missing two horses. After two more steps he could see Rose leading two back from water and tying them up. Tony walked over and said thanks he was just coming to do that, Rose said she woke early and wanted to do something to help. Rose turned saying that she will start getting a fire ready and work on breakfast so Maggie could sleep in some.

When Maggie awoke she could smell breakfast. She jumped up and found Rose had things well in hand. All she had to do is get a plate and eat. The girls both cleaned up and loaded the wagon and were ready to head up and over the Sierras. Maggie asked Tony how long do you think it will take to catch up with the other wagons? He said it will not be today, but he thinks by noon tomorrow we should be close. They have a hard pull and we have a light wagon so that should be about the right time he thinks.

Rose was back on the wagon seat, moving out, looking forward to the new day. Tony told her that he would block the wheels if needed on the climb up but he felt that the hand break would do the job. When they started up the first big hill and the team was working hard, Tony got ready to block the right side wheel when Rose came to a stop, but he was not needed. The brake did hold and that would save some time along the way. Rose was seeing new sights because Isaac and she had come in to the southern part of California and were heading north when Isaac was killed.

The next day went well with no problems and Rose was handling the team just fine. She was making good time, on the flat sections she would trot the horses and only walk on the uphill parts of the wagon road. Tony had pointed out the tracks of the heavy loaded wagons from time to time. He knew they were getting close to catching up with them. At the noon break Maggie said why don't we ride ahead and see if we can see the other wagons.

Rose was on a flat section when Tony told her to just keep coming and that they were going to ride ahead to see if they can catch up with the other wagons. Rose waved them on ahead and kept on coming at a nice ground eating trot. Rose was thinking back about Isaac and was trying to see if she really felt for him, they had slept together and she would have stayed with him but she could not come to think of him with real emotions. Was she a bad women for feeling that way? They had been on the same plantation when the owner was killed during the fighting. Isaac had got the team ready as she gathered food and other things they would need to live on as they headed west.

No, she said to herself, they were friends but not husband and wife. The time on the wagon seat had given her time to really think about just what they had been and now was ready to move on with her life. When Tony and Maggie returned she was going to ask them if she would have a place on the ranch and a job. Rose was not going to be beholding to anyone now that she was free.

Rose was about to find a camping place when she could see Tony and Maggie riding down the wagon road at a canter. Reaching the wagon, they told Rose to just keep going and they would reach the campsite of the freight wagons in about an hour. It may be dark by the time they get in but dinner will be waiting for all of us. Rose kicked up the team to a good trot, hoping to cut down the driving time. The horses seemed to know that they had some oats waiting for them.

When Rose reached the campsite all she had to do was get down from the wagon and she was handed a plate with food and told to come to the fire and meet the crew. Jack and Billy took over moving the wagon to a parking spot and took care of the team and extra horses. Tony led the way to the fire and started introducing her to everyone. All he said is that her man Isaac had been killed and she was going to the ranch with them. Rose was happy that Tony only told the crew that they found her on the trail being held by two men.

After dinner Rose asked to talk to Tony and Maggie. When they were alone Rose asked if she would have a job at the ranch or should she try to get a job in Carson City when they went through. Tony spoke up and told her that yes she would have a job and then could choose to stay at the ranch or they could bring her back to town. "Just take your time, you have had a hard time so let's just see what develops".

In the morning Sam asked Rose to drive Tony's wagon and move out with the light cook wagon so she could keep out of the dust stirred up by the big wagons. Rose asked if she could help with the cooking since she was with them anyway. Sam said it would be a great help and he was sure that the food would improve. For the next few days all went well with the wagon train and they were making good time.

Randy and Marty were in the lead with the cook wagon when they pulled in to a good camping spot for a noon break. Five Indians rode out of the trees shooting as they came. Marty was driving so Randy pulled out his Henry, hitting two with three shoots. With two down the Indians started to turn when Randy and Marty heard shots coming from behind them. Another Indian was on the ground and another was holding his shoulder as he rode away.

Rose pulled up beside the other wagon and smoke was still coming out of her Henry Rifle.

"Damn girl you can shoot". Rose just smiled and pulled forward to a good spot to park her wagon.

When Marty tried to move forward the horse on the right side just dropped down and never moved. Randy got down and could see it had been shot just behind the front leg.

"Marty, why don't you get down and help me get the harness off this horse? We can use Rose's team to pull this horse off into the brush". When Rose got her team ready she pulled the pin on the double tree and walked them over so Randy could tie a rope to the dead horse.

With the rope tied, Rose pulled the dead horse off a bit and unhooked and started back to the campsite. Marty had walked out to meet Rose to help with her team. Randy had removed the dead Indians from camp and was starting to get lunch ready for the others when they got in.

After a bit the other wagons showed up and the teams were unhitched and taken to water and put on some grass. As soon as Sam and Sean sat down Randy and Marty started telling about how Rose killed one Indian and wounded another. Both men were impressed. During lunch Rose was asked how she became such a good shot. Come to find out she had been shooting for some time. When the war started the plantation's stock was run off. Rose told them that she had learned to shoot using a small bore rifle to kill deer and other small game to feed the workers after the stock was run off the plantation, and Isaac had also shown her on the way west. Sam asked Rose if they could purchase her horse to replace the one that was killed in the Indian fight, Rose said just use him for all you are doing for me, a horse is little pay.

In Carson City, Maggie and Rose went shopping for some new clothes and other things she would need, Rose put up a fuss about spending money she did not have. Maggie told her to just sit back and let her take care of the money, all she had to do is wear them and feel good about it. Maggie told her some about herself and Sean, how broke they were when she met Tony at Mr. Brown's store.

"By the way, Rose, you might want to be looking good when we reach the ranch because you and Andy Sams might just take a liking to each other. Andy is our blacksmith and he is also black and a real nice man. Andy is a big part of the mining operation working with my dad, Sean. This equipment is going to start up a mining operation in the Ruby Mountains in Eastern Nevada".

Rose told Maggie about her and Isaac not being married or anything, they just traveled west together.

"What does Andy look like"? Rose asked Maggie.

"Well, he is a large strapping man, and you could not find a gentler man anywhere" she said.

"Maggie, how can I ever repay what you and Tony did for me? "I know those men were going to use me. I also know they would have killed me when they were finished with their needs".

Maggie said, "you just forget that the best you can, things are going to be better now that you have friends and a place to go".

With lunch finished, Marty went over to collect the dishes so he could start washing them before loading up and catching up to the freight wagons. Marty liked to take a little time so he could get a nap and then catch up to the freight wagons at a nice trot. Rose had the dishes and was walking down to the water hole when Marty joined her and said he would help. With the dishes done Marty held out his hand to help Rose up. Marty held her hand a little longer than needed and gave Rose a smile and they walked back to camp.

After a bit Marty said, "Randy let's get going. Rose was hitched and ready to start after the freight wagons, they should be able to catch up in an hour of two". After an hour, Marty came to a stop and told Randy to take over, he was going to go back and drive for Rose. When Marty stepped up on the wagon seat with Rose she could feel new energy flow through her. Marty took the reins and clicked up the team and pulled back in behind the cook wagon.

Rose turned and said, "I can drive the team just fine. You don't need to help me". Marty turned and gave her a big smile and said, "I just wanted to talk a bit with you". Rose had never had a white man pay any mind to her other than the plantation owner when he wanted her. Marty just drove and asked about her life and what she wanted. After a bit, Rose started to talk about her life on the plantation and Isaac. She told Marty about how they came to be together on the trip west, Marty asked if she had been married to Isaac, she said no.

Marty put the reins in his left hand and touched her hand with his, putting a little pressure on hers. She allowed him to hold it. Rose was feeling flushed and squirmed in her seat to relieve the warmth that was starting to grow in her core. After a few miles they caught up with the other wagons and found a spot to pass.

Tony and Maggie rode up and joined them for a while and cantered forward down the wagon road to find a good camping spot for the night. After a bit they slowed down and Maggie said, "did you see that Marty was holding Rose's hand back down the road a bit"?

"Maggie I think you have an active mind. Let's go on ahead and check out the stream we camped at last time we came this way".

When they reached the stream it was running slow but still had moving water.

Tony said, "let's go see if the deep hole is still around the bend up stream". Tying off the horses, Tony started to undress.

"Don't you think we should make sure the water is safe for the rest of the crew"?

Maggie was naked in a flash and had pulled a bar of soap from her saddle bags. Jumping in, they sank under the water, letting the heat of the day wash away. Maggie was washing when Tony came up and offered to help. With Tony's help she was washed into a very clean woman and happy woman. Soaking in the cool water was great but they needed to get back to meet the cook wagon to tell them to camp at this spot.

Dressed and back in the saddles they had only gone a short way when they met Randy driving the cook wagon and Marty was still with Rose in their wagon with the trees. After explaining about the campsite, Tony and Maggie headed back to check on the freight wagons. Sam and the crew had made good time. So far today they had not had any hard pulls and the road was well packed. Tony explained about the campsite and by the looks they should be in early.

Chapter 18 **Starting the Mine**

Ronnie got up at first light. He was thinking that the equipment should be arriving any day now. After breakfast, he told Abby that he was going to pack some food and ride out to meet the wagon train. He was figuring that they should be within a day or two of reaching the ranch and he wanted to see the equipment first hand.

Abby just looked at him and said "you can't wait any longer so saddle up and get going". Abby was starting to show that she was pregnant and she had decided that she would slow up on the riding.

"You go get Diamond and I will put a few days of food in your saddle bags and a change of clothes".

Abby heard Ronnie walk up on the porch and start into the house. She met him at the front door with his food. Abby told Ronnie that she put an extra pistol in his saddle bags just in case he had some trouble along the way.

Pulling her to him he kissed her hard and slow.

"I will be back in a few days," he said and turned and placed the saddle bags on Diamond and tied them in place. Putting his foot into the stirrup he stepped up and looked back one time and smiled at Abby. Touching Diamond with his spurs, they cantered down the road.

Ronnie kept Diamond at a good pace and it was soon early afternoon when he stopped at one of the campsites to give Diamond some rest and a chance to eat some grass. After an hour Ronnie pulled up the cinch and mounted. He would turn west about time to make camp for the night. Ronnie knew of a small spring at the tip of the mountains just a mile off of the trail, not known by many people. He had found it when he came back to pick up the horses from Sam when he was riding for the Pony Express.

Light was about gone when he rode into the spring and gave Diamond a little drink, he would bring him back later after he had a chance to cool down and eat a little. He made camp just around the point of a finger out of sight of the spring, this way any wild animals could still come in and drink at the spring. Ronnie made a pot of coffee in the small fire blackened and battered pot, then opening his saddle bag to see what Abby had packed him for dinner. Abby had packed some cold meat and a bit of bread for dinner. After some coffee Ronnie took Diamond back to finish watering him and would keep him close by on a picket line during the night. Diamond would blow if anything came close so Ronnie could sleep with both eyes closed, this is a good thing on the trail.

Morning light was just showing when Diamond started to stir, Ronnie heard him blow and stomp a hoof on the ground. Ronnie rolled out to look at what Diamond was fussing about, he was just in time to see a cougar slip up the hill into some trees. The cougar only looked back one time and was gone from sight. With the cougar gone, Diamond settled down a bit. Ronnie took him back down to drink and put him on some new grass while he fixed a bite to eat.

After breakfast of cold meat and bread, Ronnie saddled up and moved out to pick up the trail heading west to meet Tony and Sam with the mining equipment. Diamond was ready to cover some ground today so Ronnie just gave him his head and they set off at a blistering pace. After about a mile Diamond eased back into a soft canter and trot.

When Ronnie got into some low hills, he slowed Diamond down to an extended walk. This pace would be most horses' trot. With the sun getting high, Ronnie started to look for a good location to hole up for noon and get Diamond on some grass. When Ronnie eased over a small ridge he remembered a canyon that ran to the north in the valley below where he had grazed the horses that Bolivar Roberts had purchased from Sam Applegate.

He would ride up the canyon a mile or so to find some good grass. Reaching the canyon, he turned north and rode up about a mile and found some good grass and some shade along the bank for him. After an hour Ronnie saddled up again and rode out of the canyon and headed west again. He hoped to meet up with the equipment by late today or in the morning some time. Diamond was a good trail horse, ears forward waiting to see what was coming next. Ronnie was trying to think of a good camping spot in this area.

Then he remembered the little valley having a small stream that ran most of the time and set out to make it by dark. Riding in just as the light was fading he could see some wagons and a welcome fire just ahead. Calling to the camp he rode in to be met by Tony and Maggie with a rifle at the ready.

"Well, is dinner on? "he asked.

Should be ready any time," Tony said". "Ronnie I would like to have you meet a new lady we kind of found on our way back, she was in a real pinch. She was being held by two men we had to kill. The two men were in the process of cutting off her dress and had planned on raping her and would have killed her later. Maggie came upon them during a scouting ride ahead of the wagon".

"What wagon"? Ronnie asked.

I picked up a light wagon to haul a bunch of fruit trees and other cuttings from the California rancho".

"Great idea,"

Ronnie said "Now let's go meet this new lady".

Tony walked up to Rose and introduced her to Ronnie. "It is so nice to meet you. Is it ok that I come to your ranch? I hope I am not a bother. If so, I will go back to Carson City and try to find a job".

"Wo" Ronnie said, "slow down, you are not a bother, yes, you can come to the ranch. We need good people and from what I have heard you are one. So welcome to the family". Rose started crying so Maggie came over and asked her to go for a little walk, saying the boys can fend for themselves for a while.

During dinner, Ronnie got the lowdown from all the men about how things went on the trip. Ronnie was glad to get this equipment to the ranch and get started mining gold. Ronnie said, "I have another question. You seem to have picked up an additional horse or two".

"Two of them are from the two men who had Rose detained, so they won't miss them". Tony said he doesn't think they know their horses are with us, they seem to have got themselves killed doing bad deeds.

With dinner finished, all were ready for bed. The Jenkins brothers came back from watering the horses and getting them on some additional feed for the night. With everyone turning in, Rose pulled her bedroll and started out to be close to the horses. Rose had spent most of her life sleeping in the stable on the plantation, the stable was better than her room. Now the stable was a place she could find her inner peace and have some quiet time alone. The plantation had only one room shacks for the slaves. Growing up, she had two brothers living in the same room with her parents. Rose found out early about the soft hay and the smell of horses, she felt that the horses would protect her if anyone came around. Even now she loved the sound of the horses eating and they would wake her if anything came around.

Marty had eased out of the camp to check on the horses, but he wanted to talk to Rose, he had found someone he liked. In Marty's life he had never found anyone who he liked enough to bother with, now Rose was a different matter. He knew being alone with her would cause some problems with some people, but he felt the crew at Ronnie Campbell's ranch would be different somehow.

Rose walked out to her favorite horse, it was one of the team she was driving. It belonged to Tony and Maggie. Walking up, the horse turned and put his head in her hands for a good rub. Marty walked up about that time saying, "this horse sure likes you". Rose was startled at first but Marty had a way about him that didn't scare her, she felt that he would not hurt her.

"Rose," Marty said, "can I spend some time with you? I would like to get to know you better. You have had a tough time and I would like to share some of your life from the past. Tony said that you were a slave. That had to be a bad time in your life". Marty stayed and talked for about an hour then went to his own bedroll.

Breakfast was finished, horses hitched, and the wagon train moved out. Randy led out with the cook wagon with Marty and Rose right behind leading out to find the spot Ronnie told them about. They would need to carry water to cook with from the spring back into a side canyon off the trail. The pool from the spring would be big enough to water the horses, but they would need to be taken to the spring two at a time so the water could refill the pool. Ronnie had found this spring by following some wild horses on one of his trips hunting gold.

Ronnie had told Marty to be careful when approaching the spring and don't go alone, the Indians use this water so be ready even in the campsite. Marty could tell that Rose was sitting a little closer today and had touched him when he got on the wagon seat, things were looking up for Marty.

Reaching the campsite early, the three set up camp and started getting the food ready for lunch to feed the crew. Marty said, "I'll get a pack saddle, Randy you get one of the extra horses and we will load up two barrels on him for water and go get some extra water". Rose decided to go along and also grabbed her rifle just in case of trouble. The three started back into the sagebrush following a trail used by wild horses and other game heading for the spring Ronnie told them about.

Marty was in the lead with Randy leading the pack horse and Rose at the back. Marty eased his way along the trail, watching and listening for any sound that would mean Indians. Every few minutes he would walk some then stop to check for any sound, all three had a round in the chamber ready for any problem that came their way.

Marty heard a splash and stopped to listen and heard another splash. He knew that they were close to the spring. Now all three had their rifles cocked and ready. Easing up another step he could see the ears of two horses. Were they wild horses or Indian ponies? Every hair was sticking out when he took another step forward to get a better look. Reaching out, he parted the branches. At that time the wind changed and the three mustangs bolted from the spring and up the canyon at a full gallop.

Marty looked back and smiled, the three moved on to the spring and Rose and Randy started to fill the two small barrels with water as Marty stood guard. On the way back to camp all three were relieved that the scare was only wild horses. Using the small barrels from the pack horse they topped off the larger barrels they carried on the cook wagon and had enough to refill the barrel with the tree starts. Rose kept enough water to do the dishes after the crew ate lunch. Marty, Randy, and Rose were talking about how much longer it would take to get to the ranch, Marty felt it would be another two days. Ronnie, Tony and Maggie came riding in ahead of the wagons, Rose got up and got some coffee cups along with the coffee for the three.

Ronnie asked if they had any problems getting the water from the spring, Marty said that they did have a scare by some wild horses when they got right at the spring. Rose said you can eat if you want, the food is ready. "No, I think we will wait for the rest of the crew". Marty asked if they would want to unhitch the teams or just give them some oats and water to save time. Ronnie said that would be a good idea, if we can get a few extra miles over the next two days we can get home late the second day.

The cook crew had eaten a bit so when the wagon crews came in to camp, the three had the water ready in buckets and had grain bags filled for each horse. The lunch went well. The wagon crew got a few minutes of rest waiting on the horses to eat the grain and top off with water. In less than one hour the wagons were back on the road heading to the ranch.

Campsite picked up, food put away, they loaded up and started after the freight wagons at a stiff trot. In a short time they overtook the wagons and passed, heading to the overnight campsite. Ronnie rode up and gave them directions to the overnight campsite, the two light wagons would make it in about four hours if they kept this pace. The heavy wagons would take at least six hours, but this part of the wagon road was mostly flat with only a few small hills to pull. The wagons would overnight at a campground midway to Mr. Brown's store, leaving only one more hard day to reach the ranch. All were ready to get home.

Just a touch of show along the Carson River.

Photo by Ron Bell

Chapter 19 **Andy Finds a New Home**

Andy was forging a set of horseshoes when he looked up and saw an Indian woman walking along the trees heading for water. He had never seen this Indian woman before, he would ask Tee who she is. When Andy looked up, the woman was looking at him and then turned away and walked on to the stream. The next day Andy noticed the woman again and she looked at him the second time.

Later that day Andy ran into Tee and he asked about the Indian woman. Tee said that she is a sister to his wife and came to live here because her husband was killed in a fight with some other Indians east of here.

Tee said, "come to my lodge tonight to eat, you can meet her then". Andy went back to work thinking this might be good. Later that night Andy showed up at Tee's lodge and was asked in to eat and talk.

Tee and White Bird had been working with Andy teaching him Paiute. Tee introduced him to Black Dove. "She is my wife's sister, she has two little boys. You have seen them before. They are the two who watch you hit the iron. They like to watch you make things, they ask how do you make iron bend. They try but can't make it bend".

Andy laughed and told Black Dove he would show her little ones how to bend iron if she wanted him to, Black Dove said it would be a good thing for them to learn if it was ok with him. Black Dove was over her mourning time for her past husband and had given him a look that he felt said that she wanted to get to know him better. During dinner, Black Dove kept Andy's plate full and looked at him without turning away. When dinner was finished, Black Dove asked Andy to go with her to see her lodge and put her two boys in their sleeping furs. When Andy bent over to enter her lodge she offered her hand and led him to a large skin beside the fire ring. Black Dove told Andy that she wanted to have him as her new husband. Andy knew that the Indian women chose the men that they want. Black Dove removed her clothes and sliding under the blanked made of skins, she reached up taking Andy's hand. He followed her under the skins. Andy spent the night with Black Dove, and he knew he had found a new home in the Ruby Mountains. Andy had never felt so loved as he did this night, with a small fire burning in the center of the hide tent with a smell of a wood fire Andy pulled Black Dove closer to him and smiled.

Andy knew that he was not leaving Black Dove's lodge any time soon. Later that night Andy reached out and touched Black Dove in her sleep. She moved over to get closer to Andy. He knew he had found a home.

*

Ronnie, Tony, and Maggie knew they could make it home with a hard ride today. The wagons would need another day to finish the trip to the ranch. Turning to give a last wave to the crew, the three turned and rode off at a canter, the horses would get pushed hard today. Ronnie figured to ride hard today, they would eat some cold biscuits, then hit the road to the ranch.

The three passed the wagon train's campsite mid morning, they would ride on to a noon camp closer to the ranch to take a break. Just after midday they reached the small seep coming out of the hills that would provide some grass and water. Tony and Maggie started a fire to make coffee to go with the cold biscuit and a bit of meat from yesterday's dinner.

With the cinches tight, all three stepped aboard and cantered out of the campsite, Ronnie slowed down to a walk for a time to give the other horses a chance to get their breath. Diamond was still fresh, he only had a few days travel on him. Teddy and Maggie's horses had weeks of travel on them. Walking gave them a good chance to talk as they moved along to the ranch. Tony and Maggie told Ronnie about the trees and other things they brought from the rancho in California.

Ronnie asked if they thought about the different climate from California to Nevada, the winters will be much colder. Tony said he was not sure but he felt that some of the cuttings would be ok in the colder weather in Nevada. Maggie told Ronnie that she had helped with orchards in the old country and would do the planting at the ranch. She also had talked to Rose and she would help take care of the trees, she had also worked in orchards on the plantation most of her life.

Ronnie said, "come on let's see if we can get a few more hard miles out of these horses, I want to get home". Off they went at a gallop heading for the ranch and home. Ronnie knew that Abby would want to have a big homecoming. The sun was casting long shadows when they reached the ranch, Abby was on the porch keeping watch. She had figured they would be in before dark today. As she stepped off the porch she called over her shoulder for Black Dove to move the food from the stove to the table.

As the three stepped down Andy, Tee, and White Bird came over to take care of the horses. Abby walked out to meet them and gave Ronnie a real nice kiss to welcome him home and then greeted Tony and Maggie. "Come on in. The food is on the table waiting, fresh towels and water are waiting at the back door".

Returning to the table, they were met by Black Dove putting the last of the food on the table. All three looked at Abby. Abby introduced Black Dove to them and then told about how Andy and Black Dove have moved into her home in the Indian Camp. They both seem happy so all is good.

With the food on the table, Abby told Black Dove she could go home, saying that they will pick up the food and do the dishes. Maggie asked how this came about.

"As I understand it, Black Dove came over and asked Andy to come eat and he just stayed and now has all of his stuff is in the Indian camp".

Tony and Maggie looked at each other then told Abby about saving Rose and they both felt that she and Andy would make a good fit.

"Well," Abby said, "you never know who someone will like and live with. Ronnie said that you guys must be blind".

"Why would you say that"? "Well, Ronnie said that when he rode by the cook wagon. Rose and Marty were sitting real close with their legs touching. Rose and Marty may have other ideas that we don't know about. "Tony and Maggie looked at each other and laughed. We never even gave it a passing thought that Rose and Marty even were talking, I guess we are blind".

Abby said it will be interesting to see what happens when the wagons get in. If that is true, Andy's room behind the blacksmith shop is now open. I guess they could move in to that room. Dinner was a lot of fun catching up on the events of the past few weeks. Maggie started telling Abby about all of the plants and trees they picked up at the rancho in California. Maggie was telling about how much Rose knew about trees and planting, she may be a great help with our efforts trying to grow fruit trees on the ranch in Nevada.

With the dinner dishes picked up and washed, Abby and Maggie went out to sit with the men on the porch to see the last of the fading light. With a couple of lanterns glowing, they talked about what needed to be done when the equipment arrives. Ronnie said that he would ride back to the mine site and find a good location for a dam upstream from the mine. They could use the water to power the small stamp mill that was on the wagons. Abby said "why can't you put your dam at the little falls? It is only a short distant from the mine. It is a great place to swim".

Ronnie said that he would take Andy with him to see what he thought about this idea and how long it would take to build a water wheel and construct the dam. "We do have two of the new dirt dump buckets on the wagons, we can keep two teams working dawn to dark. We can bring eight horses back and only work them half of the time to keep them fresh. I will put Randy and Marty on the dirt work, we can ask Rose if she would like to help with cooking and be in charge of the planting of the new orchards and garden".

The girls looked at each other and said that they would retire and if anyone wanted to come along it would be just fine. In seconds the wicks were turned off and Ronnie and Tony were heading for the bedrooms to join their wives. Both of the girls had wash water waiting and were in a playful mood. "Another great night in the Ruby Mountains".

At breakfast Maggie decided to tell Tony that he was going to be a father, Abby was so happy that they would have babies only a few months apart. Breakfast was extended into an early morning party. Ronnie said that he would delay his little trip until the girls had a chance to tell all of the ranch hands the great news, not only one baby was on the way but two.

Later in the morning Ronnie and Andy headed out to the mine site to do the inspection of the location for the dam and water wheel project. Ronnie was telling Andy about the first time he had walked this way to find Bill and Sally after leaving the corral gate loose and the horses ran away. Andy had never heard about that day when Ronnie's father had been killed by the Indians. Andy asked him why was he not mad at all of the Indians, he said that is just how it was and can't ever be undone.

Riding at a good clip, they reached the mine location and rode past to the small waterfall to take a look at what they would need to do to build the pond to supply water for the water wheel that will drive the hammer mill. "Well," Andy said, "we do have plenty of trees that we can saw to make the water wheel. I will need to build a stone boat to haul the rocks to make the base for the dam then we can make a dirt ramp leading up on top of the rocks so we can dump the clay down on the back side of the dam".

Ronnie asked Andy where are we going to find the clay for the back fill on the dam.

"I have been working on a few things after Tony headed after the equipment and you went to Salt Lake".

"What kind of things"? Ronnie asked.

"The clay could have been a problem but after riding around I found a canyon that branches off to the left about a mile up the stream. There is a whole big hill that is about pure clay with some dirt overburden".

"Andy, you said other things. What are they"? "I figured we would need a way to unload the wagons so I built some steel rings that will go on top of some large trees I cut down to make a tripod that we can pull the wagons under and use pulleys and blocks to unload the equipment with".

"Well, I guess you did spend some time getting ready during our little trip".

"Ronnie you will want to see a tool I made to rip the dirt, making it easier to fill our new dirt mover you got. All we need to do is fill up the box on top and the teeth will loosen the dirt".

"So, from what you said, Andy, we can just bring the wagons to the mine site and you will be ready to unload them with what you have built".

"Yes sir," he said. "The wagons should be in some time tomorrow, so we will rest the crew overnight then come out and unload". Andy said, "I would like to keep the small hammer mill on the wagon until we get the dirt work ready by the dam. This way we will only unload it once, it is heavy".

Ronnie asked Andy if he was ready to head back to the ranch. With a yes, they mounted and made a quick trip back so not to be late for dinner. During dinner Ronnie told of the trip to the mine and found out Andy had things ready to unload the equipment when they get in. Tony talked about riding back into the hills to check on the cattle with White Bird and Tee, they found that most of the cattle that had been driven into the brush were back eating on the upper meadows.

Abby and Maggie had spent a lot of time with Black Dove and White Feather making sure all was well with their families. Black Dove told them about watching Andy until she felt he would make her a good husband. Abby and Maggie asked about why the women chose the men, she said that it was the best way to get the best protection for her children. Not a bad plan, the girls said. They both felt that that is just what they had done with Ronnie and Tony.

Mid-morning the wagons lumbered in and made a circle in the ranch yard, Sam had dropped off at his ranch, letting the Jenkins Brothers, take turns driving the last two days. They both had been good hands during the trip, doing whatever was asked of them, so driving was a real treat. As each team was unharnessed, Sean inspected all the equipment as it was being put on the rack for each horse on the side of the wagon. The equipment that needed any repair was set aside to be worked on in the afternoon. Andy had the Jenkins Brother's bring each horse in for inspection, looking for any loose shoes or injuries.

Andy would need to reset two shoes, one each on two different horses. That would keep them going for another month when he would need to re-shoe all of the horses. Andy had been making new shoes for the past month when he found time. He would only need to make a few new sets over the next month. It had been a hard trip pulling a heavy load.

Andy and Sean were surprised to find none of the horses had any problems. Andy was telling Sean how they would need about all the teams to move rocks, haul clay, and move dirt and gravel to build the dam to power the small hammer mill.

Sean and Andy were talking when Ronnie came over to talk a bit and find out how long it should take to build the dam using all the teams moving dirt.

Ronnie, Andy and I have been talking about giving the horses a two day rest and then move out to the mine site and go to work on the dam.

Andy and Sean, "do you think we can get the dam built in three weeks or is it going to take longer". Ronnie asked.

Ronnie, "we think that three or four weeks should get it done, by having the small drop due to the water falls we won't need as mush dirt, gravel and clay.

Sean, "are you planning to rest the teams after each day and use fresh horses every other day". Ronnie asked.

When Rose pulled the wagon into the yard with all the fruit trees, the girls all came out to meet her. Rose was greeted by Abby and Black Dove, she already knew Maggie. With introductions made, the girls all went into the house to have some coffee and talk.

Abby asked Rose if she would like to help with getting dinner ready. "We will have a full table tonight, it may just take all of us to get enough food ready in time".

Rose was up and ready to help as they worked preparing the meal Rose told Abby that she had overseen the kitchen at the plantation where she had been a slave. With Abby and Rose working together the meal was ready in no time and on the table, now they were waiting for the men to get washed up and get to the table to eat.

During a break in getting the food ready, Abby asked Rose to follow her to Andy's old quarters behind the blacksmith shop.

Abby asked Rose if she could live here until some better rooms were built.

Rose turned and gave her a hug saying this is better than I have ever had in my life.

Abby said, "we do hope you will want to stay; I know you have had a hard time on your trip west losing your man and all. Maggie told me how you were about killed by those men, you are safe now and we are your friends and family".

Rose, "I hope you know that this is your new home, we are all family and will look all look out for each other. This is some wild country, and from what I have been told you are going to be a great help in protecting the ranch all who live here".

Abby, "I have never had anything or any help from anyone but when Maggie and Tony offered me help and took care of me, I will tell you that was a first". "I just want to say thanks".

"Rose lets get back and see if we can feed some men".

"Let's go get it done Abby". Rose said.

Father and Son, I love this picture with Grant and Me. This picture was taken during a photo shoot about two years ago. Many of these pictures have been sold in and around Carson City, Nevada. They still can be purchased.

Picture was taken by Robin Travis.

Chapter 20 **Ruby Mine**

The ranch yard was alive with preparation for the last day of hauling the mining equipment, only this time the equipment was going to be unloaded at the Ruby Gold Mine. The table was set with a mountain of food for the whole crew, sprits were high.

The Jenkins Brothers were hoping to get a chance to drive the big freight wagon again. After eating, all the men headed out to hitch up and get ready to hit the trail, it would take a good hard day and part of the next to reach the mine site. The wagons could not take the shortcut over the saddle between the hills. This added the better part of one day by going around to the entrance to the canyon leading to the mine.

The Jenkins brothers, Jack and Billy, were getting the harnesses on the two teams they had driven in for Sam Applegate, they were hoping that by getting the team ready they may just get the chance for the second day of driving. Sean came out to check on the progress and finding the boys working on the team, he just walked off to check on how the rest of the crews were progressing. Horses were being led out to the respective wagons to be hitched, the wheel teams were stepping over the wagon tongue and backed up to have the tugs hooked, then the next two were led in and hitched.

Walking past Jack, Sean said to get up in the box, you boys are driving today. Billy jumped up on one side of the wagon as Jack gathered the reins. Billy released the brake. They were third in line. The day had begun and they were sitting high on the freight wagon box.

The wagons reached the campsite by the canyon opening in late afternoon. Rose had asked if she could go along and help Marty cook. Randy and Rose had talked about digging a cave back into one of the hillsides behind the ranch house. With the wagons heading to the gold mine, Randy was working on a cave in the side of the mountain to protect the trees and other plants until spring.

*

Randy was getting a good start when two of the younger Indian kids came over and wanted to help. With the extra help, the work was progressing faster than it would have without them. With the kids digging the back wall, Randy could use the wheelbarrow to move the dirt away from the cave opening. Randy was thinking about how to insulate the opening after they had the cave large enough to protect all of the plants until spring. After three days of digging they had a cave large enough to do the job. Now he had to build a cover out of wood so he could keep the inside warm during the cold winter.

Randy Jones had been sleeping in the barn but that would not be a good idea for the coming winter. He put the crew back to work to make the cave deeper by another ten feet, this would now also be his new home. He started making a wood plank front for the cave by sinking timber poles into the dirt along the front of the cave.

Then covering that with wood planks on one end, he made a door beside one of the large poles. The ranch had some extra canvas so he sealed up the wood with canvas on the inside to keep the wind from entering the cave. With the door in place he now had a nice dry place to call home. This project took about a week to finish. After installing one of the extra stoves all he had to do now is cut a couple of windows for light.

Randy had been keeping the plants watered just the way Rose had told him to do. Now he moved the trees and plants into his new cave house. Randy moved the plant into a box he had built just the same size as the wagon. Now that all of the plants from the wagon were in the cave, he was finished.

Now he had to make a bed, table, and chairs. He would then have a nice warm place to live. He had an idea that Rose and Marty would start living together soon. He knew that they wanted to be together as they were setting up the mining operation. He could start preparing the garden and orchard area in a protected area behind the house. Water would be a problem unless he diverted the small stream that came down the side canyon running by the house into the river that ran just past the barn.

If he had time he would start to build a rock dam upstream from the ranch. He would need to take that slow because the ranch house and the Indians both used this water to cook and drink. James found a nice spot to start building the damn. It was just below a little spring coming out from rocks on the side hill. This spring was never dry so it could help keep the supply of water fresh and clean. By using some posts he was able to use wood planks nailed onto the posts with a slide gate to use as a spillway. He would add a small section every few days to add to his little pond. The Indian kids liked to help with the pond so they could play in the water as they built up the walls with clay.

*

Marty and Rose had driven on ahead of the slower wagons to get dinner started, lunch was just bread and meat left over from last night's dinner. Marty was finding that Rose was letting him touch her as they worked, he had held her hand some during the ride to the campsite. With dinner on the fire and the horses taken care of, Marty had moved them to get a drink and now they were back on some grass along the creek bank.

Marty could see Rose leaning back against the cook wagon watching him, she never moved as he walked up and pressed into her and kissed her. After the kiss Rose asked him why did that take so long? Marty eased back in to make it a real kiss. Rose reached over and touched him, Marty said this may need to be quick as we don't know when the wagons will pull in. They were both ready, so it only took a few minutes before they were both over the top. Looking at each other they both laughed and got their clothes back in shape and none too soon they could hear the wagons just down the road.

Marty and Rose set up a table for the food and got the plates ready. The coffee was also ready when Sean walked into camp. Marty handed him a hot cup of coffee and said the food was ready. Taking the coffee with him, he headed out to see about the stock. This was a short day, they would eat in the daylight for a change. The lanterns were set up and ready for dark. With the stock taken care of the whole crew came in grabbing plates and filling them up and finding a good place to eat. Good food and hot coffee was a hard thing to find on any ranch. After they all ate, the clean up was done in short order and everything back in its place ready for the morning meal.

The first light was showing and the biscuits were done, meat was cooked and fresh bread was on the table. As the men came to eat they were handed a hot cup of coffee and a plate of food. Eating was a quiet time in the morning. As they finished, each man had a job to do and went about it.

The stock was watered and hitched to the wagons. As the sun was easing over the hills the wagons were heading on up the stream to the mine site. Dishes washed and put away, Rose and Marty walked to the stream bank. There was a deep pool as the stream made a bend. Clothes were off and they both were in the water.

After a short time in the water they returned to the job at hand. Hitching up the team, they would need to make up some time to reach the mine about the same time as the wagons. With the light team at a nice trot they soon could see the dust from the other wagons. They would not need to pass the other wagons today so they just kept back out of the dust. As the sun got high they could see the mine site. Sean told the wagons to stop except for the small hammer mill wagon, it would be moved further up the stream close to the dam.

Marty and Rose talked to Ronnie about a spot to set up the cook wagon close to clean water and away from the dam and other construction. Marty drove along the river to a spot just up from the dam site. He found a spot with a tree on the inside edge of a turn in the stream. The bank was undercut and had a large pool of water with easy access to the water above the pool. Marty pulled up along the tree and parked the wagon. With the wagon under the outer edge of the branches they had good cover from the sun. Rose started to put out the tables and get a fire ring made with rocks, Marty pulled out the steel support frame to hold the large pots they would use for cooking. A small rack was put on the side of the fire pit and the first pot of coffee was on and would be ready in under an hour.

Rose pulled out her Henry rifle, leaning it on the wagon wheel.

Marty asked, "what's that for girl"?

"Well, I am going to slip up stream and have a look to see if I could kill a deer or an elk. Fetch me the black, I will ride him with the harness on, I can ride him bareback without any trouble but this will work just fine". Rose jumped upon the black with ease.

Reaching over, she picked up her rifle. "Hand me that coil of rope Marty. Now you feed those men the beef we had left and you have plenty of bread. I will be back soon, they will be just fine". Turning, she rode up river at a walk. Rose had reached the upper part of this canyon when she found the spring that was feeding the stream. Checking along the bank she could see game trails leading to this part of the stream, all the game in the area were drinking at this location.

Rose worked her way up a bank upstream from the watering hole, she had ridden really slow because the harness would make noise if she rode too fast. It was getting close to high noon and it was still warm. She hoped that an elk may just want a little drink before going back to sleep the afternoon away. After sitting awhile, she heard some brush move and the sound of an animal moving down the hill to water.

Easing back the hammer on her Henry, the noise had quit. After a long wait she picked up some movement in the brush. She was thinking that by the sound it was a deer making its way down for a drink. Another pause-no sound except some breathing. Brush moved and she could see an antler above the brush but could not make out the animal. The antler moved again and a head came out of the brush looking around and smelling the air. She could not see the full body yet but it was an elk. The elk lowered his head and made one more step and turned down the trail. The shot took him just behind the front leg. One step and the elk was falling the last few feet to the bottom of the hill.

Rose eased down off the hill where she had been hiding with the black work horse. Now the fun may start when she tries to get the horse close to the dead elk. Leading him, she got closer than she figured she could when he started to pitch a fit. Looping the lead rope around a small tree a short distance from the elk, she started to gut the elk.

Every little bit she would walk over with her bloody hands and rub his nose, each time he got better until he quit pulling back. With the heart and liver back into the body cavity she dropped the tugs and roped them to the antlers of the elk. Walking to the water, she washed her hands and went back and jumped up and started downstream for camp.

As she rode in with the elk in toe, Ronnie was eating a bite and drinking coffee when he saw the elk behind the horse. Ronnie told the Jenkins Brother to give her a hand with all of that meat. "You stay until Rose tells you to come back to the mine". In short time they had a smoke rack made and were cutting up the elk into chunks that could be preserved by smoking.

Jack and Billy stayed until dinner, gathered wood for the smoking operation and helped wrap the smoke rack with canvas to hold in the heat and smoke. It would take a day or two to finish the smoking process. Now they will have fresh meat for a couple of weeks anyway. Ronnie came over and was talking to Rose about her hunting skills. She told him that she had kept the plantation in meat all during the war and some years before.

The plantation owner had let her hunt to keep from killing cattle. When the war came most of the game were run off or killed so she hunted small game to feed the other slaves. When the plantation owner was killed, she and Isaac grabbed what they could and headed west. The Henry she found on a dead soldier back into the woods. She told Ronnie that she figured he would not need it anymore and she could. I will be needing some bullets soon. She was down to only two.

Ronnie could only wonder what this girl had been through, "I will send up a box of shells if you can keep us in game. We won't need to kill any cattle". As Ronnie was getting up on his horse, he told Marty he better keep her safe. Marty said, "I think she can take care of me". Rose asked Marty how they would work keeping the fire burning day and night until the elk was finished. "Well, let's see if we can keep the Jenkins brothers for an extra day, they can keep the fire going during the night and we can take care of during the day". Marty asked the boys if they would mind helping out for an extra day. They said that would be fine. "Ok then go find a shade tree and get some sleep. You boys have the night shift".

I love this picture, the best part of this picture is I am in the lead, Grant is second, Brian is just behind Grant. All three are Bells, I am riding Dandy, Grant is on Bruno, Brian is riding Red.

Chapter 21 **A Ride with Deputy McPherson**

Jules Baster had been looking to make a big score in Salt Lake City and then head west over Nevada way and pick up some cattle on the way over to California. Jules' brother, Jarvis Baster, had a ranch south of the gold fields that could use some cattle. Jules had seven hard cases riding with him and they were all getting short on money.

The gang had camped in the high country east of Salt Lake City. They would hold up there for a few days so Jules could ride into town and find a bank that was holding some cash. The Baster gang had drifted down from the Dakotas with a few gents on their trail but slow horses make it hard to catch some with big fast horses.

Jules would only allow anyone to join the gang who was well mounted. Jules was drinking little and listening more, men at a bar were always ready to talk for a drink. With a few well placed questions he had a good idea on the proper bank to rob, many of the mining operations in Nevada and Utah kept their payroll in the vault.

Jules stayed for two days and had pieced together a plan with the best escape route. He would steal eight horses to use in the holdup. Riding back into camp, Jules laid out the plan. They would break camp in the morning and ride to a ranch southeast of town that had plenty of extra horses. At the bar one of the cowboys had told him that the roundup was starting and they would be holding some extra stock at the ranch headquarters. Only one man would be at the ranch to bring out fresh horses every few days.

The Baster gang would ease in and take care of the one wrangler at first light, then ride into town and relieve the bank of its extra money. Just after midnight the gang reached the ranch. They made a cold camp and slept some until first light. With the sun easing light to the valley, the gang made their move. As they were riding into the yard the wrangler was coming out of the bunkhouse on his way to the house to get some grub.

Looking up, he knew he was in trouble. Eight armed men were riding right at him and he had left his gun hanging on the bed post. Sid shot him without a word and just kept riding to the corrals. Sid was Jules' second in command and would take care of the gathering of the horses they would need. Jules walked on up to the house to find a plate of food ready to eat. The cook must have run off when Sid shot the wrangler.

Jules called out to the gang to come grab some food before they headed into town, Sid had Rob and Sandy take the horses out to a location that Jules told them about southwest of town about 20 miles and wait for the rest of the gang after the holdup. Sid told them to bag up some grain and take it with them.

Give each of the horses about a quart now and when you get to the spot, water the horses and give them another quart and let them graze. Sid told Jasper, Diggs and the two kids, Del and Tray, to grab some food and be ready to ride. As the gang rode into town, Jules told Del and Tray to hold the horses-each would have two. Jasper and Diggs would stand watch for trouble. Jules and Sid would go inside to get the money. The plan was set.

Sid had Jasper and Tray with him. He came in from the west with Jules. Diggs and Del came in from the east. The bank was on a corner so as Sid came in Jasper stepped off and eased up to a post with his rifle ready, Sid started toward the door.

Jules had stepped down and headed to meet Sid. Del had the horses and Diggs moved up to a post on the other side of the bank. Jules and Sid opened the door to the bank, Jules and Sid moved around the counter telling the teller to fill up the saddlebags with cash. The bank manager came up from the back of the bank to be met with a pistol pointed at him. Jules told him to open the safe and be fast about it.

With the safe open, Sid had the teller finish filling up the bags. With the money loaded and the straps fastened, they started out of the bank. Jules had told the two bankers to lay on the floor and stay put. When they reached the door the teller jumped up and went for a gun under the counter. Sid saw him make the move.

As he reached the counter he was met by a 44 bullet in the chest. With the gun fire Sid and Jules headed for the horses, each with a saddle bag full of money. Jasper and Diggs eased to the hitch rail with rifles at ready. From down the street came some bullets taking splinters from the hitching rail. Diggs and Jasper returned fire sending the men back under cover. Stepping up into the saddle, the six men headed out of town at full speed.

*

Sheriff Mackey got in the action too late to do any good. He rallied some men to get a posse mounted and get after the robbers. Riding out of town, the Sheriff could not understand why the robbers was leaving a trail leading southeast without any attempt to cover their tracks. The Sheriff felt that he was gaining and kept pushing hard.

After about ten miles he started to slow down to save the horses. The soft sand was taking its toll on their horses, all were breathing hard so he had to slow down to a walk for a mile trying to let the horses recover. Pushing forward, the posse had starting to lose some dedication; many of the horses were about finished and were dropping behind.

Sheriff Mackey slowed up when he could see some horses up ahead. As the posse rode up they could see that these horses were as done in as the ones they were riding. Mackey turned to his men saying we are finished, the gang had extra horses waiting. Turning to his men he said to gather up the horses and we will head home. After looking at the brands he knew who the horses belonged to, it was a local rancher. These horses had been stolen just for the holdup at the bank.

*

Jules and the gang changed to the fresh horses and headed west knowing that the posse could not catch them. They were safe. Now they had plenty of money and would head into the Ruby Mountains to find the ranch he had heard a cow puncher talk about. He had been told that this ranch had a few hundred head of good cattle and some great horses. The man had helped the rancher's son with some branding when his dad was driving a freight wagon picking up some equipment.

When Jules found a canyon heading up to the ridge he found a great camping spot for the night, plenty of wood and feed. Jules decided to stay for a few days. He sent Digger out to kill some game. On the ride in Jules had seen plenty of game tracks. As Digger started out, Jules told him to find and kill a young-elk-they were better eating.

Digger had only ridden out of camp a mile of so when he did in fact find a young elk and killed it with one shot. After cleaning the elk, he headed back to camp. When he reached the camp he could see that a fire was going and a smoking rack was being built. Digger started to cut up the meat so most of it could be smoked to keep it from spoiling.

Tray and Del had the coffee on and were getting ready to cook some of the elk. Digger had the back strap removed and was cutting it up into cooking size pieces. Eight men can eat a lot of meat so each man had his frying pan out and on the fire. Sid turned to Jules and said we need to get us a cook. Jules told the men that when they reach the ranch they would settle down to the good life.

After two days they saddled up and divided the smoked meat and rode back into the mountains looking for the ranch. Later in the day they reached a ridge and headed along a trail leading south. After riding a mile or so they found a trail leading to the right and down the mountain, Jules said, "let's keep on the trail. I was told of a spring and a good location to camp with grass and water". Late in the day they reached a clearing. This is the spot. "Let's set up camp and settle in.

We can scout around in the morning". With the sun coming up the gang saddled up and headed out to take a look, finding a trail little used but a trail leading down into the valleys. When reaching the valley floor, the gang headed down the canyon looking for the cattle. With the sun getting high in the sky they started to see cattle and started to gather them as they went along.

Digger turned into a side canyon. Working his way up, he found a herd of horses being held-with a fence running across the canyon. Opening the gate, he moved the horses down the canyon to join the cattle that were being gathered. Each canyon held more cattle and the herd was growing in size.

Sid was leading the way when he could see a house setting back into the trees. As the cattle came close to the house Sid could see a man and woman walk out onto the porch. As the man stepped off of the porch Sid shot him.

When the woman turned to re-enter the house he shot her. Riding up to the porch, Sid got down and walked into the house and lit the house on fire. Walking out and getting back on his horse, he rode west. The cattle and horses were moving past the burning house. Sid turned them southwest down the canyon heading for California.

*

US Marshal Johnson came into the office to talk to Larry about a telegraph message he just received from a US Marshal working out of Salt Lake City. The telegraph talked about a new gang that had robbed a bank and killed one of the tellers. Sheriff Mackey from Salt Lake City had followed the gang for twenty miles only to find eight tired stolen horses waiting for them.

When the Sheriff returned to town he found out who the leader was, he received a message sent by a telegram from the Sheriff of Deadwood. "This gang kills just for the sake of killing, so I want you to work this one real slow, taking no chances of any kind. When you catch up just shoot don't talk, that is an order".

The next morning US Deputy Marshall Larry McPherson was loaded and ready to ride to Nevada to see if he could meet the gang along the way. Larry's horse and his pack horse were ones he had picked up from the Barton gang, they sure did have some good horses. It would take him a few days of steady riding to get into Nevada, Larry would take his time to save his horses. Larry carried energy in a bag-he had a bag of oats to help keep his horses strong at all times. After five days out Larry was east of the Carson River. It was time to start looking for dust of any kind. This ride reminded him of watching out for Indians when he rode for the Pony Express. Those days taught him a lot about looking for riders. Larry was just leaving Roberts Creek heading east when he could see some dust up ahead heading his way.

Easing back into some brush he would wait and see who was heading his way. After about a bit he could see two riders easing along the trail, taking their time. Larry rode out so he could talk to the two, easing his coat back so his badge showed. The two men came forward but showed no sign of being on the dodge.

Riding up to Larry the two men pulled up and asked what he needed. Larry told the men of a gang that had headed for Nevada and they were wanted for murder in Salt Lake City.

One of the men said, "Well, they are now wanted for murder in Nevada. They killed a man and woman up in the Ruby Mountains".

"When did you hear about this"?

"Well, we had stopped at Jim Brown's store for supplies a few days ago and he told us that Ronnie Campbell was after the men and the cattle that had been stolen. Jim told us that Ronnie was looking to kill the whole gang when he catches up with them. We never saw any of the cattle, but we did see some tracks just west of the store".

Larry said thanks and started out at a faster pace, he would need to get a head of the cattle and so he could give some help to Ronnie and who else were after the outlaws.

Chapter 22 **Setting the Hammer Mill**

Andy Sams had the poles cut and he had the men load his special three rings holder for the top of the lifting A-frame. With one the teams unhooked from the wagons he had the men bring the chains to skid some trees to the unloading site. With the logs in place, he had one of the men climb a large tree and hook a pulley up about 20 feet.

With a rope through the pulley, they were about ready. Andy helped slide the steel rings over the top of the three trees. After a little trimming, the poles were ready to be lifted. Andy made a loop around the top of the poles close to the forged rings. With another pulley chained to the bottom of the tree, they ran the loose end of the rope through the pulley and hooked a team to the other end and pulled the tripod into the air.

The crew had ropes tied to the bottom of each pole so they could pull it into place as the A-frame was lifted into place. Two of the legs had been tied to the wagon wheels to keep them in place, the third leg could then be pulled out as the poles were lifted into place.

The team started to pull, and the poles started up, Andy said to be ready to run if these poles start to fall. As the horses pulled the poles up the other men kept the single leg moving out away from the other two poles. When the poles were about to the top Andy was to be ready to run if this thing gets away, "Ok now pull out the leg so we have about 20 feet opening".

As the A-frame reached the top and started to fall forward the third leg landed and held its position. Ronnie asked Andy "how are we going to get the rope off and get the lifting pulleys up to the top"? "Well, I have made some climbing boots with spikes on the inside. We will do it like the timber climbers do it". Pulling out a short rope for safety and strapped on the climbing boots, he was at the top in seconds. They would need a three-sheave pulley on top and a two-sheave pulley for the load end. Andy said to go get the single pulley at the bottom of the tree that will be chained to the single leg, now chain all three legs together so they cannot split apart.

"Now pull the first wagon under the hook and let's see if we can get some of this equipment on the ground. The trick is when we get the load picked up, we need to be able to back up the horses until the load is on the ground. Take the extra team over and pull over one of the two large stone boats, we will set the load on the skid and we then can move it close to its final location".

With the plan in place now, with the big skid pulled up close to the loaded wagon, they unhooked the horses and hooked the skid to the back of the loaded wagon. When the load is lifted from the wagon, they would move the wagon out of the way and pull in the skid to be loaded. Sean was going to drive the team and Andy would keep watch. Ronnie was happy to just watch and see how things went. Sean eased the team up to take out the slack in the rope as the load started to be taken up with the rope. Sean just eased the team up a little at a time.

The poles creaked and made some noise, but the load was in the air. "OK, pull the wagon out and the skid into place. Now the trick is to back up the team with the team holding the load". Sean eased back on the reins and talked to the horses, one step then another. They were not liking this, but they were lowering the load to the skid.

The team had to back up for a long way because of the three-line lift. When the load was setting on the skid Sean walked up and gave the team a good rubdown.

Turning to Ronnie, he said "I will give that Gary Gee his due, he can train horses".

The wagons were unloaded except for the little stamp mill, but that could wait until later. With the day fading Ronnie said, "let's go get the stock put up and fed. I think we will have elk steaks for dinner tonight, let's go". Ronnie was correct elk was on the grill over the coals, coffee was hot, the fresh baked bread was the best. For the first day things went great. The best thing was no one got hurt nor did the horses. Yes, it was a good day at the Ruby Gold Mine. Rose and Marty had a first day feast ready when the men came in from tending to the stock. Each of the men had been told what his job was when it came to taking care of the horses at the end of each day, Ronnie insisted on having the stock fed and watered before anyone could eat.

All the crew had worked a long and hard day getting the equipment staged, ready to start building supports for the mine shaft.

Sean had mined out a short section leading back into the mountain. In the morning he would start to lay the track for the small ore cars and get the first timbers in place at the opening of the mine.

When this work is done the real mining could start full time. Sean and the Jenkins Brothers will start with the single jacks, Andy will start building the timber supports for the mine opening. Ronnie and Randy Jones will start on the dam, hauling dirt and rock to support the dam face. With the plan for the next day in place, Ronnie settled back to enjoy the coming of night.

White Bird and Tee rode into camp just after dark to talk to Ronnie. Rose and Marty fixed a plate for them as they talked to Ronnie. White Bird and Tee told Ronnie that they had found some tracks of eight riders that came over the pass leading to the old Indian camp and then they turned and headed in the direction of Sam Applegate's ranch. They asked Ronnie what he wanted them to do about the eight riders. Ronnie told White Bird and Tee to ride over to Sam's ranch and tell him about the riders, then come back and tell him what Sam said.

The Indians finished off the food and took some of the cooked elk to last them on the ride, it would take two hard days ride to reach the Applegate ranch. White Bird set a fast pace riding into the black night, it was good that they knew a fast way over the mountain that was much shorter. Reaching the pass, White Bird pulled up. Tee picked up some firewood that was close at hand, making ready to spend a night in the open.

With the sun adding light to the day, Tee and White Bird kicked the fire out and started down the backside of the mountain leading to the valley leading to Sam Applegate's Ranch. The two Indians reached the bottom in the early afternoon and stopped by a small seep coming out of the hill. After letting the horses feed for an hour or so, they started heading for the ranch. By going over the mountain they saved many hours of hard riding. They would reach the ranch just past dark at this pace. With the light going away they slowed down a bit. Tee spotted some tracks of shod horses heading in the ranch's direction.

With only a couple of miles to the Applegate's ranch, White Bird halted. He could smell smoke in the air. White Bird led the way back into the brush. They moved forward slowly keeping under cover. When they got closer to the ranch, they could see horses and cattle being bunched, getting ready to start them moving. All eight riders were there moving the horses and cattle down the valley away from the ranch.

*

Ronnie was up at the crack of dawn. He was handed a cup of coffee and a plate of food to start the day. As the men came in to eat, they were all given their coffee and food.

Ronnie said, "this is a real cook crew" to Rose and Marty. Good food makes a happy work crew, this bunch should be really happy. Most of the men working had never been fed that well on any job they had ever worked. Rose and Marty finished cleaning up and getting another pot of coffee ready, Rose wanted to have hot coffee on all day for the workers.

Most of the elk was in the smoker preserving it for later use. Rose saddled up a horse and went scouting for some fish and then rode into the back country to locate the herd of elk. The one she killed was a lone bull. She would not hunt close to camp any more so as not to scare away the game. It is better to keep the local deer and elk in case you need meat in a hurry.

Riding upstream, she found a couple of pools that had a lot of trout, they could wait for a later time. With the fish located, she found a game trail leading up the mountain. She was hoping to get on the top and find a nice meadow with some game. Stopping a couple of times on the way up, she could tell that the trail was being used by a lot of animals, but it was still not what she wanted. Reaching the top, she could see some good locations to scout around some, she had quite a bit of time before she needed to be back to help with dinner. Marty would handle lunch just fine. Heading down the back side, she worked her way along a saddle that would lead her to a good-looking spot to sit and watch for animals.

Some clouds started to build, and the sky started to turn dark. With a cool breeze blowing some elk started to move out of the brush to feed. Yes, she had found a location that she could keep the workers full of elk and deer. Stepping up into the saddle, she headed for camp to help with dinner. Returning to camp, she found all in order. Ronnie and crew had lunch and Marty was getting ready to start preparation for dinner. Marty asked what she found.

Rose said, "we have plenty of meat within a short ride. I found a nice meadow just over the mountain behind us, lots of deer and elk, and just upstream lots of fish in a nice pool. We can go up and catch what we need in a few days. That will give the crew a nice change. Marty told Rose that it might be nice to walk up there and take a nice bath after dinner. "I can wash your back," he offered. Rose said, "I think you may have other ideas other than my back, but I have a few ideas of my own".

Sean and the Jenkins Brothers were making good time making holes to hold the dynamite for blasting. Just before heading for lunch, Sean told the boys to get him four sticks of the dynamite, we are going to blast this rock face. We can check it out after lunch when the dust is down. Sean waved the red flag to let everyone know the big bang was coming. With the large bang, all the horses jumped around a bit but settled down and all the men started to lunch. At lunch Sean asked Ronnie how long it is going to be before we get the hammer mill in place so we can start to process the gold. "Well, I think we can unload the mill in the morning, Sean, you and Andy can start making the gate for the water and the wood trough to supply the hammer mill. Have Jack and Billy Jenkins keep loading the ore wagon so when the mill is ready, we will have rock to run".

Sean had the a-frame moved into place to unload the hammer mill, everything was in place by midmorning. With a team hitched to the wagon, the largest of the teams were hooked to the a-frame, ready to lift off the mill from the wagon. Ronnie was standing by Andy Sams, just watching. He knew when to just watch and this is one of those times.

Sean was ready with the lifting team. Andy stepped up on the wagon seat to pull out as soon as the mill was lifted. Andy was watching as the load eased up off the wagon bed. With it clear, he eased the team forward so the mill could be lowered into place beside the dam. Sean started to ease the team back to lower the load when the big black Jake slipped on a rock and went to his knees and slid back about two feet. Rocky held his ground unmoved.

With a big push from Jake, he got both front feet under him and moved back into the load. Sean eased back on the lines and both horses took one step back then another. Soon the mill was setting on the ground ready for Sean and Andy to finish the trough to power the mill.

The gate was in place and had a few inches of water being held back. It would take another day to finish filling the dam to the required height. Wood had been split and was being cut to fit. The water supply should be ready to send to the hammer mill in the morning. The mill will only take a small part of the running water coming into the dam.

Ronnie had been hauling dirt to the mill site to build a ramp so the ore wagon could drive up and unload into the hopper on the mill. Jack and Billy had two ore wagons loaded ready to start making small pieces from larger ones. The fine material will be sent into a rocker to extract the gold.

The whole crew came over to the hammer mill to watch the water being sent to start the hammers working as the water turns the wheel driving the hammers. With the hammers working, the Jenkins brothers started shoveling rock into the mill. Dust started to rise, and the noise started to get louder. After a bit, the small pieces of rock started to come out of the bottom, ready to be washed into the rocker set up on the downstream side of the water wheel. Ronnie took a gold pan full of material from the hammer mill to test in the stream. After a bit he walked back with a big smile.

"Yes, we have good color, keep it running, we are making color".

Ronnie told the crew to make it a short day, clean up and get the stock handled then come to the cook wagon so we can make plans for this mining operation. Ronnie headed to the cook wagon to have a cup of coffee and talk to Rose and Marty about how they wanted to feed the mining crew over a long time. Marty had asked Randy if he would stay at the camp so he and Rose could go back to the ranch, Rose was going to be needed to keep the plants alive until they were able to plant them at the ranch.

Marty was a big part of the ranch cook crew. He told Ronnie that Rose and he wanted to get married if it would be ok. Ronnie said "let's get home so the girls can get to planning. We will also need to get a letter off to Zack and Betty Wilson, the preacher and his wife". Ronnie asked Rose if she could go out and kill another elk and get it in the smoker.

That should keep the mining crew in meat for a few weeks. "When you get the crew set, you and Marty start for the ranch". "We are going to head home in the morning. Sean, you are in charge. Do you need anything from the ranch"?

"No" he said, "I am in good shape. I will run for four weeks then I will bring the crew in for a few days, and we can check out the gold count".

Great bunch of friends, Pony Express riders. You can also join the fun.

Chapter 23 **Applegate's Ranch**

White Bird and Tee waited under the cover of some brush until the eight men pushed the cattle and horses away from the burned-out ranch house. Easing up to the front of the house, they found Sam dead just off the front porch, he had been shot three times with two in the back. Beth was also dead, she was laying close to the burned out front door.

White Bird and Tee had learned how the white man dug a hole and buried their dead so they found a shovel and put them in the ground under a tree behind the house. With the work done, they started looking for Little John but could not find any fresh tracks. Finding none, the two Indians headed back to tell Ronnie about what they had found.

They pushed hard heading back to the ranch, they needed fresh horses if Ronnie was not back at the ranch. Riding into the ranch yard their horses were done. Abby came to the porch to see why they had about killed the two horses.

After learning what was wrong she told them to go home and get rested, they would be needed in a day or two. She told the other girls about the Applegate's being killed. Tony was in the high country so Abby would ride to Ronnie and Maggie would ride to Tony in the high country to get him back to the ranch.

Abby was making good time when she spotted dust ahead a few miles. She kicked up her horse to close the distance. Galloping in, Ronnie wanted to know why she was pushing her horse so hard. They called the crew around and told them of the killings of Sam and Beth. Ronnie asked Andy to ride back and get the crew. This was going to be a full crew chase down and killing, none of the eight would live to tell about their stealing the Applegate's horses and cattle.

Andy returned to the mining operation and gathered the crew. Within a few minutes the crew was loaded and heading back to the ranch. They would be only a half day behind Ronnie reaching the ranch.

Plans were set in place to overtake the outlaws and kill them all. It was going to take a few days to catch up with the outlaws, the cattle will slow them down.

Ronnie planned to take Rose and Marty and the small chuck wagon, it would take them longer but they could stay on the trail longer by having a food supply and grain for the horses. Early the next day they had extra horses for each rider and an extra team for the cook wagon.

The crew was led out of the yard heading to pick up the trail of the cattle. No one had seen Little John and had no idea how to find him. They would just go after the outlaws he would just need to catch up when he could. Ronnie would take Tee one day to scout ahead and the next day Tony would take White Bird to scout the trail.

On the fifth day Ronnie and Tee felt that they could catch up late the next day. Ronnie came back to make a final plan, Tony and White Bird would ride late tonight so they could get ahead of the outlaws. Ronnie had Andy Sams and the two Jenkins brothers. Billy and Jack. They had become good shots over the time working with Ronnie Campbell and crew.

Ronnie would push from behind to close the trap. They will push up in the late afternoon hoping to catch them before dark. Rose and Marty asked if they could ride one of the saddle horses so they could help to close the trap. Ronnie told them to get saddled and leave the cook wagon behind. Rose handed out some extra food to last until the next morning.

With fresh horses under everyone, the crew headed after the cattle. By midafternoon they could see the dust from the cattle. Ronnie moved up the center, Rose and Marty took the left side, Randy moved over to the right side. Ronnie hoped that Tony had reached his position ahead of the cattle and riders.

Little John came in behind Ronnie at a gallop, slowing up when he reached Ronnie. Little John asked how close are we and what can he do. Stay with me and we will empty all of the saddles as fast as we can, Tony is ahead so watch out for him when the shooting starts. Three of the eight could be seen from behind, Ronnie waved the others to move up on each side.

Ronnie and Little John rode up behind the three. As they got close behind, the three turned. Seeing Ronnie, they pulled iron and were met by deadly fire from Ronnie and Little John. Three down and five to go. Rose and Marty had moved up outside of two of the cattle thieves, riding on the left side of the cattle.

One of the riders turned to check on what sounded like a gunshot coming from behind him, he got a look at two riders closing in on them. After the one look, he jumped his horse into the cattle herd and moved out of sight among the cattle.

Marty and Rose both fired at the rider that was still in sight, he went down among the moving cattle. Marty and Rose rode over to take a look but he had been walked over by 50 cows, not much was left to look at. Marty picked up the horse and moved back to the back of the cattle herd to check in with Ronnie.

Tony and White Bird took care of the man riding point without any problem, picking up his horse and moving back toward the back of the herd to see if they could find some of the other cattle thieves. Riding forward, they were looking for any other men. Ronnie was riding alongside of the herd. Without anyone pushing the cattle, they started to stop and mill around and to feed on the grass.

With the dust settled, the crew started to regather around Ronnie on the south side of the herd. With everyone safe and five members of the gang dead, three were still missing and would need to be run down and killed. Little John had found out about his parents being killed and the cattle missing when he had returned from scouting some new range on the back side of the mountains. Little John found the two graves and started tracking the cattle and horses, he was only a day or so behind Ronnie and his crew trailing the gang who killed his parents.

Little John asked Ronnie what is the plan now? Ronnie said he would take White Bird and Tee and will run the gang to ground and kill them. Little John said that he would join Ronnie on the hunt and asked if his crew could drive the cattle back to the ranch for him. Ronnie gave everyone their orders and asked Rose and Marty to go back and bring up the cook wagon so they could resupply for the job of tracking down the last three members of the gang. Ronnie asked everyone to set up camp while he and Little John talked. They rode off to a quiet place to talk about Sam and Beth.

*

Larry McPherson was making a slow sweep behind some hills a few miles to the west and south of where he figured the cattle would be as the sun was starting to set. A few miles ahead he could see some dust in the air so he picked up the pace hoping to get a look at the tracks before the light was gone.

When he reached the general area, he slowed down and soon found tracks of three horses being pushed hard. Larry figured most of the gang had been killed and this was the last three. Turning east by north, he figured he would find Ronnie Campbell and crew in a campsite within a few miles. It was getting late so why eat alone.

Larry was spot on; he had only gone a mile or so when he could see campfire smoke and the top of a cook wagon. Riding a bit closer, he called the camp and was asked in by Ronnie. "Well, look what dragged in just a mite late for some of the action.

Larry stepped down and a Jenkins brother took his horse and removed his gear, leading the horses? to water and some feed. Larry told the boys to get out some of his oats for the horses, they told him to keep his they would use their own grain.

After Larry heard the story, he told them he had talked to two men a few days back and found out that two people had been killed.

Larry filled Ronnie in on the information he had received from Salt Lake City. That is why he is here to try to intercept them before they could kill anyone else.

"Sorry I am a few days too late".

Ronnie said, "swear us in so we can kill them legal like when we catch up with them".

Tee and White Bird rode in, telling Ronnie that the big lawman makes too much noise, we could have had his scalp and he would never have known it. Larry asked them when did he pass them, Tee told Larry he had rode right past them when he was looking for the trail, Larry told them he had a feeling about that time someone was watching him. White Bird told Larry "they were this close like we are now".

Marty and Rose had food ready just after Larry rode in. "Now this sure is better than a cold camp," Larry said.

Ronnie said, "Larry you are the boss now, what do you want us to do and how many do you want to go on the chase"? Larry laid it out, two horses each, bedrolls, rifle and extra bullets and food on each horse.

At first light we will check each horse's shoes and check for cuts that could be problems later.

"Little John you should go home and deal with the ranch but you can come if you want to, I know how you feel".

"I am going," he said. Tee and White Bird both will go just in case they split up when we get close.

"Tony, you take the cattle and horses back to the ranch, stay a few days and see what if anything can be salvaged from the ranch house. Cut the timber we will need to rebuild the house and get them drying". Little John asked if they would move the horses back into the back pasture so they will be safe.

You are looking at a high speed mail pickup. Grant
Bell riding Red.

Chapter 24 **The Chase West**

In the morning each of the horses were checked and loaded with the equipment that would be needed for the hunt. Everyone knew this would not be an easy hunt, they also figured on at least two weeks. Larry and crew headed southwest following the trail, Tee and White Bird had been gone well before the first light.

After looking at the dead men they figured that Jules Baster, Sid and Diggs were the three man they were chasing. Larry and Ronnie felt that the three are riding three tired horses and that is a good thing. We are on fresh horses with an extra one to help keep them all fresh for days.

After checking the dead men and horses, they found a lot of money, Larry gathered it up and put it in his saddle bags so he could return it to the bank in Salt Lake City.

Ronnie said,

"I don't think any of this bunch had any time or place to spend any of the money so when we finish this, we may just have all of the money. Larry let's get on the move we need to get this done".

*

Jules had crashed through the herd to reach the far side and led the escape to the southwest with Sid and Diggs hot on his trail. Jules had heard the first shot, ducking low and crashing through the herd to safety. This is the first time he didn't have an escape plan with extra horses. The remuda was on the wrong side of the herd to make a change to a fresh horse so run he did without any extra food or ammunition. Jules pushed hard for three hours when he pulled up to rest the horses. Turning to Sid he said we need some new horses and fast.

After a few minutes of rest he pushed on telling Sid and Diggs to keep an eye out for water, as all they have is in their canteens. This was the first time Jules didn't have extra horses and supplies waiting. Sid asked Jules how long before that bunch will start on our trail. "I would say they will wait until in the morning so they can follow the trail". Diggs spoke up and told about one of the riders looked like an Indian. "Damn that is all we need. Let's get going".

When it became dark the three men made a camp in a cluster of rocks to block any light to show along their back trail. Jules told the gang to get some sleep and we will start at first light. Jules walked out a bit to check the back trail. Seeing nothing, he returned and went to sleep. As the light was starting in the east the three outlaws headed on south so they could ease around the mountain range so they could turn back west.

Jules led off at a walk trying to save the horses. They all were game and wanted to go but this was not the time to do anything but walk. After about two hours they started to make it around the end of the mountains and Jules could see a trail leading back into a small canyon. Turning down the trail he was hoping to find water and some good grass for the horses.

After about a mile he could see the trail leading up the side of the low hill. Getting off the horses, Jules led the three up the steep trail hoping water would be behind the rocks. Easing down into a small cut they found the small pool being fed by a spring.

The three men got a drink then filled their canteens. They led one horse at a time to water, just a small drink at first. After a while the horses were led back to drink their fill, then walking the horses back down into the little valley, they mounted and headed west.

Jules had been thinking how do we handle this problem, we don't know how many men we have on our trail, so do we stay together or do we split up? Sid and Diggs think it would be better if it came to a gun battle to have the extra guns.

As the three headed west, Jules found a solid rock outcropping and he headed onto the rocks to try and slow down the trackers some to get a bit of extra miles. Jules had never had to hide, he had always had enough guns to be in command. This time things could be a bit different for Jules. We need to find a ranch to get some fresh horses, but Jules knew he may have a problem. This is not the best cattle country so a ranch may not be an option.

Jules was now just west of the Diamond Mountain range. By staying to the low ground the three men had passed a series of small lakes that were only a mile to the east. As they rode off the rock shelf Jules picked up the pace trying to make up some ground. As Jules headed west looking for cattle or any sign of a ranch, they had been at a soft trot and had made some good time.

*

At noon Ronnie could see some dust coming in their direction. It had to be Tee and White Bird with information on the gang. When the Indians rode in Little John led their horses over to the extra ones and traded out the gear so they would be ready to ride when lunch was finished.

Tee told about the condition of the horses the gang was riding and felt that they would need new horses in the next day or so. If they don't get some new mounts they would be afoot soon, he felt it would take another full day to get close at the pace they were moving.

Larry felt it would be better to just stay putting pressure at the speed they were going. "let's save the horses in case they find new horses". With lunch finished, all were mounted on fresh horses. The chase was on, heading to what looked like the Diamond Mountains unless the gang changed directions. Larry and Ronnie had talked about what direction the gang would take when they passed the end of the Diamond Mountains.

White Bird told Ronnie that they could find good water by night with a good campsite. The decision was made that Tee and Larry would take a short cut through the Diamonds and gamble that the gang would head to the west trying to find some horses. Ronnie and crew would keep on the trail just to make sure that the gang did not change directions. This may take a bit longer but Ronnie wanted to stay on the trail to the end.

Tee was working up a canyon for about a mile when a sliver of a trail eased out of the canyon wall heading up. Larry asked if he was sure of this trail. It sure looks little used and very small for horses. Tee just kept climbing without a word.

Soon they were into some cedars and the trail became a bit rockier with loose gravel at times. Larry was about ready to turn back but there had not been many places you could turn a horse around so on up they went. Coming around a bend in the trail, Larry could see a saddle and the trail was heading in that direction.

The sun was going down when Tee led Larry off of the mountain and found a spring on the west side of the mountain. Larry got some coffee started in a shelter a short distance from the spring. Tee headed back up the mountain on foot saying he would be back later. Larry figured that he would look for any fires to the west. About two hours later Tee came into camp saying, "I see fire about a day's hard ride to the west". Larry figured if that was the gang, he was a full day ahead of some backup help if a gun fight started, with this bunch a gun fight will end the chase.

*

Jules was up at first light making ready to push on west, hoping to find a ranch sometime today. He knew without fresh horses they would be in deep trouble. Each mile the horses were slowing up. They were about done in and needed rest and some grain. At best the grass was poor so the horses were going downhill by the hour.

Ahead Jules could see a low hill a few miles away, Jules told Sid and Diggs to walk and save the horses the best they could. It was a slow climb pulling the horses along behind.

Reaching the top, Jules stopped to take a good look around. He needed some luck. With the horses resting under the shade of some rocks, Jules sat down to look with his glass. After a bit he decided that he could see some horses but also some cattle. This was going to be a slow five or six mile walk, they would be lucky if the horses could walk that far. A few hours later the three men found some water and grass for the horses, they were still some miles on to a possible ranch. After resting and letting the horses graze for an hour and having been watered for the second time, Jules stepped up and rode west.

As Jules rode west he could see additional cattle and horses but could not see any ranch house. He got close to a herd of horses. Each man got his rope ready to catch a fresh horse. Jules, Sid, and Diggs all had a new horse. They started to change their saddles to their new mount.

The new horses were mustangs. Jules said he sure hated to leave his good horse but we can't take them along. "Well, boys, let's see what we got, be ready when you step aboard. Diggs was the first to mount up, his mustang took a couple of steps and started to make a fuss. Diggs pulled his head around and grabbed the bridle. He made a few jumps in a circle then moved out at a walk.

Jules and Sid were lucky, they just had a little bit of halfhearted bucks but then followed Diggs's horse and the three rode west at a smart trot.

*

Tee and Larry rode south along the back side of the Diamond Mountains until then cut the trail of the three men as they came off the rock shelf. Larry told Tee we will camp and wait for Ronnie and the crew, we do not want to take on three real bad men with just the two of us. Tee told Larry that he would close up and try to slow them down.

Tee led his extra horse and moved along the trail hoping to catch up and try to steal one of the horses if he could. At dark Tee found the three horses mixed in with a small herd of some ranchers stock horses feeding by a pool of water in a field. Tee caught one of the mustangs and, tying his other two horses together using only a piece of rope around the lower jaw, he jumped on bareback and off he went at a gallop.

Tee knew that the men would only trot so they could save these horses just in case they would need to make a hard run. Tee pushed as hard as he could, he would run this horse until he dropped. His other two horses were using very little energy, all they were carrying were the saddles. Tee had run this mustang hard all day. The trail was getting fresh, he was only a few hours behind the three men. Removing the rope from the lower jaw he turned the mustang loose. Tee knew he would work his way back down the trail and rejoin his friends in a few days.

Tee mounted one of his horses and started west along the trail. It was getting dark but he could still make out the hoof prints. He got down and followed as long as he could make out the trail. Tee had seen a low rise a mile or so ahead and wanted to make the high ground hoping to see a fire. Reaching the high ground, Tee sat in the saddle for a while letting his eyes adjust to the low light. After a while he caught a flash of light then picked it up again, this had to be the gang and they were only a few miles ahead.

Tee got down and went to sleep. He would wake up in a few hours, giving the men time to get into a deep sleep. Tec had waited until the moon was starting to show, allowing for some low light. He moved up close to the camp. The horses were tied to a picket line so they could graze during the night. Tee was inching along getting closer each minute.

Each time one of the men would move he would need to wait a long time before moving again.

Tee was laying behind a bush ready to pull one of the picket pins when one of the men got up to relieve himself. Tee held his breath trying not to make any sound. After a bit the man walked back to his bedroll and laid down. Soon he was breathing slow, Tee could tell he was back asleep.

Easing his right hand forward and pulling the picket pin, the trick was to ease backwards slow enough so the horse would not make any sound that was not normal. After an hour he had moved far enough to be able to get to his feet and walk away with the one horse.

When reaching the other horses, he mounted and started back down the trail. When the sun started to show light, Tee found some cover and settled in to wait for Larry and Ronnie and the crew. Tee was sitting by a small fire when Larry and Ronnie rode in. Seeing the extra horse they started to laugh. "Tee, how mad do you think Jules is now being one horse short"?

Look what you find along the trail.

Chapter 25 **The Last Trail**

Jules woke up at first light. Looking out, he could only see two horses. He jumped up and woke up Sid and Diggs. "Why didn't you drive in the picket pin harder? We are short one horse. Now you both bring in the two horses and take a look around and see if you can see the other horse". Sid walked out and soon found the tracks left by Tee. "We have a problem. The horse was stolen by an Indian". "Ok, one of us will need to walk until we find another horse". Moving west at a slower pace, the three kept changing from either riding or walking.

Jules told Diggs to find a hiding spot and hold off the bunch coming up behind. Sid and he will ride ahead and find some extra horses and come back. This way we can make better time and get back before the bunch catches up with us. Diggs was not happy about this arrangement. He know he would be the first to die and soon.

Sid led off, heading for a low hill so he could see ahead to see if they could find some extra horses. Reaching the top, Sid pulled up and started looking for anything or anybody who had a horse.

*

Jane had been riding ahead looking for some water. Her parents were following along with the covered wagon. George and Wanda had run low on water so they had no choice but to send Jane on ahead, George was not happy about her riding alone miles ahead of the wagon but they had no choice. Jane had come back to tell her mom and dad that she thinks she saw some green trees about ten miles ahead and she was going to be gone a long time.

Jane was a trail wise girl. She had been riding with the scout on a wagon train for many weeks but her dad wanted to change direction and head north to pick up the Pony Express Trail so they had split off from the others. Jane could shoot well and knew how to live off the land if needed. This day she had ridden her father's horse. Jake was a big horse just under seventeen hands and could run. Her dad had won some money racing Jake, just before splitting from the wagon train he had picked up over one hundred dollars on a match race.

After reporting in, Jane had set a nice pace but didn't want to work Jake too hard because of him not having much water over the last few days. When the sun got high she knew she may need to camp out, hoping by some water. She came over a low rise and she could see the green trees better now, she still felt she was a good five miles out yet. Pushing on at a walk now, Jake was starting to feel the miles over the past few days.

Jane had kind of lost track of time-she may have fallen asleep, but she was at the trees and Jake was moving faster, hoping he had smelled water and was heading for it at a trot now. There it was a small stream just about dry, but it was still running. Easing down the bank, Jane got off and walked Jake to the water, but only let him have a little, only three swallows this first drink. Jane pulled her canteen from the saddle and let it fill, she then drank from it-all the time keeping watch for danger.

Jane led Jake back to the stream and let him drink his fill this time. When he slowed down, Jane got back into the saddle. She wanted to find a sheltered location to make a camp for the night. Jane found a dry wash leading back away from the stream. A short way back the wash made a turn leading back north. This would allow her to have a fire that could not be seen outside of the dry wash.

Tonight she would camp without any food but some deer jerky her father had made a few days ago. After letting Jake drink again, she put him on a picket line down in the wash, there was enough grass for him tonight. With a fire going, Jane made her plan for an early start in the morning.

*

George and Wanda had pushed on until dark hoping to see Jane riding in with Jake. When it got late they knew she could stay out overnight if needed. They both spent a wakeful night having Jane on their minds, hoping for the first light so they could get moving ahead. George had given each of the horses a little drink but held back a little water for noon, that would be the last of the water. Jane was the only hope they had at this point.

With one horse on a lead line behind the wagon, George and Wanda started west looking for Jane. Just after getting started for the day, George saw two riders looking at them from a small rise. George raised his hand to wave but was met by a 44 slug in the chest, Wanda reached for the gun but never made it. Jake and Sid rode in and stopped the team. Sid jumped up on the seat and pushed George and Wanda over the side and walked the team forward until they reached a tree. He stopped the horses.

Jules had checked the two dead people to see if they had any money, no such luck. The two men checked under the wagon seat and found two hundred dollars and some coin. Sid asked Jules if they should take the extra horse back to Diggs or just go on now that they have an extra horse. Jules said to grab the lead line and go, they now may just have a chance to reach a town.

*

Ronnie asked Tee how you got that horse, he just gave them a smile and stepped up saying White Bird and Tee will close in behind them. Tee said "we will watch, they may leave one man behind, you follow the trail, we will move wide to find him". The two Indians split up and moved wide and set off at a fast pace. Larry, Ronnie and Little John moved out at a canter to cover some ground fast. Tee said that they should only be one half day behind the killers because the stolen horses had started to really slow down.

Tee was on the right side, White Bird on the left. They had pushed hard. Just after midday White Bird saw a flash of light. Tee had stopped when he saw White Bird stop then go back to meet Ronnie. Both Indians rode back to meet the men, Ronnie asked Larry how does he want to handle this? You are the boss on this. Larry laid out a plan to have the Indians circle ahead and draw fire but stay under cover, when he shoots at you we will have gotten close enough to finish off this killer.

The two Indians made the circle and led the stolen horse out into sight, Tee showed himself for just a second leading the horse back under cover. Diggs threw a shot at Tee as he went out of sight. When he raised up to get a better shot he was met by three bullets in the back. Little John said "well, another of mom and dad's killers finished. Let's mount up and get after the next two". Tee and White Bird were in the lead. The five riders are making good time. Tee had told Ronnie that the stolen horses were not in good shape. They should start slowing down soon.

With the sun getting low, Tee and White Bird came back saying there was a dead man and woman and wagon ahead just over this little hill. Ronnie, Larry and Little John dug the graves and put up a marker with no name. Larry turned to Ronnie and said they could have just stolen the horse they needed. They never even started back to help the man we killed today, they just kept going and left the wagon team just standing. Larry said, "I just don't think I can ever figure people out".

The Indians came back riding hard. Ronnie met them and asked what is the problem? "Young person riding west and alone. Two bad men heading same way following tracks". "Ok, let's rest until the moon gets up". Ronnie asked Tee if they could track with the moon tonight. Both Indians said they could follow but a little slow.

With three hours rest the men headed along the trail with the Indians in the lead walking beside their horses. As the moon got up it was not full but was giving off enough light they could follow. When the sun started to come up they stopped and gave the horses a bit of water, each man changed to a fresh horse and moved forward. Tee said that they were getting close.

*

Jane was just waking up when she heard some horses coming to the stream. She knew they could see her tracks and would soon follow. Easing the saddle on Jake, she was just mounting when she looked up and saw a man looking at her. As she hit the saddle the second man blocked her escape. "Well now what do we have here? Looks like a nice young girl," Jules said. "You can just get back down off the horse. We need to have a little talk". Sid came down to join them in Jane's camp, Jane told the men that her father and mother would be along soon so they needed to just go on their way.

"Jules, do you think we should just help this little girl grow up some before we ride on"? Sid said. "Check her saddle bags and see if she has any food, I am hungry". Sid came back with the deer jerky and handed it to Jules. As he walked by Jane he reached out and grabbed her by the arm and ripped her shirt exposing one of her breasts.

Sid told Jane he will check out the rest of her in a bit. Jane tried to run but Sid had her in a few steps. Taking some rope, he tied her and tossed her up against the dry wash bank saying, "I will get to you in a bit" as he walked out to the stream for a drink.

*

Tee and White Bird came back telling Ronnie that we are close, they have stopped by the river. "I think they have the girl, I got a look at her tracks". Ronnie told Larry they had better finish this now and fast before they rape this girl. We may be too late so let's split up and get these two men. Little John and Tee were to make a circle to get behind them. The Indians had told Ronnie that there is a dry wash just ahead and they are in this wash with the girl.

Little John had put on a pair of moccasins and followed Tee at a jog, trying to not make any noise. As they found the dry wash they could hear the two men talking about who was going to take the girl first. Jane was crying, telling the men to just go on and she would never tell she had seen them. Little John and Tee had eased up close to the top edge of the wash just a bit more so they could see below. Jules said that he was the leader and he would take her first. Just as Jules had his belt unfasten Little John had eased over the top and Little John shot Jules low down in his back and followed with a second shot right between the shoulder blades. Sid had started to make a turn when he heard the first shot and was met with a well placed bullet from both Ronnie and Larry.

Little John slid down the bank and ran to Jane telling her it is all over both men are dead, Little John had untied Jane and was just sitting holding her, saying it is going to be ok. The Indians picked up the horses and took them to water, making ready to head home. Tee and White Bird found the rest of the money in the two dead men's saddle bags. Taking it to Larry they turned and headed for home. Little John had told Jane about her parents and told her that these men had killed his mother and father also just a week ago.

Little John told her about needing to put their names on the markers and we need to go back and bring the team and wagon to water so they could rest for a few days. Ronnie and Larry asked if Little John and Jane would be ok picking up the wagon and then heading for home. Ronnie said that he wanted to get a start for home and Larry would start back to Sacramento with his job finished.

Chapter 26 **Going Back Home**

Little John asked Jane if it would be ok if he stayed with her and get her wagon and team to water and see what she wanted to do now that she was alone. After saying good bye to Larry and Ronnie, Little John asked Jane if she was about ready to make the ride back to the wagon. She said, she was.

With both Jane and Little John losing their parents it was not an easy few days ahead for either of the two. Little John had not had time to think about his loss and Jane was just having to deal with the loss also.

"Jane can we be friends? We both need someone to talk to about our loss". Jane agreed to be friends. Filling up their canteens, they headed back to bring the wagon and team to the stream for a few days before Little John headed back to rebuild the ranch.

Riding back to the wagon was hard on Jane. It would be the first time she would see the markers for her parents. Ronnie and Larry had dug the graves and set the markers by the wagon so Little John would be close by when Jane got there. Little John helped Jane down and gave her a little hug and let her have some time alone at the two graves.

Removing the canteens, Little John gave the team some water and unhitched and removed the harness from the team and gave them a rubdown with some dry grass. He could hear Jane crying but he just let her alone for some time. Digging around, Little John found some grain for the horses and some food for him and Jane. He had seen some antelope on the way to the wagon, it was not far. He could ride back and get some fresh meat.

Walking back to Jane, he sat down until she turned and put her head on his shoulder, Little John put his arm around her. They sat that way for a long time.

After a bit she asked him, "what am I going to do Little John"?

He said, "why don't we just give ourselves a few days to get our heads around our loss. Do you want to wait here or ride back with me to try to get us some fresh meat"?

"I want to go, I don't want to be alone".

They climbed aboard and headed back to the area Little John had seen the herd of antelope. When they reached the area Little John got down followed by Jane. When they found a dry wash they turned and headed toward the last sighting. Little John leaned down telling Jane to stay close but don't step on any branches. After a short walk, Little John said he was going to take a look and see if they were lucky. Removing his hat, he eased up the bank keeping some sagebrush in front of him. Peeking around the sagebrush, he could see one only a hundred yards away.

Little John eased his rifle into position to make a clear shot. Lining up the sights, he pulled the trigger, the antelope was down. Turning to Jane he asked if she could go back and get the horses while he went to get the animal ready to pack back to the wagon. Jane turned and started back. Soon he could hear the horses coming through the sagebrush. His horse was ok with the dead antelope but Jane's horse wanted nothing to do with that dead antelope.

Reaching the wagon, Little John asked Jane to see if she could find some canvas he needed to make a smoker and fast. The meat would not last very long. Little John went out and found some dead cedar trees. Breaking dead limbs off the main branch, he now had three six-foot poles to use for the frame of the smoker. Jane had found an extra top for the wagon. Little John asked Jane if he could cut off some of the canvas for the smoker. Jane said to use what you need. "Can I gather some wood? Just tell me what you need".

Little John started cutting up the meat. Jane got the wood for the smoker and for a fire to cook dinner on. Jane unloaded the steel frame to hold the cooking pots and the coffee pot. As Little John cut up the antelope, she picked up some of the meat and put it in one of the pots. Next, she added some wild onions and other stuff. Stew was on and would be ready in an hour. Little John found some wire to make racks to hold the meat. He had not paid any attention to what Jane was doing.

When he turned, "Wow girl you sure do know how to make a camp". Jane lit up with a big smile.

With the camp ready and the meat being smoked, dinner was cooking. Little John turned to Jane and said, "thanks for being here with me, I have never had a friend my own age. How old are you? I am nineteen" he said.

"Little John, I am only seventeen, but I can do a lot, my mother taught me". Little John reached out and pulled Jane to him and told her that she was just the perfect age for him. Jane looked up and kissed him.

Little John had never held a girl or kissed one. This was the best day he had ever had, even after all the trouble. Looking over, he asked if he could kiss her again.

"Oh yes, I hoped you would," she said. It was getting late, the sun was going over the mountain to the west. "We better get some of your dinner and get our bed rolls out, it will be dark soon". Little John went out and gave the horses the last of the water, they would be heading west early in the morning.

With a bowl of stew, Little John was in heaven. This girl can cook! With the plates sand washed, Little John told Jane he had to go to sleep because the fire in the smoker had to be kept going all night. Jane said that she would keep it going until she got tired, then she would wake him and she could sleep some. Sitting by the cook fire, Jane was reflecting on the last few days, finding the water, almost getting raped, saved by her new friend. Jane remembered what her mother said when she asked how will she know who is the right man for her. Her mother had just smiled and said, "when you look at a man and you get warm all over and he is a good man tell him how you feel and don't let him go anywhere without you".

The moon had come up just after dark so Jane waited until it was overhead before she woke Little John. Jane had just added wood to the fire and the meat was smelling great. Jane walked over to Little John and slid into his blanket and pushed back into him. Jane could feel his arm reach around her. He came awake real fast.

Jane said, "will you just hold me for a little while".

Little John gave her a hard squeeze and started to get up and as he did, he gave her a real hard kiss and said we best go a bit slower. Jane told him to come back to bed just before the sun starts to come up, "I want to feel you close to me. I need that and I also know you do too". The moon was going down and Little John had just stoked the fire, it would last for a couple of hours. This time Little John removed his pants and shirt so he could feel her body next to him.

Light was just starting to show in the valley. With the light Little John could see Jane in the soft light. She started to pull the cover back over her when he asked her to just let him look. "You are the most beautiful woman I have never seen".

"You think I am a woman"? she asked.

"Yes you are a beautiful woman and I hope you chose me to be your man".

"Why Little John are you asking me to be your wife"?

"Yes, I sure am doing just that if you will have me".

"Jane, thanks for teaching me how to make you happy". "Little John we will have many years to teach each other how to be happy. You know that my mother told me that I would find a man and I would know he is the one I wanted in a matter of days".

Little John said "she may have meant hours, what do you think? "let's get loaded, I think the meat will be ok until we get to the river, we may need to smoke it a bit more". Jane handed him a bowl of cold stew and they ate it and hitched up and started for the river. They would camp there for a few days to get the horses fit for travel.

*

Ronnie caught up with the cattle in two days of hard riding. He would ride on ahead to make sure the Applegate house was being rebuilt and he needed to get back to Abby, she would be scared until he got home. The cattle were moving well, the boys said that they knew they were heading home so they would move faster. With the final instructions Ronnie told the men that Little John may or may not catch up with the cattle. He was helping a young women named Jane with her loss of her parents to the gang, just like Little John.

When Ronnie was ready to head home, he asked if Tony was going to head home with him or finish the drive back to the Applegate Ranch. Tony said that he would stay and deliver the cattle, then he would come on home. Tell Maggie I will be home in a week or so, give her a hug.

*

Camp was set up and the meat was smoking again. Little John said it would be ok but why take a chance with the meat. Little John came back from riding up stream to scout the area. It is good to know what is around for safety sake. Riding into camp, he asked Jane to climb up behind him. He pulled a foot out or the stirrup giving her a lift and she was up behind him.

As he came around a bend of the river, Little John just rode into the water and pushed Jane off the back of the horse into the water with a large splash. Little John tied his horse to a log. He sat down and pulled off his clothes and started for the water. Jane came up and asked for some help getting out of her wet clothes, Little John was more than glad to help her. As he progressed, he would place a little kiss first one place then another, causing Jane to laugh and pull away but came back for more. With each naked, they started for the water, both diving in but coming up wrapped around each other.

After a few days of getting to know each other and deciding to get married and with the loss of their parents they are looking to each other for support and comfort.

The horses started to recover after a few days and the two lovers were also ready to start to Little John's ranch. She had asked, just how big is your ranch. He had just told her it had a few cows and a few horses.

"When can we get married"? Jane asked.

"Well, I think a preacher will be at Ronnie Campbell's ranch in a few weeks. We can get him to marry us at that time," he said.

Jane asked Little John if he was sure he wanted her.

He turned and smiled.

"You are just perfect," he said".

"Besides we are a perfect fit for each other".

Wagon ready, horses ready, team hitched, they headed home to the burned out ranch.

"Jane, I was thinking that we may just need to sleep in the wagon until we get a cabin built. Mom and Dad's house was burned to the ground from what Ronnie told me. Is that going to be ok with you? This is bad, I don't have a place to live and asked you to marry me. What kind of a guy am I"?

Jane said, "you forget so fast. This is my home and now it is our home. We can build a new life in a new home when we get it built". Jane asked how many days until we get to his ranch. Little John smiled and said we should make it in about three days.

*

Tony had the cattle back in the canyons and horses in the back pasture behind a fence. Riding back to the construction site he was surprised on how much was done. The walls were up and ridge beams will be in place tomorrow by midday. With the extra help they may just have the roof started before Little John gets home. Tony was talking to Rose about Little John and Jane. Rose just smiled and said we better get another wedding planned.

"What do you mean by that"?

"I will bet they have found out they are the right one for each other," she said. "With all the hard times they both have had I bet they found each other in bed for comfort, then they will find out they are just right for each other. Get another wedding ready, I am telling you".

Rose and Tony were talking about the progress when they heard a wagon coming into the yard. Rose punched Tony when they looked and Little John was sitting really close to Jane and she had her arm around Little John.

"What did I say Tony". "Wedding" she said.

Pulling into the yard, Little John helped Jane down and walked over to Tony and Rose.

Rose said, "when do we get the preacher? They both blushed but Little John said any time would be good. Sooner would be better. Little John looked at Tony asking how did he get this place rebuilt so fast?

"Well, we all pitched in to help. You have a lot of work to do, but you do have a roof over your head".

Jane asked if she could look inside. Rose said come on. We will take a walk around. Rose looked at her saying you look happy.

Jane said, "yes we both have had a hard time but out of that we found each other. We figured on sleeping in the wagon until we can get a roof on, it looks like we can move in real soon". Rose told Jane that she and Marty were getting married as soon as the preacher gets to the ranch.

"If you want to we could get married the same day, would that be ok with you"?

"Yes I would like that, where will you get married"?

"Jane, you are going to love the Campbell's, Abby is as nice as Ronnie. Tony's wife Maggie is also great. You will love them all as soon as you meet them".

"You may not know but Ronnie shut down his gold mining operation just to catch the killers of your mom and dad, they were part of the family. Little John and Ronnie lived together for over a year, Beth would not let Ronnie leave until he had a chance to grow up some. Jane you have landed into one of the greatest group of people I have ever seen, I was an escaped slave heading west when Tony saved my live and the whole group just took me in and made me feel like a real person. I think we will all head for the Campbell ranch in the morning, it may be a good thing for you and Little John to come on up to the ranch to meet everyone".

After the walk around Jane knew she was home. Now, she needed to make this rebuilt home her and Little John's home. Jane walked out to find Little John. She wanted to talk about their new home. Tee and White Bird came riding in with an elk that had been cleaned and ready to cut up and start the smoking process. Jane went to the wagon and pulled out the canvas and wood poles. Rose and Marty came over to help. Marty asked if he could use some of this meat for dinner as they are getting low. "Use what you need, we will smoke any that is not used to feed this bunch".

Tee and White Bird had picked up the extra horses that had been used on the chase of Jules and his gang. Ronnie had left hours before and Tony would stay another day or so to help finish getting the roof on the house. Jane was enjoying Rose and Marty. The three were working on smoking the meat and getting a meal ready. Little John came up and put his arms around Jane, telling her what a surprise that we do have a home, it even has a roof. We can move in and start building our own real home together. Turning, Jane asked him if he wanted her to go meet his parents.

"Yes let's go and I will tell you about them, it is a good time to do this".

Little John and Jane walked to where Tee and White Bird had placed them. It was a good place, just past the corrals overlooking the stream with cattle walking around. He started telling Jane about the early days on the ranch and when Ronnie Campbell came wondering in with a pile of guns, riding Bill and leading Sally. How his mom talked Ronnie into selling the two workhorses and getting Dandy and Diamond in the deal. Later how Ronnie had helped Juan when he was attacked by the Indians. Also later how Ronnie asked him to help with the Pony Express horses and the killing of John Dugan the night he tried to steal the horses and kill Ronnie and me.

"Jane, you know my mom and dad would have loved you as much as I do, now let's go back to our new beginnings". Jane looked at Little John and started to cry, "I am so happy we found each other, you saved my life and now I have all of this and you. I loved my mom and dad but dad just could not make anything work, all I remember is moving from one problem to the next. This wagon had been my home for years, now look at us, we are going to have a great life together".

Mail is being handed off to the Pony Express.

Chapter 27 **Two Weddings**

A couple of weeks had gone by, Jane and Little John had driven the wagon up to visit Ronnie Campbell's ranch to meet everyone.

Little John had told Jane "we better take the wagon so we will have a place to sleep. When they arrived, she could not believe that they have a house to live in and the same crew were finishing the two homes at the ranch. Why did they finish our house with so much work to be done here?

"We are all family, that is all I can say".

Abby and Maggie were the first to greet the wagon. Little John helped Jane down and Jane was gone with the girls, he was left standing. Going into the house, Jane was led into the kitchen only to find Marty and Rose setting out cups and putting some fresh baked rolls on the table. Abby said to grab a chair, we all need to talk. "Rose, you and Marty get a chair, I said we all need to talk. Jane you look so happy. Rose told us some about your loss. You do know you have a new and different family, we are just part of it, you will meet the rest as the day goes on".

"Now Rose said you and Little John are wanting to get married".

"Yes" she said. "I just don't know how I would fall in love with a man in just so few days after meeting him". Abby, Maggie and Rose said we do, Abby said that when Ronnie came into the restaurant at Buckland Station she knew this was her man when he sat down to eat. Maggie asked Mr. Brown to get Tony to drive her out to make a delivery.

"I got Tony to kiss me on the way back, I knew he was the only man I wanted".

Rose said she was in shock from losing her man, but when Marty looked at her, she was ready to start a new life.

"Now let's get to planning these two weddings, we have sent for our preacher Zack and Betty. We say that because they have married Tony and I," Maggie said.

"We want to have the wedding here if it is ok with you and Little John". Rose said that Jane and she talked about it being on the same day. Abby asked about what would you think about just doing a double wedding and then we will have a big party.

Rose and Jane both said that would be just great.

"Now girls, we need to head to Mr. Brown's Store to order stuff. Abby asked, Little John if he would drive the wagon so us girls can have some fun riding"? Abby said this will be a slower ride because of being pregnant.

"Well why don't we use Maggie's wagon and team? We will swing by your place then you can drive the wagon. We all need supplies so we can pick up everything at one time. Mr. Brown will have an empty store when we get done". Little John said that would work great because he had to go get additional stuff that got burned in the fire.

Abby said ok, "you guys get out. Yes, you too Marty. Us girls are going to talk and fix some dinner and we don't want anyone messing with our food".

Jane and Little John were heading home. Little John asked her if she felt like she now has a family.

"Oh yes I have never had more than one other girl in my life other than my mother. How could things turn out so good after it being so bad? I am sure glad we brought the wagon instead of riding. After a short `top to show their love to each other and Little John took time to check over the wagon and team.

Back on the road Little John said, "you do know we will be getting into our campsite a bit late".

"I can live with that," Jane said.

When reaching home, they started to finish up the small details to make this new log house into their home. They moved the bed into one of the rooms, the stove was a mess but was not a total loss. With a day of cleaning it was in place and in use. Little John used some of the leftover split wood for a table. When trimming the logs for the proper length he found some rounds that would work as stools until he could replace the tools that were burned. He would start on other needed things when they returned with the supplies in a few days.

The girls came in at a trot with the trace change jingling, Little John had Jane's horse, Jake, ready to go. Maggie jumped down and Little John got up and the resupply mission was under way. Little John let the girls set the pace, he just followed along enjoying watching his future wife having fun with Abby and Maggie. With one overnight campout they reached the store, Little John introduced Jane to Mr. Brown.

"Say kids, I need you to do me a favor".

"What is that"? Little John asked,

"Well, you see the stuff that is setting out on the front porch. I was going to burn it or give it away, I would like you guys to take it, so I won't have to burn the junk".

"Mr. Brown," Little John said, "you are so full of bullshit. Yes, we will take it but let me pay you". "No," he said "it is yours. Go load it into the wagon and get it out of my sight".

Maggie and Abby had Jane over picking out other things that they will need for the wedding and also for their new home. When Little John told them, they all ran over to Mr. Brown and gave him a big kiss and hug. Jane was crying as she hugged him and planted a wet kiss on his cheek. With the orders filled, Little John loaded all the Campbell's stuff in the front of the wagon and then the furniture in the back, he could not believe Mr. Brown had given them much of what they needed to make the log cabin into a nice home. Little John and Jane had also picked up a lot of other things that they needed for the kitchen. Pots, pans, dishes all had to be replaced.

With the supplies loaded, Little John said that he would start back and the girls could catch up if that was ok. "Go ahead we will be right behind you," they said. Abby said that they had contacted Zack and Betty to do the wedding, they will stop by on the way. "Could you ask them to bring along the stuff we ordered? It should be here in a couple of weeks". "Sure," Mr. Brown said. I have a delivery man now and he can watch the store so I can come to the wedding. I will ride along with the Wilsons when they get here".

Little John was not far down the road when the girls caught up with him. They all talked about the wedding and how nice it was for Mr. Brown to give you guys the furniture. Maggie said that Mr. Brown sure helped her and Sean when their horse died and they were stuck, he gave me a job and had dad doing odd jobs to cover our expenses. He must have known that we were dead broke. Then he introduced me to Tony. Mr. Brown has been a great friend to all our families over the years. Yes, we do spend a lot of money here, but he does things that makes the difference. When Little John pulled out of the deep wash and the front wheel hit a rock, Little John said he was going to come down and dig that rock out.

Maggie said, "no way," that is what saved Tony's life by jerking the wagon, making the bullet miss. Little John said that was another time when people should not get Ronnie Campbell wound up. He chased that bunch down. They all seem to be dead.

"Ronnie is best left alone" he said.

With the wagon unloaded at the Applegate ranch, Little John asked Abby if he and Jane cold drive the wagon home and ride back. That would be no problem. Abby said, "with Maggie and I both with child that would be nice, it is much better riding a horse than sitting on that wagon seat. Give us a minute while we get our bed rolls, and I will get out horses and saddles". After about a half hour things were ready. Stowing the extra gear, they all headed for the Campbell ranch.

With the wagon delivered and a cup of coffee and some lunch, Little John and Jane headed home at a gallop, they would make good time riding fast horses.

When they reached home, Jane asked Little John just how big this little place is you told me you had.

"Well, Jane, I would say it is not that large, but it is a hard day's ride any direction to any of the markers. But when you look at the control of the water, the ranch controls it all for about twice that distance. It is smaller than Ronnie Campbell's ranch but not by much.

Sam, my dad, helped Ronnie figure out how to control land you do not own. That is done by how you file on your property and by controlling the streams and with mountains blocking anyone from reaching the back country, we control thousands of acres".

Jane was sitting on the front porch when she heard a wagon coming to the house, Mr. Brown was riding beside the wagon. When they stopped, Little John had come out of the barn to join them. Zack and Betty Wilson got down and said hi. With introductions made, Jane asked if they would like a drink or some food.

"No," they said, "we need to get on to the Campbell's, the note said that we would be doing two weddings".

"Yes, and Jane and I are one of the two".

"Great," Zack said, and helped Betty back up to the wagon seat, Zack climbed up and said, "see you in a day or so, we will get you married up proper like".

Little John said "why don't we go sit on the porch, I want to talk about some ranch stuff now that you are also my partner in this ranch. Dad was doing freight work for Ronnie, he was gone a lot. Mom and I ran the ranch much of the time. Ronnie asked me if I wanted to take over for dad, I need to be able to tell him what we want to do about the freight line, what do you think"? Jane said that she felt that it would take both of them to just keep the ranch work up. "If we both work the cattle and horses can we make enough money to live on without the freighting business"? Jane said you do know I don't know how to tend cattle and horses so you will need to teach me everything. "Jane, yes we can make plenty of money, yes I can teach you what you need to know".

"Ok, Little John, I don't want you gone and I do want to learn about ranching so why don't we just work the ranch and make it grow. One other thing, how long can we do this by ourselves without any help"?

Little John had been thinking about the same thing but had never talked to Sam about when they would need extra help. The cattle herd was growing, the horse herd was also growing, "I think we will need extra help at roundup time for branding. We can hire four extra men to help and we will need to keep two for working the horses this winter. If we have a bad winter we will need to have hay cut for feed. I would say we need to talk to Mr. Brown if any good men come by looking for work to send them our way anytime".

Jane asked if they had enough money to pay for the extra help.

"You know that I don't have any money".

"Jane, you don't need to worry about money". Little John smiled and told her she had plenty of money in the bank and with the range cattle.

"What do you think about when we go up to the Campbell's to get married, we talk to Tee and White Bird about hiring one of the Indians to just work with the horses? Ronnie seems to think they are the best he had seen with breaking young horses. Ronnie has a horse trainer for his racing stock but won't let him touch any young stock".

"Little John what do you think of Jake?

He is as big and fast as Diamond. We could use Jake as another stud, he just may add some speed and size to your horses".

"Great idea let's go out and pick some mares for him, I have another fenced pasture in a back canyon. Ronnie told me that some of the Indians bring their mares and have Diamond breed them".

With Jake out to pasture with his new girls, only time will tell if this big horse will improve his horses. With the wagon ready to go, Jane asked Little John if he wanted to try it out to see if everything is working well. Little John told Jane that it would be tested most of the night tonight, at the ranch they would not be alone and need to be quiet.

Jane said, "I wonder if all of the girls make as much noise as I do when we make love"?

Little John said, "I hope so".

"Do you want to take a trip for our honeymoon? Just what do you want to do after we get married"?

"No, I don't want to go anywhere now, we can do something when we make a cattle drive to Carson City, you said we should sell some of the older stock this year".

"I will talk to Ronnie about a drive to market this fall, then we can catch a stage to Sacramento for a few days. Abby and Maggie told me about a hotel that has a real big copper tub that two can get into, that sounds like fun to me. You do know we will need to get the dirt off after a cattle drive, don't you? Big copper tub, ok"?

Reaching the ranch, Little John was pulled aside by Ronnie and Tony. "You don't want to enter the house, weddings drive women nuts. It is better to just stay away until they call one of us". Little John was fine with that, he wanted to talk to Ronnie and Tony about a cattle drive anyway.

"Ronnie, do you have any stock ready to sell? I want to move some of the older cows to market, some of mine didn't have calves this year".

"Yes, I have been thinking along the same lines, why don't you come up here and we will brand and cull my herd then move the sale cattle down to your ranch and we will brand and cull your herd. With both herds we should have a nice bunch to sell".

"Another thing Ronnie, I want to hire one or two of your Indians to help me with the young horses," Ronnie said, "they are not my Indians they just live here".

Ronnie, Tony and Little John went to see Tee and White Bird. When they reached the Indian camp, Andy Sams came out of one of the huts.

"Andy" they said. "Little John has a problem, He needs some help and would like to get one or two Indians to help him with his young horses". Andy said that he knew one Indian who may just be a good one, he has been helping him with the forge and has started to shoe horses. Also, his wife has a brother who is coming to see her, he does not live here but is good with horses. Little John asked if he would talk to them about the job, they would be able to make a camp by the stream in the trees, I am just grazing cattle there now. "Well guys, we should know real soon, they are riding in now, I just saw them on the trail heading this way".

After a few hours of talking, both Indians agreed to come help on the ranch, Little John asked what he will need to pay them and is there anything he needed to do for them. Andy said Ronnie supplies them with flour and some other stuff and when they finish some horses Ronnie gives them one to either ride of trade. By living on the ranch they are able to hunt game and live the Indian way and they are not hunted because they are Indians. With the deal made, the men said goodbye to Andy and the Indians. "Andy, when do you think they will come to the ranch"? "Only an Indian knows, you will wake up and they will be working with your horses. You will need to learn Paiute as fast as you can. It will make life better fast. The Indian who you talked to is a brother of Big Soldier. He is the one Ronnie killed after the raid when his dad was killed. He is called Elk Man, he is a good hunter. The Indian that is working in the forge is Running Deer".

The sun was sliding down in the west when the men headed back to the ranch house to wash up for dinner. Ronnie said he was going to peek into the kitchen to see if dinner is about done, Abby turned as he opened the door and said to get washed up as they are setting the table. The three men washed up and came in to eat. The girls had the weddings planned and told the men just what they are going to do and when. Ronnie asked when we find out our directions. "In the morning we will tell everyone what to do". Ronnie loved weddings, when Tony got married Abby was ready every time they went to bed for weeks, weddings are good for Ronnie, he was thinking.

In the morning Abby was ready as soon as he woke up, with a little hand on him he was guided to heaven. With light showing through the window Ronnie followed Abby out of bed and got dressed and headed out to check on the mining operation. Tony had come in from checking on the horses. They talked about getting the cattle out of the brush so they would be easier to drive down for culling and branding later in the fall. Ronnie headed out to the mine to see how things were going and tell everyone to come back to the ranch for the weddings. Marty and Rose were getting lunch ready when he rode in.

"Want some coffee"? Rose asked him.

"Sure".

"Lunch is about ready, you were just in time. What is going on at the ranch"? Marty asked. Well after lunch you better load up and head to the ranch". Your wedding is about to start and it would be nice if you were there to enjoy the day".

So the preacher showed up, yes the girls have ever thing ready for your day, Little John should be there today and the wedding will be tomorrow around noon, if all goes well. Ronnie asked if they wanted to take some time off to go on a trip. They both said no at the same time. We do know when or if we leave the ranch, we will have problems by being married.

"Well, I was just asking". Marty said that he wanted to start on a log cabin upstream a bit if it would be ok. I feel that this area is our home".

"Rose is that what you want"? "Yes, I do like it along this creek, yes this is home if it is ok with you". Ronnie said to build any place you want. This is a good location he had been thinking he might want a house over on that bench across the stream some time. But you build your house.

By dark all of the mining workers were at the ranch. Plans were made for tomorrow, the big day, two weddings. All will be thinking about Sam and Beth but out of their passing is a new beginning for Little John and Jane. With the sun came a cold breakfast but hot coffee, the girls had things to bake and food to cook for the wedding lunch.

The men had been told what to do and just how it would be done. With everything finished, the weddings were ready to start. Andy was asked to give away Rose to Marty, Ronnie was asked to give Jane to Little John. Zack was ready with his big bible and long black coat, standing in front waiting with Little John and Marty for their wives to come forward to join them.

Rose was first to walk up with Andy Sams holding her arm. Andy handed her off to Marty and waited, Ronnie is dressed in his best as he walks Jane to his longtime friend, Little John. With the girls handed off, Zack started the marriage ceremony. Zack turned to Betty and asked her to sing two songs. Oh, how could this woman sing, everyone had been waiting just to listen. When Andy returned to his Indian wife she said better to just open your blanket.

"The End"

Book Three of - The Ronnie Campbell Series

Kill Ronnie Campbell

With the wedding finished, and the girls soundly kissed, the wedding party moved to the tables filled with food for the wedding feast. Little John and Jane were talking to Marty and Rose about what they were going to do after the wedding.

"Well," Andy said, "we are going to head back to the mine and start building a log house on the little bench above the river. What about you Little John"? "Jane and I are just so happy to have a home and the ranch. We are just going back to work and start our life".

All of the mine workers and even some of the Indians came to eat with the ranch family. When things started to slow down it was time to cut the cake.

Ronnie came over and moved the newlyweds over to cut their cake, the girls had made two, one for each to cut. Abby was ready with two special knives for the girls to use. When the cake was cut and passed out Ronnie and Abby stood up and talked about the two new families

Ron Bell was raised on a farm in Penslyvenia, many of my days was spent wondering around the hills watching the wild life. After my father purchased a tractor my time was spent riding our work horses around the mountains around my home. Moving west offered me a chance to ride race horses and help with cattle drives and branding. Hunting and fishing has allways been a part of my life, guns of all types seem to have fit well into my hands. I still like to shoot and fish. I am still active in the Pony Express in Nevada.

Ronbell.info is my website books can be purchased either on Amazon or my website.

www.ingramcontent.com/pod-product-compliance
Lightning Source LLC
Chambersburg PA
CBHW070050260626
47160CB00004B/1164